THE ASSISTANCE OF VICE

Also by Roberta Degnore

Invisible Soft Return:\

Until You See Me

The Real Connection (writing as Rachel Desmond)

THE ASSISTANCE OF VICE

Roberta Degnore

Querelle Independent
New York, NY

Published by Querelle Independent, a division of Querelle Press LLC
2808 Broadway, #4
New York, NY 10025

www.querellepress.com

ISBN 978-0-9967103-5-0, paper edition
ISBN 978-0-9967103-6-7, e-book edition

Printed in the United States
Cover design by Marshall Thornton
Typeset by Raymond Luczak

To the Sirens Motorcycle Club NYC
for teaching me that dangerous competence
and for having really cool parties

"If virtue cannot shine bright, but by the conflict of contrary appetites, shall we then say that she cannot subsist without the assistance of vice, and that it is from her that she derives her reputation and honor?"
—Michel de Montaigne, 1580, *Essays*, "Of Cruelty."

Contents

Foreword

I first wrote *The Assistance of Vice* in the stormy days of 1989. Now it is an expanded reflection of that time: A gay woman in New York City burning through the downtown *chic* of clubs, drugs, and girls.

But it was more than thrill seeking that affected our lives at that time. It was also a kind of internal flight from the plague on our community.

For Her, the main character in *Vice*, it was also an escape from success and from a lover She imagined was too perfect to keep. By not naming Her, I intentionally wanted to draw an identification with all strong women who face the world feeling alone—whether She is or not.

This is a picture of golden times later melted by AIDS. It is the story of one flawed woman's attempt to prove Herself by chasing women and excitement to feel alive in the tempest of that time. Is it autobiographical? If you know me, you'd know.

- New York 1985 -
CARMEN

Not much time, not in general and not tonight. If She was going to do it, it had to be now. The woman would turn away in a minute, maybe leave. So She, thinking way too fast, said something stupid.

"Jesus what a *crowd*."

And She inclined a smug nod toward an athletic woman in a baseball cap. The woman wore it the way men wore them these days—sporting *Bearcat* or *International Harvester* logos that were meaningless to anything in a woman's life. At least anyone who came to lesbian bars like this deep in the West Village, beyond Christopher and Seventh Avenue; this was Hudson and Morton. Yes, that deep. It was small and dark, like its Cubby Hole name, with a dyke bouncer and a U-shaped bar where the silent and strong types anchored the ends. From there those self-consciously tough looking women could keep an eye on everyone, but rarely moved to speak to anyone. And they usually proved to be softer than they looked.

These tough cream puffs, prone to dark suits and dark looks, would never wear those baseball kinds of hats. Not only were they not politically correct, with those dumb logos—although who cared—but they were ugly. And the woman She had spoken to, following Her look, laughed back to Her,

"Something against hats? You seem to feel pretty strongly."

And surprisingly, She did. A little embarrassed, not showing it, She thought about Her judgments lately. Yes, lately judgmental. But what the hell, try to get this woman into bed. Tonight.

They talked, getting a high from drinking. Wine. She focused on Carmen—that was the woman's name—her hair, her body, her face. Black hair, black eyes, a cherubic face, body a bit *zaftig*, lips turned down at the corners, so ready to be kissed. She wore a short tight black skirt, black stockings, a billowy black silk blouse with big shoulder pads and sleeves pushed up. Carmen was Her not-to-distant distaff, being so definitely femme, even though She could straddle that line when she wanted. But She was jeaned and leather jacketed, more artsy-butchy than trucky-butchy. She was almost five four and was kind of athletic, kind of in shape, kind of always watching her weight. And at thirty-four dressed down not so much to match Her downtown-ness, but to bolster forever-young Peter Pan aspirations. It was enough to fit with Carmen's younger flirty femme thing. Soon they leaned together as they talked, drank more.

"Yes, I have a lover. Bad times though," She had answered Carmen. "Do you?"

So much left unsaid. Not lied, just not said. Her lover would be back in three weeks. Three more weeks to chase girls, smoke grass—anything to avoid Her photographs. Some artist. Avoidance was her best talent so far. Or maybe it was cowardice.

But Carmen, seeing only the iceberg tip covered in snowy sympathy called Her "Poor baby." She, too, was alone even with her longtime, live-together lover most times. And she went on to add, in a whisper cadenced so sweetly, that it was "a coincidence," wasn't it?

They laughed. Intimacy dancing in the air, slinking between them. Something was right. So they could go on to pretend to talk about work, and who did what.

"Photography," She said.

"Interesting. I'm a nurse."

That was perfect because She knew, knew from experience, that nurses could be hot. Then it was, where they lived, downtown and uptown. Convenient for discretion.

And they kissed finally. She reached for Carmen's turned-down lips with Her own. The first touch was sweet, velvet. They searched, pressing slowly at first, then a quick electricity and lips parted. Tongues tasting. Cigarette falling to the floor. Her hand in Carmen's hair, pulling her closer. An urgent search of tongues, then a break, foreheads together. Take a breath.

"Why don't we go to my place," was not a question.

And they were in a cab, suddenly, and suddenly home. But who is this woman? She thought, This Carmen? Nice enough, cute, smart, but blurry now. Smoke another joint, quick, because they were so suddenly there. Together.

Carmen looked around, impressed with Her studio hung with photographs, piled with prints and jumbled camera equipment, while She watched, smoked, and had fleeting worries about AIDS. These days with all the rumors, fear spreading, the boys getting sick, you had to ask.

"I've only been with women. You?

"I've been with my lover for two years," Carmen said.

"But not only her?"

"But only women."

What the hell, word on the street was women were safe except for junkies, and Carmen was smiling, sitting on the couch now. And She went, thinking to kiss her lightly. To re-probe, re-think. But Carmen grabbed Her around the neck, pulled their lips together. And She was suddenly on Carmen, Carmen moaning, moving under Her.

Jesus. Unbelievable. So hot, so ready, so wanting. Young, and what tits. *God, feel that.* Get beyond the skirt. And Carmen helped, grabbed up her tight skirt, fought to open her legs.

Prying Her mouth off Carmen's She bit at the silk blouse. Ripped off a button with Her teeth. Moved the bra away from soft, overspreading breasts. Her lips locked on a nipple, hard, reaching. Carmen made a sound, thrust up so her open legs caught Her thigh, jammed it between them. Working it, Carmen moved her body under Her. Gasped, screamed, and came. But they didn't stop. She freed a hand and felt Carmen through her filmy underwear, soaked, steaming to the touch.

And Carmen whispered, "Oh God."

Sweat poured off Her, dripped between Carmen's breasts. And Carmen licked it off Her neck, licked Her sweat. She felt Herself going, giving in to letting go. Who would do this? This younger woman, ten or twelve years younger probably, but no child, and so hot. Suddenly Carmen's tongue in Her ear, the moaning constant.

And then, "Come to me baby," urgent, breathed into Her ear.

And She did. In heaves She came hard on her, made Carmen come again. In the sweat, in the juice, through soaked clothes. Long once ... and again, and again. She clung to Carmen, Carmen to Her, almost shrieking now.

She wants me. I can do this to her. And my lover, that bitch, doesn't want me? But look at this. I'm good. Oh my God. She won't stop, can't stop. She wants more of me. Of me. Me?

They disentangled themselves, not slowly, and stood. Still kissing, still clinging together. She told Carmen against her lips to "come to bed." And like an obedient child she moved from Her arms only just enough to walk there, get to the bed they hadn't needed so far. Then Carmen stepped away, looked into Her eyes and began to undress. She watched until Carmen's breasts were fully exposed, torn blouse and big bra for their fullness thrown aside. Then She had to have them. Her lips, slow and soft, brushed over the naked nipples and Carmen took in a breath. Light touch, cool breath on warm skin. Carmen shuddered, tried to put her hands on Her head to increase the pressure, but She would not allow it. Held Carmen's hands at her sides and used only lips, tongue, face and hair to explore her. Lightly on Carmen's face, her neck, down her sides with those touches until Carmen tried to twist away. Then Her lips soft on her round stomach, tongue playing in rapid, erratic licks. Carmen's knees began to buckle but She held her up at the hips and stopped, pulled away.

They had the courage to stare into each other's eyes. Such desire. Their eyes fully open, talking silently, wanting. She could see Carmen's wetness through them, the lips that opened with their own need for Her. And Carmen strained but She held her in place.

"Do it," Carmen said to Her. "Come on."

"Yes." She answered, but thought of her lover away again, travelling again. For a moment, a second, wondered why she, Her lover, couldn't do this anymore. Why? Five years together, was that the problem? Time? Goddamn dyke drama, dyke closeness, too close for sex.

"Come on." Carmen leaned her big breasts against Her. And through the tee-shirt She still had on felt Carmen's hard nipples, the exquisite softness around them.

They kissed a hard kiss. Tongues shoved deep into each other's mouths, one and another again and again, fast. And Carmen still made inspiring sounds even after all they had done, and pushed her hips against Her. They held their sex tight against each other, pushing hard through the clothing. And the wet flowed out of Her. So hot, fire between them. It must be now. She pushed Carmen away gently, told her with her eyes to undress completely now. And Carmen did, their eyes locked as she loosened the skirt, stepped from it, bent to pull down the lacy stockings. She watched her, saw the smoothly clear flesh exposed, the lovely triangle. And this time it was She who made a small sound from her throat, unplanned.

Carmen was naked, standing in front of Her. Reaching, she took hold of the waistband of Her jeans and unbuttoned it. Smiling, her pouty mouth playful, sensual, eyes burning, promising, she turned away and lay on the bed. On her side, one arm under her head, her breasts falling one on the other, legs slightly crossed to hide her dark patch partially from view. She watched Her undress. It was quick, but not deliberately so. When She stood at the side of the bed, unafraid, Her kind of sleek and kind-of worked on, but not to excess, gym-worked body exposed for Carmen, they both smiled.

"You look like a Rubens painting," She told her, and meant it.

And it embarrassed Carmen a little so she said "You're too good to be true yourself."

They laughed, then She went slowly to the bed. Carmen rolled onto her back at the last moment, her legs spread. She held Herself above her and slowly, slowly lowered onto her body. Her breasts touched Carmen's. Then it was very fast. The superb feeling of nakedness, that easy, wondrous woman-skin on woman-skin, every time, but especially the first.

Her hand found her wetness immediately. One finger thrust hard, deep inside made Carmen yell. Her hips moved up while She worked hard, unrelenting. Carmen came, thrashing, calling out, but She did not stop. Hard inside, a rhythm of urgency still, beyond her coming. Carmen's nails dug into Her neck, Her back, the back of Her arms.

"Yes, yes."

She came under Her insistence twice more, three times. A longish moan, then a cry of constant spasm that closed around Her fingers now deep inside her. And when She felt this her own burning begin. So She went deeper into Carmen then pulled out to make her cry out, disappointed. But Her fingers went to her clit and brought a sudden shout before the shock of the emptiness was complete.

She fucked Carmen hard like that, deep inside, out to that sensitive skin, then in, out again—but softly—to tantalize her. In partway, make her buck and strain then out and send the voltage through her, and back in before it was over. Carmen was loud now— She thought about the neighbors, only briefly—and kept giving all that to her.

"No more."

Carmen said it while she pushed away. But not too far.

"Now you," she said as her fingers found Her down there.

"Oh God yes," She tongued the words into Carmen's ear.

She was ready, coming hard, lunging against Carmen. And as Carmen's arched hips met Her, Her fingers found Carmen's ass. She slid Her hand between the cheeks and pressed against the tightness. When She pounded down on her, Her finger moved inside and Carmen called out until the room filled too much, too much with her sound and again She thought of the neighbors, always too close in New York, feeling their invisible *there-ness* now. But even knowing She'd have to pass them in the hallway sometime or other after this sonic sharing didn't stop Her. Coming, coming together—and separately—constant, continual.

When it was over She took Her finger from her deliberately, slowly, making Carmen grab at Her, clutch Her from the receding depth, and the feeling. They kissed long and intense. Gentle. Bodies soaked with sweat, breasts heaving. And their lips parted finally, sweetly.

She disentangled Herself to get a cigarette, a joint, go to the bathroom. Returning, Carmen was almost asleep. She opened her eyes a little and smiled. Opened her arms and received Her.

"You just don't stop, do you ... so good."

And She held to Carmen's lips another toke of good grass to send the last burst, the waning colors of falling sparks—illuminations they had created with each other. Then Carmen was asleep. She, however, was too awake. Thoughts of a lover who had stopped doing this for Her, or because of Her. She would come back in just three weeks. She would be happy to have her back, right? Three weeks. Three more weeks of days and nights to prove Herself, to Herself. To chase girls, to smoke grass—to avoid working on Her work, Herself.

Young and fair and on my mind. A separate night from everything. Strong and fair. The sensation that will not leave or even lessen. Nothing to be done. A night separate from everything.

- Another Day Gone -
MARY

Feeling fucked up, not really fucked somehow, She wandered alone in Her studio. The city summer heat, the noise suddenly loud since Her lover was away. It yelled at Her, *you're alone you're alone you're alone,* on stifling sidewalks and from subway screeching metal wheels. They hadn't made love in months. She would not admit it was a year even to Herself. But She had tried. Had She? She didn't know anymore. All She knew was She needed the release, the sense of value, the wanting from another woman.

She tried to work on Her photographs, the fine hand-tinting She was experimenting with for the feeling She was trying to get into them. She painted on the prints, delicate, trying to make something, something visual there in the washes brushed over grainy grays or crisp blacks. Couldn't do it. She confused it all, everything in her life. No matter how good it was with someone else, like that sweet Carmen. She missed her, Her lover, *goddamnit.* God damn her. She couldn't work on Her work, Her art. It was her lover's fault. Yes, lately judgmental. But no worse on anyone else than Herself.

So She looked awful when She went out. She was only going to buy film, more Kodak Tri-X 400 at Duggal or B&H over on the West side, but somehow ended up at the bar again. The Cubby Hole again. Early, a little after five, there would be the after-work crowd that was not enticing to her. Their severe skirt-suits, panty hose and too-low high heels were not a turn on. She would have only a drink. That's all. Oversized crumpled white shirt, paint stained studio jeans, funky sneakers. So what? Only one drink.

There were a few women in the bar, no one interesting. She left her drink, went to the bathroom, and returned to find a blonde sitting next to where She had been. Very striking. Not beautiful, too round-cheeked for classical beauty but somewhere between cute and striking. Cool and confident, buoyed by blondness and style, she smiled. She wore a white belted, baby blue sundress with spaghetti straps—the only things covering her very white skin above the dress's loose top that allowed glimpses of décolletage. Sexy, and—when she spoke—Southern. South Carolina.

"My, I knew it was early but there's nobody here, not really. Except for me and you, hon-ney. And I've never seen you in here before. What do you do?"

She told her, and Mary, so blonde, was impressed. So She bought her a drink. This insured her easy banter, observations and bad opinions about almost everything would keep coming. But She liked it, the easiness, because She was too depressed to contribute much anyway. All She could think was that Mary was a dish but probably not Her type. Besides she was too tall for Her at about five foot seven and too full of herself. She was an actress, had an older lover who kept her, and she bragged about it.

"But no, honey, I got to have your number. I know a lot of people who'd love your pictures. And they buy."

So She gave her a card and left. Just another nowhere, sexy, flirting encounter.

But She could still feel Mary's hands on Her, where she had made certain to touch Her as they talked. Her hand, upper arm, and once so tenderly on Her cheek when She had made a joke. So She felt hopeful in spite of Herself going home, going into Her studio to try to work. Maybe, maybe if this one ever called She would get it on with her, this leggy blonde. But She was only hopeful, maybe walking on air a little because she was so attractive, so damn alluring. Southern women; She had a weakness for them. It didn't matter if they weren't Her type—She ran after the exceptions. There had been another, two others, the one not worth recalling because the sex was terrible, selfish. Almost as bad as the stewardess She had gone with to her uptown hotel once. Simply insensitive, unconnected fucking. The other one was also too painful to remember because that particular Southern woman had gone seriously crazy after She left her. Serious suicide attempts (yes, plural) and so demanding that She had to turn away from the control. She still couldn't think about it.

Mary was on Her mind more than She wanted. An actress, that Southern accent, those seductive looks, the sexy talk like, "I'll do about anything on a first date, honey." And She believed her. Couldn't get her out of Her head, hoping.

She smoked a joint when She got home while she tried to work, got very stoned, and blew off the night with mindless television. Kate and Allie—why weren't they gay? The Golden Girls? Too old, but at least they were feisty. When the news reporter Pat Harper came on Channel 4 with her story about disguising herself as a homeless woman, She had to turn it off. Too depressed to see the plight of homeless people. Never mind work on Her photographs. Lonely. She thought about it once, that was all. Lonely.

At nine the next morning the phone woke Her. Was it real or stoned fantasy? Why hadn't She remembered to turn on the answering machine last night? Who could it be? Not finding out was not an option so She hung over the side of the bed, reaching around in the direction of the ring until Her hand hit and knocked the white Trimline phone off its base. She pressed the curved receiver with its glowing keypad to Her ear, untangled the cord. *Hello* was only mumbled.

"Hihoney,canIseeyoutonight?"

What? Where were the multi-syllables? Where was the usual languor in this gust of words? She collected Herself and muttered She "had plans" because She did, to have dinner with a friend. But *well,* Mary said she was going to the country the next day.

"I really want to see you tonight, honey."

She was at Mary's East Village door at seven with a newly-bought half-ounce, a packet of Bambu to roll joints and a bottle of painted-by-Warhol-in-an-ad Absolut—what Mary had drunk at the bar. Just west of First Avenue on 10th Street only two doors beyond the Russian baths, it was a normal funky red brick building with a fire escape climbing up the front. The static-y buzz opened the door and, after four narrow flights, Mary's greeting was warm. She was wearing a nothing kind of checkered sundress—tight halter bodice with a flowing skirt—through which She could glimpse a bit of bare tit now and then when Mary moved. The shiny wide plastic belt helped keep that revealing top tight, and the skirt below alluring. But Mary chattered incessantly and after her first, lingering kiss at the corner of Her lips she stayed away, showed Her to a seat at the small, neat dining table. From there the living room was open before Her and the bedroom could be seen through an open hall door. It was sparse, all of it. Clean and neat against the usual tenement eighty layers of paint globbed over every light switch, and obscuring the fine old molding's details. She was nervous, dry mouthed from the grass as Mary chatted, actually telling bad jokes. But still She was intimidated. This woman was beautiful, She decided. This was going to be it. How should She approach her? How obvious to be?

She rolled another joint that Mary declined except for one hit. Too much the lady, too straight despite gayness. So She ended up getting more stoned than She wanted. A trip to the bathroom, and on returning—steadied only a little—Mary was sitting on the couch. God, did She look good enough to compare to *that*? –Mary's blonde perfection?

What now? How soon to get to her? That, it seemed obvious, was what Mary wanted. The flirting was heavy; the provocative looks intense. But Mary kept to her end of the couch. She did not respond or touch Her hand so nonchalantly placed near her. Mixed signals, yes and no.

Come on, honey, but don't touch, was what She saw and felt. And this was bad because She hated to be wrong. Worse, being so stoned and therefore paranoid didn't help.

No rejection now, please. Be careful, She told Herself. *Careful with this one.* Leggy blonde beauty, actress, vivacious—and, maybe vicious.

"I got lavender contacts today. You didn't eee-ven notice."

Mary smoldered unquestionably blue eyes at Her.

"Well ..."

"Well, come over here. Closer. See?"

She stumbled over Mary's foot as She bent to her upturned face. There, like that, the glare of a lamp on that gorgeous face that was in no way adorned by lavender eyes, She was paralyzed. Mary's look was too intense. The play was so obvious it couldn't be real. And there was no stoned-ness in hell that could make Her could get over the fact those eyes were only watery blue. No lavender, contacts or not. Struck by this sudden reckless honesty, so stoned, She sat down again.

A pout sprung onto Mary's lips. She was bitter and suddenly monosyllabic without pauses.

"Well what'll we do now?"

And with that kick to the head of daring in the face of defeat She got it together. She had to, or else—or else it would all be over with Mary.

"There's always this."

She said it and moved onto the couch to kiss her. Confidant now that the game was called, stoned or not, She finally moved.

Mary received Her enthusiastically. Deep kisses, her hands everywhere. Fingers darting between their lips, into Her mouth or running over Her ears, or her hand pushed hard over one ear to excite Her with that turn-on roaring sound it makes. So primal.

Mary was a biter. She bit Her lips, Her ears, and nearly swallowed Her ear-cuff earring. And she bit Her breasts through Her t-shirt. Frantic movements touching Her all over through Her clothes. Squeezing hard on Her crotch. Mary hurt Her, but so good. It wasn't like being attacked by the drunk straight woman last year who wanted to be fucked so badly but turned hostile at the last second. It wasn't like being really hurt, but it was wild, intense, and a little kinky. Mary was suddenly the sexual predator, taking absolute control. Unbelievable. She had not expected this, the hurt, the bites, the already bruised lips. No sweet kisses here. Not until later, after making Her cry out from a nipple bite. Then Mary calmed, sleeked back their sweaty hair and looked at Her with a shrewd smile.

During this break She had a suggestion, a wish, a need. It was time.

"Let's go to the bedroom," She said. But Mary wanted dinner.

"I know just where I want to go, darlin'. I need the energy, and honey, I want time to think about what I'm going to do to you. Later."

They had sushi on Avenue A. Mary, in the midst of her vapid

jokes and shallow stories about life in the South, would lower her voice suddenly to say how hot Her breasts looked under Her shirt and how much she wanted them. So She, of course, could barely eat, but Mary cleaned both sushi boards effortlessly. She could only be clumsy, however, and drop every cigarette She tried to light. She was generally an anxious wreck—waiting for the *what next*—until they were walking together through the rain to Her studio. Mary possessively, romantically, linked her arm through Hers. In the rain, sharing one umbrella, She felt Mary's body pressing against Her's. Mary moved so her breast rubbed against Her shoulder. She knew exactly what Mary was doing.

Once inside, though, Mary cooled again. Sitting apart from Her, she put her feet up and kept up a steady stream of her stupid stories. But She stayed, laughed appropriately, and obsessed over what might happen next.

An hour went by with more stories. Mary was apparently at ease but at the same time She was bored and still waiting. Waiting. Bored with the talk and the game but still trying to figure it out. *The what next?* Rejection or just a play, another game? Should She grab her or just forget about it and suffer the boredom, call it a night? Mary yawned. *Disaster!* But no, she suddenly wanted to watch a movie on TV.

"Is your TV in the bedroom, darlin'?"

Of course it was, although there was no real bedroom, only a shelf-partitioned area. They couldn't move fast enough.

She remembered then what Her lover always said about the "tube," the "hideous tube." Her lover constantly complained about the television being on, although she avidly watched it. And now Mary was riveted to it, approaching the bed without taking her eyes from the brightening shapes. She playfully pulled Her down along with her as she jumped onto the bed. They fought over the remote and zapped through stations. When they clicked around and landed on the same black and white 1940s film with Barbara Stanwyck for the third time they agreed that was it and settled back. Mary's arm went under Her shoulders and she kissed Her quickly, hard, but no tongue.

"I'm hot, honey," she said it as she leaned forward and peeled off her dress.

She wanted to know why She was "still dressed." So She obliged—under Mary's scrutiny.

As soon as She was naked, Mary pushed Her down and rolled on top of Her. Mary's fingers went immediately inside, made Her flinch from their force. Hard, hard thrusts. Bites on Her neck, bruises on Her upper arms, nipples sore from teeth raked across them. She pounded on Mary's back, part in passion, part pain, part to avoid the worst of the bites. The deep jabs of Mary's long fingers made Her arch, try to get away. But Mary was taller, pinned Her, slammed the heel of her hand against Her clit while three fingers probed deep up inside and curled into Her.

"Come on, baby, feel it," she was growling at Her. "You're so tight, honey. Come on, you got to take it. Come on ..."

The demands were in Her ear with Mary's tongue, saliva hot then cooling like a million pinpoints. She was lost, overcome, pinned down and pried open by the Southern belle. Surprise might have blunted the intensity of the fuck, but it couldn't because it was an absolute fucking, a fucking-your-brains-out fucking. She never expected this wildness, the power of Mary's greed.

Suddenly she was out of Her, grabbing Her legs, lifting them high in the air. She cunt-fucked Her so fast and hard her blonde hair matted with sweat. Slammed into Her, hurt Her pelvic bones. She grabbed for Mary's arms in defense, felt pulled apart. But, still, it was good. Didn't want her to stop: Mary, the graceful Southerner who suddenly flipped Her over to ass-fuck Her.

"Come on, baby, feel it. You're so tight, honey," Mary said it low and dark. "Somebody's not been loving you right."

She said it as she fought one of her fingers into Her. One hand was on Her neck, holding Her down. It gave her full access to taking Her from behind.

Explosions went off in Her. Never, never had She been fucked like this. Tough, ruthless and all the while with Mary's honeyed voice coaxing Her, opening Her, preparing Her to take more. Another finger, thrust in with the force of Mary's hips, and She clawed the sheets. She had to yell for her to stop, but it did no good.

"Darlin', you need this."

Mary heaved into Her with all her weight and She came with a force that made Her buck back so Mary was nearly thrown off Her. But she was a strong girl, that Southern belle, and kept her fingers in Her from behind, grabbed Her with the other hand and slammed in from the front. She wouldn't let go, didn't stop her heaving fuck until pleasure turned to a cry. Then she took her hands from Her, from in Her, and turned Her over to cradle Her like a baby. She was shaking and Mary cooed and rocked Her, kissed Her with tenderness for the first time.

But She felt the tension in Mary and knew She could not rest. Mary was ready. She rolled over her and Mary spread her legs. She pounded and slid cunts with her until Mary started to moan.

"Come inside me, honey, come inside," she commanded it.

And so She shoved as much of Her hand as She could into Mary, pushing with Her hips, rocking, until Mary came. Then Mary bit Her so hard on the neck that she drew blood.

Whatever movie had been on was now off. There was something about palm trees in the Caribbean in lurid color instead of the black and white oldie. It made Her think of her lover, the good sex, the closeness they had on Virgin Gorda. She remembered She had tried the most gentle ass fuck with her then and Her lover, shy, hadn't wanted it. Fine. But She remembered what Mary said, that She was tight there. Someone hadn't been loving Her "right." That's for sure. And She turned and kissed Mary.

"Why darlin', you're sweet," she said before she pinned Her again.

She dragged her tongue down Her body and went down on Her with a force that stunned. Mary's tongue was as experienced as her fingers and She found Herself coming again. She tried to turn away from the iron grip, and the hard and soft tongue sheathed inside of Her. But Mary would not stop until She had come twice that way, under her demanding mouth.

It was nearly daylight when they finally stopped. They fell asleep in each other's arms and She remembered somewhere in the slumber that She was released, satisfied deep within Her *self*. It was a sense of some true but ineffable *self* somewhere deeper inside. She was aware of the rush hour traffic noise outside only when She noticed She had turned away from Mary and clung to the edge of the bed. An unconscious defensive move because She ached and felt bruised over Her whole body. But as She was about to drift off to sleep again She heard something, felt movement. Mary was rubbing her eyes hard—that was what She thought—but then felt the movement, unmistakable, that Mary playing with herself. She dared not move, but listened to the swift juicy sounds, the short insistent stabs. A little gasp, and it was over, a hesitation, and then Mary turned quietly and curled against Her back.

There are still aches in muscles, sweet aches. Some bruises. A bite. Such abandon. Meaningless for labored-over emotions but so elegant for a fleeting presence that will ring in memory for all my life.

No encumbrances. An isolated joy. A memory.

And the sensations pull as if they were hands. The insides of me move, go toward them. Willing, asking. Ready as few times before. Ready to allow whatever will happen. A trust. It allows the abandon, maybe spurs it.

The feeling is inside beyond any control. It responds on its own to the memory.

I walk down the street and remember. Inside I move and a little cry comes. A moan, a sweet breathlessness. How can this be, this adolescent purity once more? The feelings as if never felt before, but they have been. It's only the newness, relived. And the one who gave it. Fresh. Again and again.

- Then A Week Went By -
GIRLS

I wonder if it's all over. I'll never see her again. That's all right, too. There's no reason to go anywhere else, to anyone else. And yet, diversion—and more than that she is. She is just too much on my mind.

She remembered Mary saying, "You're special, darlin', I had so much fun with you." She remembered it, but it was worse than that. She believed it.

And She, sore, surprised, smitten, couldn't pry Mary from Her thoughts. Trouble.

Her lover was coming back in two weeks. Mary would be away in the country for one. And of course Her emotions were getting fucked up. The thrill of that, that Southern belle turned ruthless in bed, was something She could not shake. Mary wanted Her. Not like Her lover, leaving with no goodbye lovemaking. And when she returned, would it be all right? Some welcome home romance would make everything good again. *Would it?* She wanted to look forward to that because She loved her, of course, deeply. Of course.

Her lover was a socialite turned political activist. Margret. The easy grace of breeding in her movements, her laughter, her look made living with her like handling fine crystal. Light as air to the touch, flawless, fragile. Like that, like fine glass Margret could be held and appreciated, but there was a correct way to do it. Like putting down a champagne flute carelessly or too rough, it could break and cut you. But for Her, Margret was resilient and indulgent of Her and Her escapes from success … well, until recently anyway. She, the scruffy artist, was in love as soon as She saw Margret at some loud meeting for some gay action for some offence or other in the basement of the still new Lesbian and Gay Center on West 13th Street. That was before. But now, She liked not to think about it, how serious it was, the deaths from what they finally labeled AIDS. The number was increasing scarily and now everyone was getting organized there in those meetings, men and women together. But She, in Her usual defensive way, signed the petitions but cruised the crowd.

Lithe, thin, not too tall, Margret had thick red hair and delicate fingers that moved like music. It was those elegant hands that got to Her, wanting to be touched by them. They were like a photograph her friend Sam had of Edna St. Vincent Millay. A photograph by Genthe of Millay lightly touching the branches of a Magnolia tree. The photograph's feel intrigued Her and something in it, sparked in Her too. It was Millay's hands. And you couldn't even see them clearly—the tapered fingers, more than touching, so gently holding those branches, showed a vulnerability exposed, but secret. Edna St. Vincent Millay's hands. When the mystery that was Margret went home with Her and was so tentative but so open to anything She wanted, it was as though the photograph of Millay had come to life and was Hers.

But now She was so fucking needy, needy for fucking, affection, being wanted. Margret had not even kissed Her, really kissed Her, in months.

"We have more than that," she would say.

And they did, maybe they did. Something deeper. She wanted to believe it.

But Mary, God, what she had done to Her. And She was a sucker for what Mary was: actress, blonde, striking, leggy, effervescent if a little stupid, and that Southern drawl—the three or four syllables she could get into a one word. She was a slave to all that, the image. All that and wanton, greedy in bed. She could almost come just thinking about her, what she did, what she was, all those imaginings of her and of them together.

She couldn't work. Her photographs stayed in piles, untouched.

She couldn't confide in friends because She didn't want to hurt Margret. Besides, one doesn't do that with simple affairs no matter how hot they were. What to do? If only Margret would love Her in an emotional way instead of retreating into intellectual arguments. They didn't ever really talk about "it." Margret simply rejected Her every time She tried to make love. It was as if she was exasperated, maybe turned off? No, that couldn't be. It was as if Margret was more engaged now with the rowdy beginnings of the political action group they said they were going to call ACT UP, all those boys and cute girls there at the Center. It was important, Margret said, to get involved. There was this bizarre disaster, this AIDS. Yes, but still ... Why the hell did She still love her? But She did. She only needed to feel valuable, to know She was still attractive. Besides, what was Margret doing about her own needs, Her no-lover?

I don't know where I'm at. Worked great before, need to work on my work. Today I can't, won't.

Sitting, watching the sun from the fire escape. Burns intense, simmers and dies just a little.

The crazies, crazy voices, were buzzing. Couldn't work, couldn't eat. Restless, unfocused, smoking too much, and smoking too much grass. Would Mary call? No, not from her girlfriend's place in the country. She suddenly couldn't stand the aloneness anymore. The aloneness She had craved before Margret left was only empty now. Her lover had made Her empty. Was that true? Probably not. On impulse, she returned Carmen's call. At least someone, and such a delicious someone, wanted Her. Anytime, anywhere. Time was running out. Margret would be back home in, what, less than two weeks? She didn't want to look at the calendar.

She bathed carefully in preparation for Carmen. Concentrating on her, her responsiveness, made Her forget Mary for a while and made Her wish Margret wanted Her like that. Two weeks. Never mind, Saint Carmen of the Screams would be there soon. And she was. Deep kisses at the door for a very long time, bodies pressed tight, Carmen's ample breasts against Hers. She felt the relaxation and the tension that comes from letting go, happy to be with a woman, to feel each other.

Carmen was too perfect for words. If She moved Her hips against her, she sighed and responded. If She grabbed her ass and squeezed it, she leaned into Her. If She put Her thigh between her legs, she rode it eagerly. There seemed to be nothing She did that was not appreciated, nothing Carmen wanted done any differently to her body than what She did to her. But of course there were times when she wanted Her tongue out of her ear and so she would turn gently away, offer another part of herself. Her mouth, her breasts, she would offer with ease ... and soon it was her cunt she offered. Carmen pushed gently on Her shoulders, and She knew—fell to Her knees, and through Carmen's jeans heated her with hot breaths.

Carmen leaned against the door, hands pressing Her head down there with, "Yes."

She ran Her fingers over the zipper first, watched Carmen react. Then She found the button and loosened it, went back to her covered crotch with Her mouth. Carmen gave little cries. "Let's go," She said and stood up. Carmen fell against Her and they went entwined, as fast as they could, and fell on the bed. She wrestled down Carmen's jeans, left them knotted on one leg, and plunged into her.

Carmen exploded a sound when Her tongue drove straight inside of her, retreated, dove again. Over and over, with her cries, She entered her, took her with Her tongue. When Carmen started to come she reached for her clit to touch herself. When she did, She freed a hand and entered her ass. Carmen lifted her hips off the bed, screaming now, churning. She kept giving it to her after she had come two, maybe three times.

She pursued Carmen up on the bed as she tried to get away from feelings that were too intense until her head hit the wall. Then Carmen grabbed Her to push Her lips, Her tongue further inside. The last thrust was hard, deep, then a slow withdrawal and suck over her clit. Carmen whimpered a little, and then they were embracing, kissing with a softness unexplored before.

"Do you do this with everyone who just walks in the door?" Carmen was gentle, stroked Her face as she spoke.

"Only with cute ones," She said and made Carmen laugh.

"Yeah yeah yeah, you probably line them up."

"Never." She said it while She played Her tongue over Carmen's breasts.

They fucked only once more before Carmen fell asleep. It was good to see the girl so satisfied, so peaceful. But it left Her stuck with Her thoughts. Her lover, Margret, and Mary. How could She do it, even think of them with this lovely in Her bed? —their bed, really. She was crazy. You would have to be nuts somewhere along the way to not appreciate what was naked next to Her. Although it wasn't that She didn't appreciate Saint Carmen, She was simply starved for affection. She wanted Her own lover, Margret, to do this, to make love like this.

Why didn't they talk about it? But she thought they had, Her lover, with her logic of so grounded, so logical activism. And, after all, if a woman wasn't interested in sex—relationships change—so what? They shared a life: worries, bills, friends, all the mundane things that were the essence of life. That was what was so fucking deadening: living. It was true that their life was usually high-pressured. It was New York, crises abounded in just getting through the day. And of course She was most times preoccupied with it all: the city, her art, problems, money. But why should sex have to dissipate? Dyke drama. Goddamn dyke relationships. Too close, too intense, too loving. What happened to joyful, fun, weird sex?

She took Carmen's arm off Her breasts and placed it gently on the bed. Still asleep, she reached for Her but She moved away, threw on a shirt, adjusted a fan and sat down to have a cigarette with Her thoughts. She watched Carmen sleep and thought about sex with Margret. It had been fabulous, at first. The first two or three years, She couldn't remember. It was, what, five, really five years now? It pained Her to think about it. Why didn't Margret want Her anymore?

- Time Was So Short -
INVOLVED

Mary grabbed Her as soon as She walked in. On the couch immediately, they wrestled through clothes. Mary ravaged Her, hurt Her again. But she would not remove Her trendy denim coveralls nor go into the bedroom. She came with Her thigh pressed into her crotch and biting Her tongue. Then she sat up and flipped her hair.

"You're so special, darlin', you really are. I wish I could stay with you."

"What do you mean, I'm not spending the night?" She could not be cool enough to hide the hurt. "That's what you said on the phone—that I was."

"Well hon-ney, I just got to visit a very good friend of mine. They need me. I wish I could stay with you but I just can't."

And Mary launched into telling Her some long story that was unfollowable. After a few minutes, She didn't even bother to try. Pained, bewildered, feeling ripped-off, She didn't want to make a scene. She didn't want to act like a jerk, or like it even mattered.

She said something like, "Sure," and lit a joint.

Mary, offhand, reached for a toke. That was unusual for her and She noticed, noticed it but swallowed any comment.

"So when will I see you?" She said it like it didn't matter while She watched Mary get ready to leave. She watched her. Mary was dressing with concentration, attention to detail.

"Why as soon as I can, honey. Let's go. Walk with me."

She wished Mary wouldn't drape her arm over Her shoulders, possessively, routinely. It wasn't that She minded walking the streets that way, across Saint Marks to Second Avenue. She didn't care who noticed. It felt so good when she did it. This beautiful woman's arm laid over Her, easy and firm with such ownership. She wanted it now. But the problem was that She dreaded when it would be gone for good. She still wanted her, bruises and all. It wasn't the kinkiness, it was her. She craved Mary's consuming attention when it was focused on Her, and cringed from the awful dreary distance when it wasn't.

They crossed Second Avenue. Too soon the tattooed and pierced, cigarette and joint littered East Village would be behind them. But She didn't worry about that, leaving home turf. The problem was leaving Mary. And as soon as there was the thought, suddenly, just past the Gem Spa on St. Marks, Mary turned and kissed Her, lingering, fully on the lips.

"Bye honey. Call me. I want to see you again."

And she was gone. *Now what?* She should go home to work. There was a huge pile of prints She had to sort through. A whole spread for a magazine and She was going to blow the deadline if She didn't shape up. Her lover, Her Margret, back in a week and She was fucked up over another woman. Infatuated. Stomach-lurching smitten and doing nothing but smoking grass and drinking. Yes, and being crazy. She needed to talk to someone, a friend She could trust. Drop a quarter in the phone in the nearest *bodega* and hope she's home. Get off those depressing East Village streets. Everyone was too colorfully hip. Self-appointed vendors were selling old leather vests and combat boots on the sidewalks, students leaned against their portfolios while they talked at the public phone half-booths, everyone seemed on their way to something, and too many smiled in that benign stoned way that made Her feel She was missing out.

I must learn to allow things, to follow things. Accept. When I know what ought to be done I don't do what matters--except to do that, to learn I shouldn't push. It looks too hard. But I need to work, should work on my work.

The ratty corner *bodega* was playing WCBS oldies on the big silver boom box stuck on a shelf above the cigarettes. "Be My Baby" blared out at her and deepened her misery. *Somebody*, She thought, *be my baby*. Old songs were the worst. "96 Tears" came on—could it get any crueler? Luckily, Nance answered the phone. Salvation. She headed for her place leaving Dion singing "The Wanderer" behind Her. "... never settle down ..." *Oh shut up.*

She told it all to flame-haired Nance, pacing the floor, smoking. Nance looked bored, as usual.

"I know it's nuts. I don't really want her, Mary, for a relationship, I just *WANT* her, know what I mean? She's too fabulous."

"She's a blonde, right?" Nance yawned. "You're so fucking predictable."

"What? Come on—"

"You have a type when you cruise the bars and you're feeling sorry for yourself. Predictable."

"Thanks. You think I pick up blondes for revenge affairs? Sounds like male bullshit."

"Just bullshit," Nance said it between hits on yet another joint. "And you're nuts, period. What're you going to do?"

Who knew? That's what She wanted Nance to tell Her. She tried to explain the images, because that's what Mary was to Her. Mary was what she looked like—like every senseless stereotype of a desirable woman, a sexy woman, a prize. It was embarrassing, and Nance agreed with Her.

"Just stop it right now, asshole." Nance turned from where she was heading for her apartment's ancient window to sit on the fire escape outside. "Before Margret gets back, your lover, remember? It's only another week 'til she's home, right? Or what are you going to do, leave her?"

"Christ no, never. This is nothing, Mary's nothing. I just *WANT* her."

"You keep saying that. It's boring. And you better get rid of those hickeys and bruises and shit before next week. You look like you've been locked in an S&M basement. And liking it. Girl, look at you, you've really been bit."

She had to admit, mumble it, that all the marks were "uncomfortable."

Then She told Nance She wished her emotions could be as unruffled with Mary as they were with Saint Carmen of the Screams.

"Who?"

"Carmen. She's really cute and—"

"Eat shit and die! You've got two girls? You crazy bitch. I've got no sympathy for you. You've really flipped out this time. What about Margret? Stop it right now, asshole. She's coming home to you. What about her?"

Yes, what about Margret, Her lover? Her life was getting too complex for Margret to come home so soon after being away for so long. At least it seemed long to Her.

"Just forget about those other women. Or at least keep it in perspective," Nance said. "A couple of fucks, ok, but don't get involved, don't get crazed."

But She knew She was already over the edge. She hadn't had enough of Mary. Not enough of Mary telling Her she was "special, darlin'." And not enough of what Mary did to Her. She wondered if Mary fucked with everyone like she did with Her. How could she? What energy.

She left Nance feeling not much better and decided to go see "Before Stonewall" at The Public. As luck would have it, She ran into Teresa, a woman She had known for years from around the bars. After the movie Teresa asked if She wanted to hang out and smoke some killer grass. Why not? They drove to the piers and parked. The grass was excellent and Teresa was horny. She said her lover had just dumped her and she couldn't figure out why. Teresa was a tall thin woman, dark and handsome. After they laughed like mad over what flaw it might be in her, in whatever, or in everything, they started to make out. It was fun but that was all. It didn't go anywhere.

They laughed harder about not being into it. They hooted like only stoned freaks can, and enjoyed it. They liked what they were doing. Having fun. But it didn't help Her mood when Teresa dropped Her off at home and She was alone again.

I need to be alone. There are times of disconnection that take you—just take you away from yourself. You need them. I get back together when I am disconnected. Get out and get in. Stop this noise in my head. Get in.

She called Carmen. No answer. She called Mary. Her fucking answering machine was on. She was with a "friend," right? Maybe she would call Her later. She had checked Her machine as soon as She walked in and there were only assorted calls from friends—and the editor for the photographs She hadn't worked on. *Damnit.* If only She could stop Her mind, stop the restlessness. But why shouldn't She be restless? She was getting laid for the first time in maybe a year. There was a lot pent up. And Her lover, Margret, what was she doing about it? How could she stand it?

And She wished She had some coke. That would lift Her mood.

She took off all Her clothes in the heat, lay down on the bed and smoked another cigarette. Got up again, put on a cassette and laid down again. Another cigarette. Why didn't Mary fucking call? She lay like that, thinking bizarre darknesses and weird goings on exaggerated by the long throb of the tape. It was Burning Spear's "Resistance" album.

He was wailing about the "Queen of the mountain" and getting married sometime. God, how She loved the sound but ignored the words.

Where were Her politics? Politics? She didn't care about any of the Jah stuff the Rasta men were into, but She loved their reggae sound—never mind that God stuff. She knew Rasta men thought women were only good for sex and singing backup. Didn't matter. She couldn't resist the beat. The politico-correctos would require an explanation for it. That's what those friends of Margret would want, a justification for love that was off their restricted charts. They were so "correct" and so fucking disconnected. They didn't know how to live—most of them—meaningful, emotional lives, so they hid behind rhetoric and dogma. Actions, marches, political stuff, and always in a group—but not for sex. They were always together for some freezing fucking march. Or, if they did fuck, it was such fucking superficial fucking. At least that's what it seemed like to Her—so judgmental lately. Those girls didn't do drugs, it seemed to Her, or hang all over each other, feeling up each other, or have to hid cute bites and such. But those were Her mean thoughts, never to be voiced. Thinking of Mary on Her, and on and on and on Her, made Her stomach twinge. Exquisitely.

She toyed with the hairs of Her crotch, feeling them, pulling at them. It amazed Her how sore She was, still sore after being with Mary. The entire area of Her abdomen, thighs, hips and that layer of flesh under the pubic hair showed various yellow and blue bruises. All of it was tender, sensitive. Still She might have played with Herself had She not been so rubbed and nipped raw. Her own lightest touch burned.

Why didn't Mary call? She had to have her again. And only a week now. One lousy week to stock up on some kind of weird attention, attraction, validation.

A cool breeze for the first time all day. And I notice I am tan. The clouds are mackerel scales, but puffier. A jet has a silver-icy belly and looks unreal. A reflection moving against the current of scales.

It's something I had a word for a minute ago but now it's gone. My fire escape, piece of civilization.

I worked a little but well today. It's scary. Solitude is the only answer. The only one. You can't do it with other vibrations around. Maybe later. Maybe sometime when it's easier, if that will ever be, ever can be.

Suddenly a cloud cover moves in and the wind picks up.

Solitude. You need to be by yourself—for days and weeks. It's been four, almost four and a half weeks. I'm just settling down. Almost five weeks and just beginning to settle. I need more time. Oh god I need more time.

I should plan what I can do when Margret gets back. She'll want to be alone too. Probably here—in my space, our space. Where should I go? Where can I?

Being alone you have time. That's what's so good, for everything it seems. At least a day like this.

Sunday, up at seven, out on a little run to the Gem Spa for a Times *at seven-thirty. Out on the fire escape by eight-thirty with coffee. Working on my photographs by eleven. Finish a draft layout. Clean the kitchen, straighten up, vacuum. Eat a little, clean up. Work on the collection of pictures to say something, mean something ...*

- Tick Fucking Tock -
CRAZED

"Honey, you're so tight. Somebody ain't been loving you right."

Mary had been right, was right. It mortified Her. *Why not, goddamnit?* Why no "right loving"? Why the fuck not?

Other women wanted Her. She had been fucking Carmen regularly and loving it. No complications except for some with Carmen's lover evidently having wanderlust as well, and Carmen getting upset about it. So she was pulling back a little on meeting Her to protect her own relationship. Again dyke drama, games, needs, fears. It didn't bother Her because She couldn't offer saintly Carmen a so-called relationship. They had talked about it, neither wanted to lose her own lover. It barely tainted their innocence and exuberance in bed.

But Mary, Mary was meeting Her only in restaurants and bars now. Holding Her hand openly, suddenly leaning across a table to kiss Her full, hard on the mouth. She was ecstatic to be with Her. But never to fuck. Always an excuse. After all, she had a lover too.

"Honey, we can't get too serious now."

Who wanted to get serious? Just fucked.

But it was serious for Her because She was uncontrollably under Mary's control, trapped in a push-pull spell. Just like in experimental psychology classes She had taken, the strongest influence on behavior for rats is random, intermittent reinforcement. The rat, or crazed dyke, never knows when she's going to get rewarded so she keeps doing, or trying to figure out, whatever behavior it was that earned her the reward in the first place. But the "whatever it was" kept changing.

Fucking rat in a cage was what She felt like. With what reward exactly? Mary? Her lover, Margret? It made Her wish she had a lover like Alice again, a very carnal nurse. Alice had been into toys, devices, equipment to use in bed. Christ, she had been fun. And loving. That was some years ago—what, 1979 or 1981?—and both of them had lovers at the time, same pattern as now. Was it Her, or the women She chose to run around with?—or who were receptive to it? They had "primaries" neither of them wanted to lose.

They would meet in the afternoons when Alice finished her shift at the VA Hospital on the East Side at three, or she would leave early because she was a unit supervisor. They would talk on the phone during the day, tantalizing each other in code, not trusting VA operators. She would be in the darkroom and know that Alice was sitting in a glass-enclosed office, the big nurse on the ward. But because she was a psychiatric nurse she didn't wear a uniform, and that disappointed Her. She had always wanted to seduce Alice in starched nurse's garb—more male bullshit, but titillating because it shouldn't be. And the politico-correctos can go shit themselves with that one.

Those were excellent days. They would have undressing races, and Alice always won. She could never get Her stylish cowboy boots and tight jeans off faster and Alice would lie back waiting, taunting Her. It meant that she got fucked first. A full woman—just enough— Alice liked revealing her body, and She liked being buoyed on it. Alice loved being fucked whole hand and could take Her inside, crying out every time like it was the first time. Sometimes She could slip in past Her knuckles when Alice was really relaxed, really hot. And Alice went crazy; so did She. They would fuck for hours every time they met. It would start most times with the fist fucking, actual or attempted, then progress to Alice going down on Her and then to the toys.

Alice liked the double-headed dildo, loved feeling filled up. She would fuck her long and slow with it, working it by hand. It was such a turn on just to see her respond. Most times She came just by fucking Alice like that. Other times Alice would want her on the other end of the thing, and that was good too. She had to use her inner muscles to clamp down on it to push it into Alice, pull it out. It was hot, very free and very affectionate.

She missed Alice. They had simply grown apart. Schedules changed. And there were always those primary lovers each of them had. Primary relationships. What the fuck was She doing in yet another one?

Why didn't Mary call? Why wouldn't she fuck Her anymore? Maybe just a bad week. And Margret, would be back in two days now. Two days! Two fucking days. Two days and no one to fuck. She had to get out, get to the bars. There must be someone who would have Her, take Her. She wanted to be taken. She didn't want to act, She only wanted to be fucked. Like Mary did it, someone who would take over for a change. Her own Margret rarely acted independently when she had, or did, or would fuck Her at all. Now She wanted to be the recipient, the real recipient.

She called Mary. Sam, Her good friend, had given Her passes to the VIP room at the Palladium where there was always shared coke in the bathrooms. Then they could move on to The Saint and the Paradise Garage where She was one of the few women to have a membership card.

But, "Sorry honey, there's ..." some story that Mary gave Her, sweetly and polysyllabically told, but a story. She could not stand to hear it. So She went alone to the Palladium. Sam would be there anyway, and maybe even Nance. No one ignored VIP room passes. Not Her, not tonight. Only two days before all this had to end.

Mary, maybe She would call her again from the clubs. And maybe she would invite Her over later to spend the night. She wanted her so badly She burned, way down in the pit of Her. And only two days before her lover returned. Return of celibacy.

- Making Last Seconds, Last -
CINDY

The flashy, loud, crowded, three-story dance floor, exclusive private rooms, fabulous Palladium on East 14th Street was disheartening. Enough straight people, decent number of gay boys and only a few girlies—mostly in couples. The strobe lights and black lights in the corridors downstairs weren't as pulsating tonight, it seemed. She went up to the quieter, darker and more discreetly packed VIP room and started drinking Jack Daniels to work into an even fouler mood. Mary, the fuck. Margret, the no-fuck, fuck. To get them off Her mind would be worth a fortune. Although it turned out not to be a fortune but the price of a dime bag of coke. Johnny, an acquaintance, one of the nice gay boys She knew from just around was more than willing to share some snorts. But She wanted Her own. They did it in a stall in a bathroom, mostly unisex because no one cared. They snorted up from his supply and he generously insisted that She save Hers. Well, at least somebody thought She was worth having as a friend. Or maybe it was because he gushed over the white leather Vanson motorcycle jacket She wore, the one She got at Trash and Vaudeville, the hippest place for clothes on St. Marks Place, just off Third Avenue. Or maybe it was because she was wearing so little under it. Christ, what a mood She was in.

I am numb today. Haven't worked in too long, not on my pictures, pictures that mean something. The stupid wonderful clubs I hang out in make me sick. The openings I go to, a lot of women artists—who are these people? Strange people to me. Successful people. They swarm in my dreams, no, in my nightmares. They are my nightmares.

I've been doing a lot of coke, some bad coke from the street. It felt like there was a cold poker shoved up between my eyes. Icy searing in the middle of my forehead. Walking lobotomy. And the bouncers at the club were selecting people to go into the private room. I stared at the guy and walked right in while everyone handed in their little special cards. No mood to be messed with. I ambled through the crush and settled at the bar, standing near an attractive bare back. She talked to me instantly. I wish she hadn't. So much better to see than to hear.

I lit a joint and decided to make a stand. A young man in a leather jacket with the word SEX painted in white on the back came over and said hi. One missing tooth.

Buy me a drink, he said. Big smile.

No.

Let me have some of that, he meant the joint. So I stubbed it out, put it back in my cigarette pack.

He couldn't believe it. I saw him later on another floor and he made lewd gestures at me. He didn't know I was too needy to give, wouldn't be forced. I saw him telling his friends. I felt cursed by him. Boy with a line, a smile. Not enough.

It made me sick. The whole place, the contacts that wanted making. And I saw people who needed to see me, there, in the trendy Palladium at the moment. Who cares. I can't stand it anymore. I need to be heard. What for, I don't know. I need to be heard. To tell stories. Who cares? I do, more and more. But I don't know why.

The next night is an opening, and after that is another. I'm already angry.

I sit on the D train going uptown. I just saw Maximillian, a kind of friend who's a performance artist of mostly silent encounters, and he said I looked great, but down. That's it. Great but down. Why should I be so down? Because I'm a failure.

Keep saying the fears and they'll go away. Like hell.

But with Johnny, getting a drop off the coke, She suddenly felt like dancing. He and two other boys went with Her and blew away the dance floor. Nina Hagen was there performing that night with her signature "*African Reggae.*" It was electric. On another night when

Hagen wasn't there, She remembered how the DJ had stretched out playing her wailing tough plea, though, wanting to go to *Africaaaa*. He extended it forever, like it would never end. She had danced and *whooped* to it like there was no tomorrow—or, that was Her hope. And a couple of cuties started dancing with them and were not a couple from the vibe She got from them. One of them, tall, light and lean danced near Her, sexy. They teased each other, bumped hips together, eye contact, and then they grinded away to be with the boys and yell *Rastfariiiii* with Nina Hagen. Bad politics. She didn't care. She loved her reggae, although She did make a point to never back down to a Rasta man whenever they pulled their superior sexist shit.

Right then, She didn't care. The new girl from the non-couple was pretty cool, interested in Her, and that was all She needed. They danced a few more cuts alone then went together, the woman's arm around Her waist, off the floor.

Her name was Cindy but She thought it was too cutesy for her. She had a more regal posture than a Cindy. And that wasn't the only misfit: her voice was nasal and heavy with a Staten Island flat, punctuated accent that She associated with the bar types who came into the city only on weekends with their cars, were very married to their lovers and had little houses in the suburbs. Cindy drove Her home and accepted Her invitation to come up. But when it came to it, She couldn't do it, and neither could Cindy it seemed even with her wife away on some business trip. They drank and talked for an hour, Cindy edged closer on the couch. The girl did want it after all, She decided, but was out of practice in pick-ups. That was exactly what She didn't want, didn't need. If Cindy were so damn butch let her do it, take Her. She waited. After one more Staten Island story and no lip action, She got up and said She was tired. Cindy was surprised, started scrambling to find her shoes, and apologizing.

"Well, I guess ..." she kept saying without ever finishing.

At the door they finally stopped and stared at each other. She reached up and touched Cindy's cheek in goodbye. In return, Cindy bent to kiss Her. The touching of lips was a miracle, a revolution. Accent, life-style, Cindy's too popular model American car, none of it mattered anymore. She had been too judgmental. Those trappings, bad taste or not, didn't matter. Not for one night. The girl could kiss.

When she started to caress Her, though, rubbed Her breasts, it took Her out of Her dream. She didn't want this woman, never mind the wetness seeping out of Her. "No," She told her and, "goodnight." Cindy was hurt, angry. But better now than later. Suddenly She couldn't lie to her, to Herself. She closed the door behind her, and then She started to cry.

Where was she, Her lover, Her Margret? Where was her head? Why wouldn't she love Her, love Her body? She looked great, could get other women. She had proved that. She had been forced to prove Herself—and being forced into that proof helped the guilt. But not completely. Through Her tears She found the scraps of paper with all the girls' phone numbers and tore them up. But She knew them, all of them, by heart—well, She knew the important ones anyway.

She cried and thought about the people who used to fight over Her. It was when She had been fucking—at the same time—Ann, Paula, Carla and because it was so many years ago, Justin as well. He was a painter who was a wild, dedicated, single-minded artist and druggie. He was still a friend now. But he had been the last man eight years ago, maybe nine or ten. Out of all of them She had finally chosen to be with, Carla, an intense, vibrant dancer focused on her career, her art. Sex was had always been good for them. But now it made Her cry harder to think of how She left her, left her for Margret. Left her to be alone, but left her for Margret really. She hated that responsibility, the onus of having left Carla. But She was always the one to leave any relationship. Some sense told Her when to get going, an early warning system. It kept Her protected.

She didn't feel the system was working now because She didn't feel like leaving Margret. She only wanted steamy sex, excitement, or maybe it was adoration. *What's wrong with that?* Things were too hard all around to also have to feel worthless at home, in bed. That was the worst.

"No," Margret would say. "It isn't like that. We share so much. Don't make a big deal."

And She would grumble, "Ok, ok."

It's so good, so alone. Why do I fight it? Alone without feeling I'm judged—it's easier.

I'm in love with one, have a case for the other. "Tonight You're Mine Completely ..." is an oldie track. I've had that. Should be happy with it. Memories, more than that. Experience, part of my soul. Is that what it is? Part of my soul, all our souls. That's why the fucking media is so potent, it becomes part of our souls if we let it.

I want to say something with the photographs. To talk about my life. Is that so important?

I'm so fortunate. Get so depressed. Margret says, why are you depressed, you're not getting shot at. Yes. But it's all relative to where one is, isn't it? Bullets or bullshit?

Night comes. Slowly. Pink in the sky, and the blues. The blues. In love with one and, without censoring, in love with the other too. Feel so needy. Give so much, to the people who trust me. Feel so responsible. Where do I get it back? Where do I, how do I? Will it ever be enough?

I've been alone, am alone. Give myself pleasure alone. Don't have to wait.

She couldn't stop crying. Not until She told Herself to *fuck this*. Coke time. And she dressed and headed for East Village haunts. Buy another dime and do it all. Buy a dime and hope it doesn't take too long.

Find Constance Never Connie and she'll do it, she'll know where to get some dope fast. But she'll want to share it. Maybe that would be better. And it was.

Constance Never Connie was in her street-mama mood and *yo-baby*'ed her way along to Avenue C. Tall, screaming-head of blue hair, long legs ending in big black Minnie Mouse shoes, she rap-talked about digging girlfriends when she had the *girl* dope—cocaine. And what about some *boy*—heroin?

"Mama, you want some boy too? All right!"

Another dime, a little *girl* and a little *boy* dope. Very all right. And Constance Never Connie copped for them while She waited on the corner, looking as normal as She could as the police cruised by.

"We cool, girl."

Constance Never Connie said it without breaking stride heading back to the rock and roll record shop where she worked on Avenue A. Where girlies hung out. Where, in the small dark back room where Constance lived, they snorted up the *girl*, then some *boy*. Cocaine and heroin, but She always got the terms confused no matter how many times She snorted each of them. Who cared? Forward and backward in whatever order didn't matter. It was all the best. And the dish, the dish flew among them—the girls in Her club of the mind who hung out together in Alphabet City on the Lower East Side. There was Constance Never Connie, Nance, who liked her snort and a good time, and little Deb, who always wore leather and never said much but who idolized Constance Never Connie, trying to get her into bed. But she only played with Deb, teased her.

"You wouldn't believe the tits on that Flo girl," Constance Never Connie laughed it out. "The kind you don't know what the hell to do with. Move them out the way! Know what I mean?"

"Give it a rest, CNC," Nance said between snorts, feeling sorry for little Deb.

And Constance Never Connie laughed her bitchy laugh and turned the attention to Her instead. They started poking Her about what She might be doing while Margret was still away, but She denied it. Only Nance knew and she would never tell. But even Nance joined in, ragged on Her without spilling Her story, just to give Her a hard time.

"I know you, asshole, what you get into when you run around alone," Nance said.

"No way," She lied.

Everyone laughed at Her. Raucous.

"You got to be messing with somebody, cheater. Slip us the dish."

"Shut up," She pretended to joke back.

But it made Her feel lousy, and She shot a look at Nance. Constance Never Connie picked up on it instantly.

"Something's up," she started demanding. "Who you seeing?"

"No one."

"Yeah right, liar."

"Shut up and pass the stuff." She said it to deflect Constance Never Connie.

"No way, girl. And you," Constance flicked her cigarette ash at Nance. "You know something. I know you know."

"You're high."

"And?"

"You're holding up the lines," Nance said and everyone cracked up.

"Bitch," Constance passed the mirror with the rows of white and yellowish powder. "Girl on the left, boy on the right."

"About time."

"And I still don't believe that shit. You doing something."

"Yeah. Doing some lines."

And they giggled at Her coolness, passed around the mirror, snorted. The lies that were obvious to everyone were forgotten behind the rush of drugs, the good time and raspy arguments over who took bigger lines. A little *girl* and a little *boy.* Coke and heroin. Forward and backward. And She thanked the universe for the diversion from Her friends' questions, and from everything.

"Whose is that?" Constance Never Connie pointed at a line.

"Not yours," Nance laughed, not at all funny.

"Come on. Split it."

"Fuck that!"

So Constance Never Connie and Nance fought over the last line. Little Deb quietly pulled another bag from somewhere in her leathers and tossed it to them. And all remained right with the world.

"How many lovers you had at one time?" Constance threw it out to everyone.

"Two," Nance said.

"One," from little Deb.

"And you?"

"What?"

"What, what? Come on." Constance wasn't letting go.

"Me? Ok, so four, a long time ago," She said. "Happy?"

"Not as much as you were."

And in the laughter their little world was brighter. Later they all would be on the semi-nod—that not quite true junkie head drop to the chest—but no nodding now, and it emboldened Her.

"Funny," She said. "I was just thinking about them tonight."

She told them, being high, about having Ann as a lover and Justin at the same time. She told them Ann was a little out-there, could be morose and possessive—not horrible, but it made for a better story. Six months with her and seeing, but not with any meaning, Justin at the same time. And it was only now and then. And that was in the early 1970s, long before the whispers of AIDS.

"Then I met Paula at a party," She said. "And I was getting tired of being on Ann's leash anyway."

"Some people like that," Deb murmured.

Everyone rolled a look at Deb, but She didn't skip a beat in telling them how Ann would sulk for two days over a woman who had paid attention to Her in a bar, or wouldn't speak for an evening if She were a half-hour late for a date. That was when she started Her affair with Paula. Paula was very ready and very hot.

"The first date I had with her we sat around and talked in her apartment, uh, more like a closet."

"Like they aren't around here?" Nance growled it.

"Hers was worse. Avenue D. Anyway, we were just smoking, drinking and suddenly she blurts out, 'Well is this all we're going to do?'"

"Damn, you are so lame!"

"You weren't there, CNC. I jumped her and we fucked 'til we had sheet burn on our asses and knees. And she was a talker, you know, like giving instructions while I fucked her."

"Eeew."

"No man, she did it with such, like, passion it was great. Like porn, I don't know ... great."

"I hate you," Nance said it slowly, lit a cigarette.

So nothing stopped Her now that She was in coked-up story telling rabid mode, flinging Her words. She went on, telling them about how She was still seeing the suspicious Ann, staying with her in her penthouse—which made Nance throw a lit cigarette at Her. But She kept on telling them about it. How Ann fucked with slow, thorough neediness. She peppered Her dry-mouth rapid-fire story with snippets of being with Justin in between.

"Then I went to Montauk alone to get away from it all. That's where I met Carla. She was something. Wouldn't go to bed until the third time we saw each other."

"A record for you, bitch," Nance yawned it out.

But She wasn't telling them all of it. How with Carla it was a quiet, deep lovemaking. Serious, although Carla did like a little light bondage. After a week of lust, she demanded fidelity from Her. But She hadn't been sure if She was ready for that and headed back to the city to find out. Ann was morose, and only wanted Her in bed and patiently waiting for her when she came home from her some kind of big deal stockbroker job. Paula was more passionate, and Carla kept up an intense long distance romance with Her. They masturbated together on the phone. Carla talking, urging, asking how it felt from the other end of the line. And She could do it that way. She came, listening, doing it to Herself and knowing, hearing, feeling that Carla was doing it to herself at the same time.

She had been neither confused by it all nor frightened, not even worried. Everyone got what they wanted form Her when She was with each of them. But one day Paula was anxious, said she had something important to tell Her.

"It's about Ann," Paula had said.

And She knew that Paula knew Ann was Her lover because of that party where they met her. But Ann didn't know about Her having Paula on the side.

So She tried to act calm, "Ok what?"

And Paula had nervously told Her, "Don't get angry."

Then she said that she had been fucking Ann while She was in Montauk "and after." And she said she would stop, and that she was "sorry."

"Cold!" Constance Never Connie shouted.

"You got what you asked for," Nance shot at Her.

"Fuck that. It hurt," She said.

She tried to explain through Her friends' critiques. She told them that "Sorry" wasn't enough coming from Paula. Sorry, but why? Why do it? Knowing their involvement, why fuck with Ann, Her lover, of all people?

"Because," Paula had told Her. "Because of how you're always strutting around with her it made me feel like I don't mean enough to you."

She said she had wanted to "get to" Her to get back at Her, but now she was "sorry." It was only a euphemism for hurting Her. Paula had kept saying she was sorry and that she only wanted Her, badly.

"Shit. What'd you do?" Constance Never Connie coughed it out, high pitched from the attempt to hold in a toke.

"I never touched either one of them again."

That was when Ann tried to kill herself, but She didn't say that now. Only Nance knew. Ann survived a very heavy bottle of sleeping pills that nearly left her in a permanent coma. She still remembered seeing her on a breathing machine when She went to sit by her at St. Vincent's. But Ann recovered and continued the affair with Paula for years afterward. In the wake of all that, She had let Carla move in with Her. Carla brought the iron discipline of her dance and her expertise in setting up housekeeping. She did everything from shopping to stocking the fridge to nicely diversified and appreciative sex. A good wife with a serious art. It lasted years.

"You cold bitch," Constance Never Connie said. "You left Paula because she cheated on you but sounds like she was the one who really wanted you, risked for it. So who did you fuck while you were with wifey Carla?"

It was a good thing the coke spiked Her mood and the smack laid Her back, because sometimes Constance was too hip for anyone's good. She at first wanted to slug her but was too high and mellow for any strenuous action—hell, for pretty much any movement at all.

"Only a few."

"Yeah right, only every blonde She could get Her hands on."

Nance made the joke to break the darkness. It worked. Everyone laughed and remembered the various bright-hairs, natural or not, they had seen Her with.

"I remember," Constance said. "I saw two, and a brunette once. No, wait, three brunettes! What happened there? But shit, you had something like five other lovers in like six years. That's cold, girl."

Constance threw a lit match at Her in fun, but not really. And she had to throw one more invisible, verbal jab at Her.

"I could never do that," Constance said, too quietly.

"But they were only affairs," She said. "I never left Carla for any of them.

"Yeah right. Not except for Margret, the fourth darky—ok, red— then you dumped her," Nance said, quietly, too.

"No. I wanted to be alone for a while was all. To work."

"Bullshit."

Constance jumped up and yanked open a drawer there in the cluttered back room that was their clubhouse, and her home. She rummaged and pulled out another bag of dope.

"True confessions get a little reward—for us who got to listen— not you, bitch girl."

So they snorted up, put on lipstick and went to the after-hours clubs. They got higher on more of everything and fuck confessions, true or not. And She decided not to think about Her life again for at least another year if She could help it.

There was that one-night stand a while ago. Don't remember her name. I laid back, took. I took very well, very hard. She never knew the gift she had—maybe a little. She was too stupid, very good in bed, though.

Where are they now, those who need to give? Because I sure need to take.

- Times's Up! -
HOMECOMING

"Exhausted. *Merde*, I'm so tired." Margret kept saying it when they got back from LaGuardia. She didn't mention the roses stuck into jars meant to be immediately seen and appreciated on the low square coffee table, cleaned of Her usual mess of books, papers and just stuff.

And Margret took only a few steps to look into the studio, but She gently prodded her along to the darkroom. There was Her work, there—at least one piece. But Margret's exquisite fingers did not pick up Her vivid welcome home print, a black and white photograph of two woman seen from behind at the end of the Christopher Street pier, staring into a sunset across the Hudson. She had painted their hands in a delicate fuchsia wash—they were almost, almost touching and were outlined by the crimson sunset She had brushed in ahead of them. It was good. Ok, so She had painted it for Margret in a rush in the darkroom at the last minute that morning. Still, it was an offering. She tried to kiss her welcome home.

Margret's lips turned aside. Slowly then, slowly, she allowed Her's to find them. No tongue. An embrace. No more.

"Sit down."

Margret said it as her willowy arms were already disengaging. No hand holding on the couch—the fabulous jacket was moved aside. But She put Her arms around Margret, pulled her close. And yes, then Margret relaxed against Her, one elegant hand resting lightly on Her neck. It was chaste, but it enflamed Her with the image of her friend Sam's Genthe photograph come to life. The feel of Millay shown there, that smartness and rarefied world that was here for Her now. She tried to kiss Margret, sought her lips, but Margret laughed and nestled delicately against Her neck.

"I just walked in."

"That never mattered before."

"Not now. There's time."

But there never was time. Margret let what looked like a brand new, custom fit, diagonal-cut, seamlessly draped, python-skin, long jacket slide from her arms and onto the funky couch. Everything was so smooth and elegant—the movements, the jacket taken off and then hung up. Margret, slender fingers already reaching for the stack of mail, wanting to talk. What had She been doing for six weeks?

"You finished the photographs for the *Shutter* layout, I'm sure. Can't wait to see them. Just give me time to breathe…then, then I can't wait. I'm just too exhausted now to really look."

"Ok."

Fucking ok? She wanted to tell her She had been fucking Her brains out. Women wanted Her, other women. So what the fuck was the matter with Margret? She tried again. Went behind her, kissed her neck while she looked at the mail. No response. She tongued her ear lightly.

"Don't."

Margret said it gently, but she ducked her head, pulled away. She smiled with an indulgent kind of look. Or tender exasperation.

"Tell me what you've been doing. Sit here and stop that." She said it like a mother.

Don't start a fight. Swallow the hurt, the want. Swallow the anger. Margret just got home so She shouldn't push. Margret hated feeling pushed. But what about a request, gentle and sexy?

"Hey, come on, babe … ?"

"Really," Margret said, sounding final.

She heard what it meant, the "really" that was more than that. It wasn't a word but a tone that communicated so much more.

"What's the matter?" Margret said it like a sigh. "That's not necessary now."

"Ok."

"Ok."

"Jesus fucking Christ, aren't you happy to see me?" She had to explode. "Don't you want to see me?"

"Really," again the tone. "I just walked in, don't start. Please."

"You've been gone for six goddamn—"

"I got a show for you."

"What?"

"I wanted to surprise you. That gallery you heard about in Berlin, *Essen*. I went there when I was visiting my mother. She knew someone who knew someone. So I showed them all I had, the few photographs I have of your photographs. And … You're invited. You're in! But you have to send them more work, by next month. I thought you can send them what you've already done for *Shutter*, that you've just finished. See? Don't I love you?"

It left Her without words. Margret kissed Her sweetly, then, full on the mouth. Firm and intense, more than sexual, beyond that. Then Margret pushed Her away, playfully. She waved a handful of mail at Her, and she smiled, warm and deep at Her.

Without words, head spinning, She got up and left Margret to deal with weeks of mail. She managed to smile at her. A show. Berlin? She felt nauseous at the good news. No, worse, She felt like She couldn't breathe.

She went and turned on the TV in the bedroom, lit a joint. That seemed to alert Margret to Her mood, to something being wrong, and it brought her into the bedroom space. She thought She read these things in her because Margret came and curled up next to Her. She seemed to want to soothe feelings she knew she had hurt with her refusal right now. Still, She wondered if Margret was being real—or did she think Her reaction was overdone, a little silly? Didn't matter. Margret's softness made Her feel like She had been too demanding, shouldn't have asked—or even expected sex. After all, Margret got Her a gallery in Berlin! *Holy shit!* She was the one who was wrong. Margret loved Her. And Her feelings were wrong, again, not Margret's.

"Just relax. You're so tense."

Margret said it softly, and with the earnestness of true caring. But she got up from the bed. Clearly she was showing her love for Her, but not how She wanted it, not how She desperately needed it.

She should tell her, tell her about Her affairs, the women who wanted Her. Enough of the bullshit.

"Relax, why don't you? Don't get scared about the show. I'll help you," Margret said it like it was going to be easy and went back to the couch and her mail.

Go to hell. She wanted to say but didn't. It would start a fight. There would be nothing but Margret's logic after that, her talking. Nothing but talk. And She would end up being convinced Margret was right somehow. No sex. She was fucking other women out of need, primal shit, avoidance shit that She couldn't even see Herself, or admit—why say anything? *Fuck honesty.* She didn't want to hurt Margret, didn't want to lose her. She loved her. Margret frustrated the hell out of Her but She loved her so much that maybe she was right, maybe sex didn't matter.

Jesus fucking Christ, she takes care of me. She got me a show. She wanted, and She knew deep inside, that She wanted Margret forever. There was no one who compared. *So don't fight it. Don't fight.*

After putting her mail in various piles to deal with, Margret came back into the bed. She edged in next to Her and fell asleep in Her arms. Mind racing, fear building, She continued to smoke and think of the others. Mary the Southern belle made of steel, and Saint Carmen the responsive, the appreciative, the screamer. She wondered if She could keep seeing her, even with Margret in town, maybe even telling Margret. That would be something. She remembered how shocked She had been when an ex-therapist who became a friend told Her over lunch how she and her lover fucked other people. They did it regularly and would come home to trade stories about what the other women were like in bed. She had been shocked and a little scandalized, and the ex-therapist had laughed at Her.

"You really couldn't do that," she said to Her. And laughed. "Not surprising. You're not honest enough. You're willing to experiment with any street drug and anyone from junkies to judges. You like sex with strangers but you could never share your 'lover.' Too much honesty in it."

How She had hated that woman for being right. No, She could never do that. She knew Herself—half-assed as it was. But affairs were affairs, little things you kept private that didn't hurt a lover. But that openness? No. That would sully a purity She cherished with Margret. Those delicate hands ...

Margret embodied Her idea of clarity, a rareness, the exclusivity of genius—or was that just Her escape into the image of Millay and wishing She could create that, that piece that was for Her too frightening to even attempt? The thought of Margret—who was maybe Her own creation—with anyone else was excruciating. Any vibrant and swiftly squashed fantasy of it could torment Her.

A double standard—She could but Margret couldn't. Yes unfair, but not really. As long as She didn't know, as long as it was meaningless—a once or twice fuck—*that* maybe She could handle. Still, She didn't want to think about it.

Margret slept peacefully, delicately, against Her and snored not quite inaudibly, but gracefully. She was always embarrassed about that and denied it when She confronted Her with a tease and told her she snored, as if it were something she should control, something well-bred European-educated women did not do under any circumstances. But Margret did snore, even if it was as stylish as she was in every other way. Refined, even features, crystal skin and blue eyes, inflamed-hued hair and a firm body, beautiful legs. Hands, though, her hands were art. She was especially caught by Margret's fingers, always so graceful in movement or still. Paintings.

The first time they made love She kissed her fingers afterward. It had been good, not the greatest, but She had gotten off on bringing Margret out, her first time with a woman.

And Margret had whispered, "It was how I knew it would be."

So good. She couldn't get enough, didn't even want Her to leave the bed. And if they ever fought then, in the beginning, they could always fuck to make up. But not anymore, not for a year, or more than that. Anger, no, hurt cramped up Her stomach.

She wanted to wake Margret, shake her, tell her about the women, about the terror in Her being with them helped cover up. *Tell her. The truth?* Instead She moved stealthily from bed and went to the bathroom and cried. Then She played with Herself, leaning between the wall and the tub.

- The New Now -
WASTED

She tried to see Mary over the next few weeks, but the fucking was done. It finally dawned on Her that this must be the way the girl conducted all her affairs. A few fucks with a new woman, then back to her lover. That was all right but what was all that bullshit about being "special, darling.'" Just that, Southern belle-shit.

Just blow it off. Fucking blow it off. So unsatisfying. Not an artist. That's what it is, she's not an artist. No sensitivity. Is the other any better at it? I don't know. Don't care.

Why did I call her? Fucking bitch has my number. Yeah she's got my number all right. Keeps me strung along. Her lover's going out tonight, she'll call. Fucking bitch. Is anyone satisfying?

I need more, more than any human can give. More than any one woman. They should fucking wait on me. Just wait. And hand and foot, that too. Fuck them all. So I go out. Maybe she'll call. Who cares? I need someone special. Someone who knows me, who can care. Fuck it.

But Mary wouldn't have mattered so much if Margret had been different, if she wanted Her. She needed wanting.

Monday after a heavy but brief storm, the story of my affairs. Heavy and brief. At least that one, Mary. Pretty girl and used to it. No good, not for me. Now there's the sweet little one, Carmen. So sweet. And my Margret, the best. But the pretty girl is too much on my mind, too blonde from the beginning. I sit here in the silence and dripping rain and wish she'd call. That's the problem, the unfinished end with her. The bitch.

Carmen kept calling, even spoke to Margret on the phone once, asking for Her. But She didn't want to jeopardize the relationship with Margret, such as it was. So She said, "let's cool it" to the girl. And She settled in to try to make it better with Margret. Make it better. Life conspired to patterns, though, boredom and old ways of relating.

They got back to work. Margret reminded Her about the Berlin show she had negotiated for Her. But Margret didn't know how behind She was in deadlines for delivering Her prints, of course. Believing Her, that prints were already sent to *Shutters* magazine and She was getting Her work together for the show, Margret took up a temporary advisory position on a philanthropic board focused on public art. While she did, she wrote poetry and poured herself into activism with needle exchange programs, fighting anti-abortion groups, fighting anti-gay groups, fighting racist groups and generally getting involved to resist bad shit by fighting on the front lines to bring about good stuff for all by working with any intelligent lefty, super-progressive, ultra-egalitarian political action that came along, domestic or international.

Mauve thoughts on mauve paper. I found out that Carmen has taken another lover. Strange feeling. Why should it matter at all?

But I had the best offer in weeks, the most generous maybe. On a chance street encounter, Alan, who I knew from SoHo openings, tried to hit on me in clumsy male fashion, but nicely. He invited me for a joint and computer-played-on games, and to walk his neighbor's dogs. Irresistibly interesting. His factory loft just across the Manhattan Bridge in Brooklyn must have been 1830s vintage. Arched hallways and arched windows. Inside it was with dogs and cats with fleas not so bad— mostly it was with the sleekest, newest computer. Good dope, too.

Friday the thirteenth, weird day for sure. Saint Carmen of the new girlfriend—
is she just shaking me up?

So I sat by the fire at Alan's waiting for him to return from the local bodega
with dog food. A fire in a big stove at the hint of a temperature drop in the summer's
evening. Nuts. But I made it myself. Feels good and felt good. I provided for me.
Again.

The intimacy with Margret was as it had been, no fucking, and it
had never even happened for welcome home. Only cuddling, falling
asleep together. They could pop pimples on each other's backs, She
could trim their twat hairs in sleek, thick haircuts, and they shared
the focus on Her career and the increasing news over friends getting
sick with AIDS, still so fresh. All that, everything, but still they did
not fuck. When She tried, Margret would never kiss, and when She
moved on her she would never respond. She would work like crazy
trying to excite her. But no.

"Never mind me," Margret would say. "Take care of yourself, get
off. Didn't you do it yet?"

And then She would jump out of bed, hide that She was starting
to cry. Margret would ignore Her or embrace her later, even rock Her
to sleep.

"This isn't important," she would whisper. "We have so much
more."

More? Worries, especially for Herself, for the bills that were Hers
even though Margret paid for most everything. She didn't tell Margret
about an eviction that was looming over Her studio. Pretending
things were as usual She could depend that Margret would want Her
to work and not be upset by too many daily worries. Margret wanted
to invite people over to Her studio. If they did have a party, though,
all the arrangements were, as usual, Hers to make. If Margret had no
faux job to go to, or didn't want to, it was She who called in with an
excuse for her. If it was reversed and She wanted to stay in bed one
day Margret guilt-tripped Her. So She withdrew from her, regretted
the girls She let pass by, and believed this love would get better. That
She could make it better.

How the fuck? Most mornings being alone was all She wanted. The boredom, the asking if She were working enough for the Berlin show, criticism, the feeling of being valueless because she wouldn't fuck Her that oozed from Margret was always there. They had some good times, of course. There were the looks, the meeting of eyes heavy with warmth, a small smile. The easy brush of hands, the leaning into each other on the street—nothing telegraphed to others but they felt the sweetness of their touches, so subtle. The comfort, the security of being together. After all, they loved each other.

A friend with a loft just down the Bowery gave them his getaway house in Provincetown for a week. Truro, really. Nice guy.

"Get away, relax," he said.

He tactfully avoided commenting on their mismatched moods over dinner at a subterranean Bleecker Street spot. What he did do was insist, and so they went. They had a great time, relaxed. She wrote, She photographed, She drew pictures.

Drizzle morning, drew. Went and walked on the salt marsh. Saw a dead seal. Walked in the dense woods holding hands. Walked a lot.

Provincetown, Cape Cod Bay, low tide. Snails like a million black dots, black stones all over the sandy bottom. Snail trails, long shiny tracks in the damp sand.

Snails, a black scatterplot until there is water deep enough to hide them. Low tide. Men walk out to boats lying on their sides in the sand. Rake for clams, hear them.

The salt marshes, salt ponds, they smell sweet, fresh. Crabs rush into holes, they feel you coming.

Clumps of mussels cling to clumps of soggy sea-something plants.

And the million snails look like a million stones strewn by a fast stream, like mountain streams that cut a channel. But this is a small channel in the bed of a Cape Cod salt marsh. A big one, at Wellfleet.

At night some animal makes a loud shrieking sound that is like a child or a calf screeching for help deep in its throat.

But no sex, only closeness. No sex, still.

"Don't say that," Margret answered Her plea. "It's not 'only' being close. We have so much."

"But ..."

And when they returned to the city it was the same. Same friends, heavy work, heavy worries about it—Her art. The eviction was drawing nearer, and even if She told Margret it would be expected for Her to handle it Herself, or try to. Margret's money was her money, separate—although she gave to Her, supported Her really. Legal fees mounted and She handled them somehow, borrowing or shifting balances from credit card to credit card. She handled it with anxiety and sweat and Margret helped by talking, talking, figuring out, telling Her the "shoulds."

"You should handle it before the end of the week."

"Jesus, enough!"

"Don't get upset. You should stay calm, and ..."

Should. Always the "shoulds" for Her, nothing else. It made Her feel valueless, like nothing, like Margret was a keeper instead of a lover who lusted for Her.

She wondered if She could be alone, live alone. Ever. Not just live alone, as in assuming one knows how to live already—but She worried over if She could really *be* without the structure of another person: rising, washing, working, going to the movies. When She was alone She didn't know time, had no schedule She did not make Herself. No work that had a pattern imposed from outside. Only doing Her own work, photographing as She chose. The life of an artist, or a misfit. It frightened Her, and She craved it.

She lied to Margaret about the rent and about Her mounting bills. Her bills were getting insurmountable now—credit card charges for paints, print papers, chemicals, film, drugs, liquor ... Her debts became immortalized in envelopes She stacked unopened when they arrived. She laid books and magazines over them so the return addresses wouldn't stare at Her—those credit card logos, the austere bank fonts. She supposed She could get a real job to help pay them. But how? To do it, make Herself perform the motions, was as foreign sounding and feeling as packing a bag and moving to Paris. Use the fucking beloved American Express card and just go. She wished She could. But there was the career-boosting piece for the magazine She still had to finish. And the show! Margaret had set it up, like it was easy for her to give, it seemed, to make Her career. A lifetime's work finally given an imprimatur of acceptance by the art world's ruling body. Reviewers reviewed *real* gallery shows.

Her own show. The pain of that scrutiny, the opening of Her work to criticism, and of Her, too, began to have a vibrating effect on Her nerves, Her behavior. Not having sex didn't help. Like standing in front of speakers too loud and bass too high, throbbing in Her chest—like that. Her moods became jerky, pushed by the energy of psychic noise.

She had to work, and threw Herself into it. Yet the distractions of the big sickness that was growing all around Her. Acquaintances were starting to die, then friends. *What?* The growing terror took Her away from Her work. More clatter, compelling, conquering, maddening uproar just beginning. And Margret's voice.

"You are concentrated on your work for Berlin, aren't you? Don't get so involved in everything else, anything else. But after, you might get a job. You know, work from the show? Some sales? Something."

What? Get a job? No matter what Margret actually said, She only heard that. And Margret's volume was yet only on a low setting with her finely tuned sense of equality, anywhere she thought it should exist.

The first three months were hell. It took that long for Her to negotiate with the gallery in Berlin to wait for Her work, for the deadline date to be firmly set for the definitive collection of Her work. And that was when Her friend Sam—big photography collector with old WASP money, but Her friend who stunned Her, showed Her the image of Millay—that was when it started happening to him. AIDS, the thing no one knew enough about.

That was when She was still feeling guilty over Her affairs, and that was when Margret started to get angry and to show it. Angry at the way She led Her life, angry at all the responsibilities that fell to Margret, and angry that She wasn't paying Margret the kind of attention she wanted, like adoration and pampering maybe? Was it with good reason? Maybe Margret was right to be angry because

She was no prize in mood, money or companionship. Margret was Her support and, of course, cared deeply about Her crises. Yet she somehow did not respect their severity even though they affected her too. She didn't want to see the weakness they erupted in Her. Instead Margret wanted to see Her handle everything, see Her conquer—be tough, do Her work for god's sake. And suddenly over those three months it was not only the crises in Her life and the toll they took, but it was that weakness, the shrouding, sucking weakness—unlabeled— that She battled alone.

I don't feel like a failure anymore. I am one. I'm no good to anyone. My uncle died and here I am, not at the funeral, not with the family because I can't afford it. They'd pay the plane fare of course, but why can't I? I could never say, take five thousand dollars, Aunt Mary, to help take care of Uncle Bill; go on a trip, mom and dad, I'll pay. *Oh I said it, couldn't deliver.*

Fucking failure. Walk through raped SoHo and see it. The young clean ones who have made their careers already. The chubby scrubbed ones who are suddenly collectors of photographs that are more like snapshots. I'll never make it with my work. Who cares about the tints I paint on monochrome prints? Who cares that I want to make my photographs like sculptures of women together, to break the surface, layer it with transparent washes, thick coats of paint, parts of other prints to create textures. No, not a fucking collage—a movie. Impossible, what I see in my head to make real, visible.

Why do I bother? Submit shit and because that's what it is I'll get shit back.

I'm alone with stupid grief. My uncle who was so good to me. But my grief is for me. I cry for me. My failures.

"We never do anything anymore," Margret complained again. "You're always too tired. We should go out more."

"Yeah right. We don't do anything anymore, like fuck."

"That's not it." She was disparaging, condescending. She used the mother tone.

"It's not? Do you realize that I'll never approach you again, I'll never take the lead again just so I won't be rejected by you?"

And Margret would *huff* away, making her classic insulting gesture of dismissal. She evidently forgot the real threat that came from Her hurt. But it was no threat. She did stop approaching her, stopped trying to make love to her. She was not certain, though, that Margret even noticed.

"And how the hell are you taking care of yourself, getting off? How can you not?"

Margret never answered, turned away as if the question was crazy. And beneath her.

But She had to take care of Herself, release all the energy of all the hassles. Sometimes when Margret fell asleep turned toward the other side of the bed, She would play with Herself, get off. Many times She had to stop halfway because Margret would turn. Even that, even that she thwarted without replacing it. It was like watching television. If there were something She wanted to watch, get into or was into, Margret would start a harangue about how She was always watching "the tube" instead of talking to her. The truth was that after the pressures, the work for Her photographs in the magazine, dealing with lawyers and eviction, her Sam so sick with that goddamn enigmatic AIDS, after all that in a day She was a zombie. Just trying to figure out what he wanted to eat, what he could eat, sent Her down to Chinatown or up to the East side. Lychee? *That's what you want for breakfast, Sam?* If that was his whim, that's what She sought out. And when it wasn't exactly right, those lychees from Pell Street in Chinatown that were too fresh (not the canned fake ones he was used to), or when his taste had changed from one hour to the next She went back out. By cab or by subway She'd head for the fancy emporiums off Madison Avenue around 74th Street to get ginger that was individually wrapped and cost a fortune.

After stressed out days a little sex would have been nice. But since that was impossible, escape in TV was all She had. Margret would never let Her enjoy it. She would take the remote and flip channels. Or turn it off.

"Can't you just be with me? Talk to me?"

"Ok, ok."

And another desire, simple and unimportant, was trampled. But if She came home and Margret was watching something, well, then that was all right, inviolate. Just like sex, she would not enjoy it with Her, but if She played with Herself she would turn toward Her to interfere.

Interference. Noise in Her head and static from Margret. Margret who thought, who demanded that she was a help to Her. By nagging, lecturing and wanting Her to take time to live her life for her as well. Still, Margret did help. Her logic, her talking through problems with Her, helping Her keep Her head straight—it helped. But she tended to repeat herself, degenerate into lecturing Her instead of discussing anything.

"This is real closeness, like this, just living together, being," Margret would say. "But you have to calm down. I can't take it anymore."

She couldn't take it? That was funny when all the real responsibility was Hers.

"A relationship should be a base. A source of strength that gives you confidence to go out and be in the world."

Then why didn't she do it? Why wasn't Margret more independent? Why now when She had no time for helping her with her life, family issues, her poetry—why was she so demanding now? And with no sex. That was what She needed, sex, while Margret only wanted Her for the daily grind, the strength She had to fight for Herself every day. And She began to think it was Her weakness Margret was really angry about, not paying enough attention to her was only its symptom.

They did go out, though, when there was time and they weren't fighting. They had Nance and Kelly to deflect being alone together. Many times they went to the boys' club, The Paradise Garage on King Street. There was always drama. She did something stupid every time, worthy of being yelled at by Margret—who actually raised her well-bred voice.

"What do you mean you can't find them?"

Margret was loud in Her ear, leaning close without touching Her. They were stopped at the top of the club's truck ramp. Stoned, partying men jostled around them to get in the door. Uneven lines of more men, loud in high party mode or too high and in the glassy eyed zombie stage, were coming up behind them on the long ramp and were clumping up behind them.

"Find them, or try to get new ones," Margret, veins on her patrician neck suddenly too defined, couldn't stop. "It's a hundred feet, how could you lose them? Again! Look in your pockets! You know they're not going to let us in without passes. *Merde!*"

She punctuated her disgust with a dismissive gesture that She could read above the thumping beat of Grace Jones from inside. Margret had reprimanded Her right there in the line of stoned men waiting to get into the club. She tried to laugh it off, of course, pretending Margret was making a joke and only acting so angry. But it was obvious she was serious. The mother-tone in front of not only strangers but Nance and Kelly, Nance's, new cute girlfriend. They looked away, pretended they were very involved in taking together although no one could hear anything there with the music blaring.

She cursed out loud to Herself into the pounding loudness of the bass. Then She turned and threaded Her way through the ramp-ascending gay boys back down to the street door.

Fucking bitch. Fucking embarrassing bitch.

It was no problem to get another entry pass from the meaty guy at the door. He remembered Her, winked. That was nice, made Her feel better on Her way back up the ramp. When she got to the top the line had moved along and Margret was hysterical because they were about to go in. She always got crazy going into clubs or parties, scared probably, but what a pain in the ass nonetheless because she would never admit to it, then dump her irrational anger on Her instead.

Always so logical, Margret could figure all the angles, could help anyone see a totally new perspective on any issue, but not on herself. She was a coward about revealing herself but was so damn comfortable telling Her that She had to change. But She had to try to stop this, stop Herself—lately too judgmental.

"You're too emotional. You get so involved in everything, these crises that you make yourself."

"I make? And what makes your way the best? So I'm emotional, so what? At least I don't talk everything to death, I act. Talking is all you fucking do."

It was true. Margret was not a person of independent action, just independent means. She always tried to connect their different art pursuits together in spite of knowing that She liked and needed to work alone. Margret required the support of another person, always. Everything important she wanted done together, except for fucking.

There is quiet outside. Now a horn, and again. Motors and tires going by. Silence never lasts long enough. Not here. Maybe dying or in death, but probably not. I feel sure of that.

I wish I could die, I think it. Not that I want to be dead. I'm afraid of what exists in death. But the process of getting there without being there is comforting. It means simply not being here, not necessarily being anywhere else. That's anarchy. I don't know what I want but I know I goddamn don't want this.

How can I work without being alone? I'm here in bed, she is at the other end of the studio, working on her writings. But there are no barriers. I need to be alone. I need to listen to me more. I love her but it's distracting. I need to be alone. Big deal, if I just keep thinking it, will it happen? Like the portrait of Dorian Grey, be careful what you wish for. The cat might be listening.

Why did She love her? Margret was magnificent, majestic, rare, divine—and she was devoted to Her in her own restrained way. She was an incandescent presence, smart, caring, giving—and a bitch. Things were not good at home when She met Judy. Judy was the editor assigned to work with Her on the photographs for the big journal issue. Tall, sleek, ebony skin and hair, with strong, competent hands, full lips and the smallest wrinkle lines at the edges of brown eyes. Her manner and speech were slow and deliberate. Judy was as solid and substantial as Margaret was crystal filament brittle. Not at their first meeting, but at the second, Judy asked if She were attached to someone.

"Yes, but ..."

"I see."

Judy smiled, did not laugh. She smiled, maybe a bit embarrassed. Or was it disappointment?

They watched each other across the cluttered desk in her office, asking with their eyes, afraid to say it out loud. *Are you?* It was the unspoken question, the need to know. But they knew. Judy with her trendy butcher's jacket, tight black pants, cropped hair. She with her tight jeans and Margret's silk tee-shirt, braless, beneath and the oversized men's dress shirt unbuttoned down the front but belted at the waist. And one earring. They knew. They were suddenly shy, these obviously experienced women so drawn by that unfathomable just-out-of-range-of-admitting electricity in the air between them. The paralysis of words went through their heads.

Is she? Would She? Should I?

They cleared their throats and shifted their feet. They were both standing, waiting.

"Maybe we could have a drink when we finish here," Judy said.

"It's a date."

Then, damnit, She remembered the plans to have drinks with Marla, Margret's friend, a very boring poet. She would be in trouble if She didn't show up because Margret would be there.

"But, honest, I can't today. Sorry. Next time for sure?"

They would be working together for the next two months regularly. So much time, putting the first drink off was suddenly a nice tease.

"Next time."

Judy smiled full into her eyes then. And She felt that wetness ooze from Her, just enough, and She had to look away. *Months of this?* She would have gone to bed with Judy in two minutes for two years with another look like that one.

So She was late meeting Margret and her friend, but She was in a very good mood. Unfortunately, so was Margret, the kindest she had been in weeks. She guessed from their looks and the way they stopped talking when She arrived at the Mogador that they had been talking about Her. Maybe Marla was telling her to tone down her critical barb slinging. Certainly something was different. Margret was soft again, like when She was sure she loved Her and wasn't just a whip-cracker to turn Her into the artist who maybe Margret really wanted. So soft again. It warmed Her instantly, those blue eyes, those delicate fingers that just brushed over Her hand. She really loved this woman when she was like this. It all came back, visceral—no explaining it. And She felt guilty about Judy, Her Judy fantasies. So She ricocheted from the prospect of exciting salvation for Her lagging self-concept to the realization, the admission, that Judy could not be Her diversion now. Not with Margret like this—so damn dedicated to Her with a stinging love She could feel. Maybe there was going to be no diversion from girls for Her anymore, not with Margret like this—or maybe not like any possible way she could ever be. She loved her.

She pressed Her leg against hers under the table and Margret did not move away this time. All bitterness was forgotten. All Margret had to do was be soft and it brought back how good she was to Her, how devoted. She forgot the quarrels, the hurt, the need for other women. It crossed Her mind that She was a wuss, that She was fogged by the image She made of Margret rather than seeing the reality of her. Why did it take so little from her to get Her back into wimpy lover mode again? Was it only sex? Really sex? Was that really all She needed from Margret?

Her mind would not be still because She felt it in Her body. Maybe tonight they would actually do it. But Her head reined Her in. She would not make the first move, still. Not again.

- Sliding Back to The Old Now -
FIRST WOMEN

"We had a good time. It's enough."

It wasn't important to her. A good time over drinks was "enough" for Margret as she curled against Her, falling asleep. But She wanted her. Hot, desire and need, too hot. It had more to do with Her than with Margret lying against Her like that.

"Come on?"

She said it gently. There was silence—the unspoken "no" in response. Face turned away, softened by a little smile.

Only memories. Was the problem time, too much time together? Too much closeness, dyke closeness—goodbye sex? Truro, Provincetown had been great for them, relaxing walking with fingers hooked together. That was intimacy. Yes, and aloneness.

It's a lot of very small things, inconsequential by themselves, that keep you in existence. The importance of a notebook now, a lecture, a gallery, a trip, a "something" keeps you in the world. But it's nothing.

Small things, the heaviest weights. Nature is economical.

If we thought about it, how insignificant it all is, we'd end it. End us.

Whales, see them but lose them. Quick slippery things. Big and elusive until they suddenly leap from the water so near you could touch them. Breathtaking.

Whales very black, blacker than I thought they'd be when I saw that first one, its side so near in the water, black. Easy water.

Only memories. Was the problem that She was Margret's first woman lover? Should She show her more—more experimentation, more sex, maybe threesomes? How? Margret didn't want to try anymore. Never tried it, except for in the Caribbean, a little bit from behind—just a little. Only once, only a little way in, to make Margret tense and question.

"What are you doing?"

"Loving you ... just loving you."

Was it that, because She was the first woman? What about Her? She looked at Margret asleep, holding Her, and thought about Randi from years ago. Randi taught at the downtown Detroit ghetto university, Wayne State, when She was a student and "ghetto" was the condition that radicals sought out. It was the time of fighting for Civil Rights when it was unquestionably what had to be done. March, fight, be heard, protest the war in Vietnam, get arrested at sit-ins, join Students for a Democratic Society, support the Black Panthers and idolize Angela Davis and Flo Kennedy.

Flo Kennedy, a forgotten icon. She was only nineteen or twenty when She actually had breakfast with the famous Flo. What an honor. Black feminist lawyer and activist Florynce "Flo" Kennedy was a giant in the Women's Liberation and Black Power movements in the 1960s. She had breakfast with Flo Kennedy, gone with a California activist to meet her, in the Palmer House Hotel—was that its name? They were all staying at the hotel anyway for the New Politics Convention in the hot summer of Chicago in 1967. They met in the hotel's small, darkish breakfast room where there were probably only four other activists scattered around, waking up with coffee at nearby tables. Flo was loud and proud and bold in her cowboy hat and she was definitely letting it be known that she was not into the boasts of Her friend—a California white boy Cesar Chavez activist boyfriend (everyone was doing it). She had met him milling around the hippie-student-women's-black power-student group. They talked, shared a joint, planned revolution, and She moved into his hotel room. The next morning at breakfast, he was lifting his white boy shirt to show off the scars on his abdomen from police dogs in Selma.

"You can do that in your own neighborhood! We don't need you doing our thing!"

Poor guy, he had been so proud of his righteous scars—She felt sorry for him. In that exciting time of believing in change for the better when She was in school in Detroit, She remembered how impressed She had been with Randi, with her strength of character and her no bullshit attitude about art and everything, telling everyone whatever she thought. The attraction was intense. They would drink and talk. Randi was a young professor, but She was only a student And because of Her infatuation, nearly lost the job. Reeking of beer, of marijuana, they met whenever they could, given their class schedules, every day and throughout the day for whatever time they had. Nothing sexual then, at first, just the attraction. That unnamed and ungraspable wanting. Wanting.

Randi toyed with Her a little, hinted to Her she had a woman lover before. Leaving her hanging on the words and the mysteries behind what Randi wasn't saying. She was curious and ineffably covetous, wanting. Wanting a woman for that forbidden secret knowledge. But Robert was there, the guy She was fucking. He was cool, an SDS activist into firebombing police cars and living '60s radicalism to the fullest by doing acid and every drug that came around. He was not a very good fuck, but he tried. He was a good guy.

Robert. She had not thought of him in years either. Twenty years? How many had there been, women and men, for Her? She had made a list before, like everyone does at some point—usually adolescence— She made a list of who She had fucked in Her life. Twenty-five women and thirty-three men, up to that time. Women were more difficult to get into bed. Twenty-five women. Why didn't Margret want Her? Randi, She remembered, could be cold like Margret. Was it the challenge that attracted Her to this kind of woman? She had chased after Randi without knowing quite what She was going after, but She did it. And Robert knew, at least suspected. He gave Her the keys to his apartment because Randi wasn't feeling well one day and She wanted to take her there, the most nearby place, so she could rest before she had to teach another class that afternoon.

They hadn't been there more than ten minutes before Randi pulled Her down. Fully clothed, sweating, She came in seconds. Feeling her, a woman with that incomparable softness for the first time, exploded in Her mind and body. Randi wanted to touch Her, take off Her clothes. But She was petrified with too much trembling need, had to be coaxed. And when Randi put her hand on Her cunt through her soaked underwear and She felt the heat, the throbbing, then when She was about to come again from the ecstasy of that feeling, that was when Robert walked in.

There was no scene. He apologized, went into the other room. Randi left. Robert, of course, wanted to fuck. Guilty, confused, She tried to do it for him. But She ended up in tears. It was so false, so stupid. She couldn't prove anything to him, but he didn't mind. No, he didn't mind. He was excited by it, the fucker.

But he wasn't important anymore, not after that. Randi was. The next day She ran to her, found her at home. They fucked like mad and She was transformed, transported. Randi, She thought, was beautiful. Luxuriantly blond with chiseled and somewhat hard features, she was beautiful to Her. She could still see her face just above Hers, lovely, reddened from coming, coming into Her, in Her—that feeling. She would always remember her face like that just above Hers, eyes closed, coming, coming.

She felt so differently suddenly, so fulfilled. Happy. She had always watched the hero get the heroine in the movies and She identified with the man—getting the woman, just for that. That was what She always wanted without wanting to admit it, not wanting to be one of those, one of those dykes. Butches who looked like men. She never wanted to be like that, but She found She didn't have to be. She felt more Herself, more real than She ever had before. She got Her woman.

She was so in love ... or was that a lie to justify what She had done? Was it just the sex, that first-woman sex? The terror and wonder? A lot of the feeling was that, the sex, and at the same time a lot of it was really because She disliked so many basic things about Randi so quickly. Good sex, but everything else ... ? What She had perceived at first as strength She came to view as rigidity. What was once Randi speaking her mind, She came to see as limited. And She found her to be an embarrassment in front of Her friends. Too loud, too rough, too argumentative. Too straight—as in unexciting, not hip. It got so that staying home and fucking was all right, in fact She couldn't stop.

But going out with Randi was either a bore or uncomfortable.

The relationship got rocky fast but She could not break it. There was all that lust, and the guilt it brought. So much guilt. Do it with a woman? *You sick, twisted misfit.* Society's readiness to bludgeon dangerous dykes to death one way or another was in her head. And there was still Robert who she'd fucked. He stuck around, still liked Her—and She liked him. He was cool. He still wanted Her but She couldn't do it, couldn't get into it now. She wouldn't do it because She couldn't lie anymore.

She still wanted to hang out with Robert because they understood each other and the politics and energy of the time, but Randi started dogging Her about it. She wanted to be with Her more, but Randi didn't fit in with Her acid-taking crowd. She was too insensitive to trip with, too uncool for the hippie druggy student scene where other professors had easily fit into, but not Randi. It came to a head when She learned—after one very magnificent trip—that Randi actually believed there was only one reality.

"Oh for God's sake, this is it! This is what there is in the world, what we're seeing. All this exists, period. Nothing else. Where? What are you talking about?"

"Like the Beatles even ... like, life goes on, you know, within you, without ..."

"What are you on?"

Who can explain about tripping to anyone who hasn't done it? The pictures, the wavy melting stuff, the realities, the lifetimes you saw in the spaces of the world between the bullshit that only exists because we're conditioned and lied into an artificial, lockstep trivialization of the universe. No, She could never bring Randi to Her friends where acid omniscience ran high and deep.

But that was so long ago. She was young, nineteen or twenty. She had already left Detroit once for The Haight, went back and forth to a Mendocino commune, dropped acid at fifty cents a hit on West Coast streets, smoked tons of grass, fucked with hippie guys. She had done all that before meeting Randi. She was melancholy, remembering it all. It was too long ago. There had been gentler drugs than cocaine and crack, gentler drugs for the gentle '60s. She absolutely believed those were gentle times and drugs, and for Her, they were.

There was always pain, though, even with the first one. Even then. She left Randi for a weekend to drop acid with Her friends out at some Michigan lake. Although She told her She was just going to stay at a friend's parents' cabin She knew that it was an excuse to take some LSD in a really cool place. She made the mistake of calling Randi from the cabin phone to let her know She had arrived safely. Unfortunately, it was just as She and Her friends were starting to *rush* from the blotter acid. She didn't need to hear Randi's jealousy at not being there, not being on the edge of tripping.

"I can hear it in your voice. Why don't you ever do it with me? I want to try it once!"

Being screamed at when you're *rushing*, starting to trip, is not pleasant, and it breaks every unwritten code of druggie conduct. Her friends could hear the voice screeching from the receiver.

"Forget that." Somebody muttered it as they hung up the phone for her. Funny, She didn't know it was gone from Her hand. What a creep Randi was to give anyone bad vibes when they're about to *rush*.

"Yeah."

It was said from behind Her and was appropriate to nothing She could think of, not that She was exactly thinking of anything. She realized, though, it came from Jerry—maybe. He was just back from the Peace Corps and wore some kind of South American village straw hat tilted on his head. His green eyes seemed to be thumping from the drug starting to hit and he had a benign, goofy grin.

And Julia, Her old friend, she seemed to be running around the cabin manically, blue flames coming out of her heels. Blue flames. Everyone laughed until they cried sweat, or sweat tears. And they sweated and cried and laughed until they scared themselves. Then everything started to move. The rug pattern danced, the walls folded inward toward them. In the bathroom the eagles on the gold shower curtain flapped their wings and stared at you with mean eyes while you peed, for hours it seemed. And it took hours before you could get away from them, or someone came to get you, or just came upon you there on the toilet as they were wandering around. Sometimes someone would tell you everything was all right and make you laugh about the bathroom tiles singing such cool music in there.

You had to laugh. Laugh until you cried and felt one with the indescribable universe that flowed through you. In pinpoints or streams or colors, or sounds or something.

They kept each other from freaking out. Jerry and Julia and two other people She didn't know but who seemed to be gods. It had to be done from time to time. When the music came and attacked you at the throat too much, or like when She wanted to drive into town to get some privacy to talk to Randi maybe, to make it better. It seemed like a good idea to apologize so She didn't have to feel guilty, so Randi would understand. Then it passed: she would never understand Her, not this kind of interwoven cartoon super-unreal reality.

"Go ahead, take the car," Julia told Her. "Just watch for lions on the way."

"Getting to the car." She was so thoughtful, serious. "Or driving?"

"Where?"

"When it's ... you know—"

"Inside. Saw them inside."

They all went out to look, but forgot why. Instead they walked on the midnight frozen lake and scared themselves into sweats and hysteria that felt great.

She remembered how lucky She felt then that She was not hit with the bad news until She got back to Detroit from the lake the next day. It would have been unbearable while She was tripping so hard. Randi and Robert had been to bed together. And She was shocked, hurt. Julia, on the phone, laughed at Her.

"What did you expect? They're both jealous of you. What else could they do to get back at you for dropping acid and stuff with us? Fuck them."

Instead, She stopped fucking them. Both of them. She had to. No trust after that. Besides, who cared? She had touched the universe, and the rug. She had tasted music ...

- Time Doesn't Stand Still. Does It? -
ALWAYS MARGRET

Her days started at five in the morning. She and Margret were together, again and still, the assumed love and the silent complaints were the same. She had to steal the mornings to work in the darkroom to get ready for the big magazine piece with Her work. Judy, dark, sleek and delicious—Judy was a taskmistress. She would accept nothing less than Her best work. That was fine with Her, but She couldn't really concentrate on it.

Sam, her friend Sam, was changing every day, so quickly but so slowly. He was Her high-class buddy, Her otherworldly insider in the New York art scene. He was Her personal museum, Her own viewing room, Her wallow with rare photographs he was making more legendary just by making them his. Like the Genthe of St. Vincent Millay he bought and She was able to hold in Her hands. Sam, the collector, collected Her and She loved it.

He was pure WASP chisel-cheek-boned handsome. But the way he looked lately, the effects of AIDS that no one understood were horrifying—his palms purple one day, his complexion green-tinged the next. With all that and his body shrinking because he hated to eat, it was worrisome—no, it was terrifying. Every day She would bring him soup or sliced peaches, whatever he could get down, whatever he asked for. Maybe tomorrow, maybe by the end of the week he would be better, or worse. Or he might be gone. That was the joke of the disease that was getting louder and louder in the city. The joke was how it could drag on and then, suddenly, not long enough—they died. It happened to Her friend Billy. She saw him at an opening, his cheeks splotched with red over an unnatural, bilious whiteness. That was a month ago, now he was dead. He was twenty-nine.

It was getting hard for Her to sleep. She dragged Herself from bed and accidentally woke Margret, who was sweet, but with an edge.

"Why can't you stay with me?"

"I have to work."

Besides, She thought, what for? Why should She stay in bed with her at all? *You won't fuck me. I won't approach you anymore, can't take another rejection, not now.* She wanted to say it again, but not really. She was tired of talking. And She couldn't think clearly, wasn't working well. Worries. The eviction was progressing: the thousands for lawyers She was shifting onto one credit card and another, not doing much good, and Her regular bills were going unpaid.

"Come here, your coffee's ready. Right now."

Margret projected her mother-tone from where she stood at the darkroom door. A surprise—not the tone, but the coffee. How could She fight failure with her so near in Her space and invading Her private time?

"In a minute."

"I made it for you, goddamn it," Margret snapped at Her. "You wake me up all the time and don't even care that I did this for you. At least say thank you."

Thank you? She had been up since five and it was ten now. She had already guzzled all the coffee She needed. But She did not want to fight so early, feeling so lousy. All She could do to get away was leave Her work.

"Can't you be a little pleasant? You're always so negative, can't you get out of your mood for once, have a decent breakfast with me?"

What about you? Can't you ever be decent to me, stop attacking everything I do?

The words were only in Her head, again, because Margret's anger and that tone stopped Her. She couldn't fight it, didn't want to add another battle to Her life. Too weak, too vulnerable, too down. They were all the traits Margret hated in Her because she wanted Her energy for herself. So She pretended to smile, tried not to talk about Billy being dead. But She knew She had to say something, respond to something or else Margret would condemn Her again.

"So how is the work? You will make the deadline?" Margret said it, and it was not a question.

"Work's fine."

There was no balm in honesty. She had given up because it always opened a diatribe of righteous "shoulds" from Margret. The truth was that She felt empty in the work, paralyzed.

Looking at my cold plants still outside on the fire escape. Still worried. Feel alone. And the landlord, eviction. I need to be alone, being apart when I am evicted until I find another studio—a place for both of us really, even though she has her place uptown she doesn't like—moving will put distance between us.

The landlord is a jerk. Stupid hassles. What happened to art? To meaning? Where are the meaningful days again? Alone.

"I'm tired of your bad moods. Can't you be a little pleasant? Pleasant at breakfast at least, that's all you have to do. I make breakfast because you wake me up and you can't even be civil?" Then Margret turned softer. "Come on, things aren't so bad. We're healthy."

How can you fucking say that when the boys are dying! Her rage had no energy, couldn't speak. She swallowed the toast, stingily buttered, and drank the coffee that was never filled to the top the way She liked. Never enough. But She swallowed and smiled. That was Her relationship with Margret, swallowing and smiling. And not getting enough. She remembered "someone ain't been loving you right, honey, you're so tight ..."

It was true. So tight. Her ass. Her emotions. Her needs. *Thank you for nothing, Margret.* But She kept going through the motions of a relationship.

"Don't you ever dance together?" Constance Never Connie shouted over the bad band at the Pyramid Club on First and Seventh Street. "Margret's just sitting there. Go get her to dance, girl."

"Doesn't want to," She said, pretending it didn't matter.

Margret liked to sit, watch and critique. And because the Pyramid was so small—not like the spread out levels and rooms of the Paradise

Garage—in that kind of small space Margret's isolative behavior was more noticeable. She wouldn't embrace in public, wouldn't hold hands. All she was really good at was pulling away from Her so that tonight Nance noticed and even her still kind of new girlfriend, Kelly, noticed. She was humiliated, as usual, and danced with other women or just danced. Margret didn't seem to mind. It was only when Nance and Kelly and She were having a good time dancing together that she came out onto the floor, stiff, never relating to Her. No sexiness, no eye contact, no fooling around. One lousy night that She wanted to take a break from the pressure and Margret was still a cold bitch.

It was enough. *Enough of this shit.* So She asked Constance Never Connie to get Her some heavy drugs, soon. But it wasn't soon enough and She went home to another loveless bed with Margret. She tried not to know She was missing the fun that other women were having with each other right then.

Smacked again. And smacked again. In the face, and up the nose. Snort some smack, feel great. The way I felt, un-alone, infringed on at home is, what? Hateful. Hate. I hate who robs me of aloneness.

Run around, be down. Yesterday I saw her again. Airhead actress at her new apartment. As shallow as a plate. Plate face, smooth soul, no feeling. Tonight a junkie is more interesting, more rewarding, warmer and more giving than the pampered manipulator.

Had to borrow money from friends for bills, for drugs. Demeaning. I got drunk, hit the girl bars. My life runs out in ooze. I know what time I wasted, do waste. It is Monday again and I'll go out with Saint Carmen. Carmen who's with another girl now.

How can someone become interested in anyone else when they're with me? Everyone must feel the same way. The risk of caring. The risk of dying, the risk of showing. The risk of not being seen. The risk of dying? Mauve thoughts.

Incessant disco music. Depresses me because I wonder who's dancing with whom now. Who's seducing when the seducer's at home, sweet Carmen?

I need:

Drugs, Sex, Devotion, Money.

Courage, Devotion, Drugs, Sex, Money.

Courage, Drugs, Devotion, Sex, Money.
Courage, Sex, Drugs, Devotion, Money.
Devotion, Drugs, Courage.
Devotion, Courage, Drugs, Money, Sex.
Humility, Patience, Fear.
Humor, Ease, Satisfaction.
Fun, Confidence.
Confidence, Acceptance.
I need to sleep.

Margret worried about Her. She worried about all the pressure She was under, and she had reason to.

"You shouldn't get so involved, don't get so upset. Just don't."

When She cried over taking Sam W to the hospital again Margret held Her. And she understood when She went to the bars with Nance, when She had to so She could talk to a friend who was special to Her. Margret understood. And when She came home a little drunk and a little hot and Margret was smiling playfully in bed, waiting for Her, it was nice. Warm. But when She lay down and tried to make out with her Margret only giggled, turned her lips away after one kiss.

"Go. Get undressed and get some sleep."

"No, come on ..."

Margret only took Her in her arms and rocked Her. That was all, again. Again. The pressure knotted in Her stomach and tears nipped in Her eyes. But no, She wouldn't ask again. She had already broken Her threat by approaching her again, and been rejected again.

Maybe there was too much pressure in both their lives for sex. Maybe. *Cold fucking bitch.* But that wasn't true. Margret was no monster, and she loved Her. She was still the best She had seen in so many ways. Smart, attractive, an activist, an arcane intellectual way of looking at the world so that She learned from her. She grew with Margret. She thought, She believed it. Or was it because that's what Margret always told Her?

It was none of that. It was because Margret was the image She had made of her in Her mind. Margret was Her Pygmalion. Margret was the ethereal, the unattainable, the quest that was always out of reach. It was the perfection She ladled on Margret like a syrupy torrent. She needed Margret there, with Her, to be perfect so that She could fail and never have to blame Herself.

- Time Stopped -
THE WORST

There was a gaping hole of death that was his mouth. It breathed on me. I taste sweet death still. Sweet death, sweet smell of death. It stuck in my nostrils all day. But I learn, like I told him, learn from everything. Teach me like you always did, Sam. How to enjoy. How to be excellent. How to be a little bit the bastard, the bitch. I need to know that more, you told me. I'm too easy to shut up. And you told me that to encourage me, to tell you what I thought about making things go smoother for you when you went home from the hospital that first time, that time I took you in, one of the times with a 104 fever. I felt so terrible because you didn't want to go, were afraid of never getting out again. But you got out, three more times, and lived three months after, exactly. Three months.

A gaping hole of death. Already death was inside. Still you fought. I could feel it. I saw it. You did not, would not relax. You were too afraid before, I'm sure you're fine now. How silly we seem to you already. But we will be, are already, empty without you.

But I can learn from you. That is what I take. Let the callow social climbers take the money, suck from your fame. I'll take the knowledge and run. Seeing, touching, holding the treasures you have—it's so much more than enough. It needs no fanfare, it is in my mind and soul because of you. All the images you gave me, dreams, real or not. Now all that matters is how it comes out. And that will take time, I know. You liked all those cute young ones, but you bloomed a little late yourself. I'm not so young anymore either, but very young too. I have time.

Or maybe not, maybe that's arrogance or ignorance talking, the two usually go together. Who knows how much time there is? That's the trick, isn't it? Not knowing. We must know everything else as fast as we can because we can't know that, when. Good.

And when your friend, your heart, has died, why does it seem callous to yawn, even when you must? No sleep, no work.

Sam died when She didn't expect it. She thought he would get through the bad spell. He had so many times before over the last year. So many bad spells, so many rebounds. Rebounds to a lower level each time … eating, walking, talking, thinking. The collector never got off his back again. She was losing a soul mate. He was disappearing. But She could not mourn—enough, or too much? There was enough and too much crying, enough and too much anger.

Finally, there was too much hopelessness, the void he left too much. Finally, days were turning to weeks and Margret had to tell Her it was "enough." She reminded Her that She had a show coming up. She told Her that She could not give up any more of Her life for him. It was so like Margret: it was true and she was saying it for Her own good. And of course, of course, that was too real for Her. Margret was right again, and caring again, and so She could blame her for an imagined perfection—again—because then She could take refuge in never being good enough. So She cried alone, sobbed when She was alone. That was the only time it really came out of Her— Her grief for Sam, and for Herself. *Selfish bitch.*

She was a failure. She couldn't save Sam. She couldn't work. The show, the magazine piece, would never be done. Judy kept pushing Her, laid down the law, demanded She work. There was no time for romance between them, and She didn't want it, couldn't handle it. Judy sensed it and was all business. Besides, She could not cheat on Margret, not now, not anymore. She loved her—She had to, didn't She? Her life was grounded on Margret and all Her fantasies of her. And Margret helped Her. Their lives were intertwined. Daily living, the phone calls, always knowing where the other was, what the other was doing. Dyke relationships, close, no cigar. Close, no sex.

She didn't see anyone anymore. Not Nance, no drugs from Constance Never Connie, no Saint Carmen, not any diversion from any other woman. Although Sandy tried. They had fucked years before, one nice night in bed. It was during the first year She was involved with Margret, and Margret had wanted a break, to be alone for a few weeks. She didn't understand it, chalked it up to a straight woman freaking over her first affair with a woman. And Sandy happened to come by, a friend, available and wanting Her, so they fucked. Sandy could only be touched in a special way. The lightest pressure on her clit was all she could take. Quick, light, one fingertip brushing. Sandy hung onto Her, called out when She went inside saying, "No." Relaxed only when She withdrew, touched outside again. That was all she wanted. No tongue on her or in her. She wanted only that. Light, fast, constant just touching it.

But She had played with her anyway, gave her more than she wanted. Instead of constant motion She would hesitate, make Sandy feel the sudden absence. Then She started again, the rapid lightness, then a stop. She worked hard because Sandy took a long time to come, needed that playing for a long time, to relax, to get hot. But she came finally, hard, crying out. And She came with her, came short and hard just from watching Sandy, feeling her intensity build. A decent fuck.

Now there was no time for anything. The deadline was getting close for the magazine. Sam was dead. Dead. She couldn't think, had to keep moving. There was no money, the lawyers took it all and lost the case. She would be evicted in a month, the day after the deadline for Her photography collection. She thought She might go crazy. Although Margret kept her own tiny apartment that she owned, she rented it out. It didn't help Her at all. Besides, She hid how bad Her finances were anyway. She had to, and She would, find a place to live for both of them. It was on Her. Margret never really worked at things like this, that wasn't her style.

"We'll find something."

But something was hard to find. It always is in New York. Only friends would take them in, and only one at a time. So while She was working toward the deadline, they packed up and put their things in storage. They would split up and stay individually with friends.

I cried about my grandmother today. After fourteen years. It doesn't matter. It seems like I've done nothing since she died. The failure dream: sounds like you could have been somebody.

The failure dream. My grandmother. I promised I would return to her grave only with my success validated. But I never did. Do I keep myself from getting success, so close now, because of that? Then she will really be dead. I will be alive with no one. No family anymore, not the myth it was. What problems they are in for, these TV media Christians. Family hawkers. How funny it will be. And I will be there then, the sage old lady, to put together the pieces, give them my iconoclasm. My courage. Do I have any? I think I do for some things, great courage. Like a lioness. But for other things, pain, that of others mostly, I am a terrified, whimpering beast. Helpless. When I am helpless I am a coward. Let me have the strength to see I must always try, then I will have the hope to have courage. Is it a prayer? But only to me. Who else is there?

My grandmother, I miss.

I cried with control. I could not give into it.

"Light griefs can speak; deep sorrows are dumb," says Seneca in Montaigne. Montaigne who I forgot I was reading so avidly a year ago.

The beating of the wings distracts me more than the blaring horns outside. The cars are gridlocked but the dragonflies hovering at the windows in back make a terrible din, much worse. They beat their heads, those bulging eyes, into the dirty glass. One pane is already broken. The one with the iridescent blue wings has cut himself. I throw a brick and break another pane ...

She was burned out, in a foul mood that seemed permanent. She moved into a friend's storage room in his Bowery loft, the extra room, and slept on one of those plastic chaise lounges intended for the beach. Margret moved in with Nance because it was a better, more comfortable place. The unspoken split was that She did the harder things, was more butch without really being butch. So when it came time to move again it was She who moved. Margret stayed in easier places, moved fewer times with less discomfort.

Sandy offered Her a place with her and her lover, but neither of them wanted the temptation of getting involved again. She wished She had more money, or Sandy did, so they could have gone to a hotel to be together—a fleeting craving. She had done that with one of the nurses She used to fuck, Ester. It was a while ago, some years, a time when She was still having to rent darkroom space from someone else because She did not have Her own studio. Ester lived in the building where She would work and they always ran into each other. Sometimes Ester was alone, sometimes with her boyfriend.

Ester was cute, gamin-like, and She thought She might be getting looks from her but She discounted them because of the boyfriend. One day, together in the elevator, Ester turned to Her with a glittery smile.

"How much longer do I have to flirt with you to get you to take me to bed?"

Words almost failed Her. But She recovered.

"Right now?"

"Good."

That was that. Simple. Hot. But there was nowhere to go because he, whatever the boyfriend's name was, was at home and She was living with Carla then, who was also at home. So they went to the Waldorf, the Waldorf in the middle of the day.

Ester held Her arm while they checked in. The clerks were efficient, took Her credit card for one night without blinking and didn't bother to ask if they had luggage. They went quickly to the elevators and up, arms intertwined, Ester leaning into Her. The room door closed behind them from the weight of their bodies against it. Instant tongues, instant sucking, Ester probed Her mouth passionately and then opened up to take Her, suck Her tongue deep inside. She moved so that she pulled Her tongue first from one angle, then another, her lips kneading over Her extended tongue. *Like a cock, sucking my tongue like a goddamn cock, but Jesus!*

She attacked Ester, pushed her back into the door, tried to force her leg between her thighs and felt the skirt material stop Her. She sighed into Ester's mouth and she responded from with small wanting sounds and sucked Her tongue with new energy. It seemed she was driven to getting Her off with only Her tongue. Ester clamped her lips

77

around it and pulled on it, rode it with her lips, around it, caressing it, licking, loving it with her own tongue. She switched from hard and fast to slow and long drags on it, slow and hard. And damn if She didn't come right then, right there jamming her against the door.

Ester clung, held tight and melted against Her. She stroked Her face, purred in Her ear that She was "so good," so good. But She knew Ester had not come.

"What about you?"

"You're wonderful," Ester whispered it.

Ester pulled up her skirt and put Her hand on her through the underwear that was soaked, and She yanked it aside, tore the leg elastic and went into her with two fingers. Ester sucked in her breath and dug her nails into Her shoulders.

"Yes!" She kept her fingers in her, put Her other hand under her from behind and picked her up. The weight of her body against Her fingers made them move deeper inside and she moved against Her in little spasm while She carried her to the bed that way. Ester was happy with that.

"Fuck me, make me come, make me come ..."

And She felt something was wrong suddenly and left her. She took Her fingers from inside her.

"No!"

And She was already working her clit. That's when Ester breathed, "Yes, oh yes."

And She teased her, moving in and out of her, feeling the tension build so that her body stopped bucking and she trembled, muscles rigid, waiting, wanting to come, to get over. She worked, worked hard, feeling Ester almost there. Almost. Ester made small sounds, shaking, waiting, wanting. She worked harder, feeling her at the edge, so ready to come, so tense, so ready to get over. Her hand moved over her cunt fast, and in her, over her clit, a little probe at her ass. Pressure, release, quick, then a sudden stop. Ester gasped, and then the lightness, tender caresses, and Ester's head raised, her body arched. Still she didn't come.

She was soaked with sweat and panting. She stopped, tore off her clothes, left Ester shaking and not wanting Her gone. She knelt between her legs and made her look at Her nakedness. Her breasts exposed, Her flat stomach, Her cropped black bush.

"You're beautiful," Ester said and reached for Her.

She pushed her hands away and took hold of Ester's top, yanked it over her head. She was wearing a bra built for large breasts on a tiny body, reached behind and unhooked it while She unzipped her skirt and tossed it aside, pulled off her underwear and flung them away. She was a little wild, feeling the challenge to make her come. She fell on Ester, ground their breasts together. Sucked, bit, made the nipples hard and red so She could pull them between lips, hold them with raking teeth and fluttering tongue over nipples. She held Ester's legs wide open with Her own, moved on her, found the spot, the hard clit, and pushed, rocked, thrust hard.

Ester went tense again, "Yes yes ..." She clawed at Her back with long nails that hurt.

"Yes," through clenched teeth, "yes" with rigidity shaking her body, "yes" holding her breath. Then, suddenly silent, stretching, straining to come.

And She felt her stirring in that stillness, the only sound now Her own breathing as She worked over her, on her. Ester's clit was slippery and She lost it from time to time with the bone above her cunt. She switched hands, trying to shove entirely inside as she used to do with Alice. Ester was there, at the edge, grabbing at the sheets, gasping now, bucking her hips, trembling. And then the quiet, holding her breath, at the edge. Right there, right there. She could feel it and slammed into her, out, bore down, tantalizing her clit.

And, "Yes yes." But no. She couldn't do it. Ester told Her to stop and She collapsed on her, her arm and lips and tongue numb from the effort.

"What's wrong?" She asked it gently. "What do you need that I'm not doing?"

"Nothing. It's the best. That's the closest I've ever been, ever. It's me. I never have, but now I know what it must be like."

She put her arms around Her neck and kissed Her. She put her tongue deep inside.

"You were wonderful. It's the best, really."

"But not enough."

Ester gave Her details. She had never had an orgasm. She submitted to unfulfilling sex with her boyfriend until she realized and admitted that a woman might solve her problem, a woman she was attracted to like Her. And She didn't know quite how to feel about being used like that. Flattered? Ester didn't give Her time to figure it out because she began, shyly, to explore Her. She had never felt another woman before.

With wonder, with curiosity, she started to touch Her softly. She kissed her breasts with tenderness, took Her nipples between her lips with care as if their hardness might explode if sucked without concentration, concern, feeling. It was an innocent touch, subtle, searching. She relaxed, gave up Her body to Ester's explorations.

Ester's hands moved down to Her and played, touching short black hairs, moving her fingers over her, feeling through the valley almost to Her ass, always softly. Ester moved down so she could see Her there, watch her own hands as she taught herself about a woman, about herself. And she spread labia apart, put a finger, then two into Her wetness. Very slowly then Ester moved inside. Her fingers looked around it seemed, took joy in exploring Her, did not miss any part of Her inside.

"This is so wonderful," she said and probed in Her hesitantly, then deeply, found the shelf so high inside and hooked her fingers onto it. Then "Oh my god" she breathed against her down there and She could tell Ester was rejoicing in her own awe at this newness, these woman secrets.

Offering no instruction, no comment beyond the wet flow from Her and Her deep breaths. She allowed Ester to do whatever she wanted, and Ester took the opportunity to love Her well. Her hands, her face, her lips were used all over Her and especially down there, opened to exploration and communion only guessed at before. She centered there, concentrated on feeling inside of Her, and being completely inside of Her.

She started to move under Ester, reacting to her touch. Ester encouraged Her and got excited by Her excitement.

"Do it, show me," she insisted with her hands, her mouth.

Her fingers went deeper inside, deeper, and sought Her ass. Her mouth sucked Her clit inside, her tongue stroked with a long motion. A curl, a valley formed in her tongue that fit Her clit into it and pulled it between her lips and into her mouth. And She gasped an "Oh Christ" and came in Ester's mouth, holding her head on Her, moving against her. And Ester made some kind of sound but kept sucking and stroking, rode with Her, brought Her off and would not stop. She finally had to pull her by the hair to put an end to her perfect moves, Ester's suddenly expert enticements to make Her come.

And when it was all finally over and they had draped over each other as long as they could, relaxing, they had to leave. They had to try to leave or it would start all over again and they had no time for that, for more of each other.

"When can I see you again?"

Ester said it softly in Her ear. There were other people riding down in the Waldorf's dark and deco elevator with them.

"Soon," She said with a laugh She could not control.

"It better be," and Ester squeezed her ass with both hands, not caring who saw.

They checked out four hours after they had arrived, and the desk clerk did not blink. The bill was half the room rate, half of what She had signed for when they checked in. She had to ask if it was correct.

"Sign here, please," was said without a glance, "for the adjustment."

- Stop the Clock, Stop the Clock, Stop … ! -
FRENZY

Memories of fucking helped block out the memory of Sam being gone. Being gone? Shit, being dead.

They're going to die. They're going to die. Today. Tomorrow.

Why are we sitting here? Why aren't we screaming through the streets? Why aren't we heaving great logs of wrath against stone walls, sweating our terror.

Is anything else important? Should anything else be? A life. Lives. People we know, yes, and the knowledge they have and we have about it. They're going to die!

Is there any way to be polite?

What to say? We know. They know. No surprises. This is the end of your life. Who cannot feel it? The very stupid or the very, very smart.

Why is there so much time to sit with the knowledge, and so little—of both.

I hate knowing the end of a movie but not knowing when it's going to end. I don't know what to take seriously anymore, if anything.

Why should I care so much? Because I'm afraid of the knowledge. Knowledge is death. Knowledge is freedom? Not with this plague.

Never revise, knowledge is death. So afraid of dying to be free. Dying is free. That's why so many poor people do it in wars, house fires, on the streets, of starvation. The boys are too well fed to die, but they do. Too well fed to die, too scared, too stupid, me. I am only afraid of me. Who taught me that, to be afraid of me? They all did, it all did. Does it matter to affix blame?

Still fear, claustrophobia. Fear of self?

Why is the moon so clear, the cold so cold? A specific kind of night. The best kind for rattles of spirits deep in your ears. These are your own, alone, no one else hears.

Howl at the moon. They're dying. They're dying.
Say it loud. Make it a horrible example of its medium, make it meaningless.
Scream it too much, blunt it, erase it, try to forget. Forget the way he looked
when he was dying, the breaths he reached for, fighting.

So the months fly past and the boys are dying and the girlies are running around fucking each other. As least that's what She heard, or saw, or got propositioned for but ignored because of Margret and because of Herself, their conditions. A week on a beach lounger in a friend's Bowery loft junk space, then find a sublet for three weeks, and then what? No money, no prospects—unless She actually finished the work for the Berlin show, which She so far was not working on enough ... hardly at all. She had pushed back that deadline, a little, by two weeks, not enough—all She could get. She smoked cigarettes like breathing the air and ate candy and junk, alone. She wanted to be alone, without anyone, without Margret. Her mood was so rotten that Nance couldn't stand to talk to Her on the phone. Depressing.

It could have been better. *Shutters* magazine did publish her work, along with a review that was much shorter than Margret had expected, really, that she had set up for Her. But then again, She ended up giving them only six photographs to choose from—even with Judy pushing Her—and they chose only two to print.

It had been two weeks since that deadline for Her photographs in the magazine, since that moderate success, but it didn't feel like any success at all. Margret was both furious She had not delivered all the work She should have, and jealous, too. She was brusque with Her, mean, snide. And yes, it was true that She got a kick out of calling the guys at Her film supply places, like Duggal, and accepting small *kudos*.

"Yeah that was my work in *Shutters* ... Yeah, thanks."

And Margret would say, "Two prints and you have to tell everyone? If there had been all you were supposed to do ... ?"

It hurt Her feelings. She found it hard to answer beyond, "You know I tried." But Margret seemed hurt, too. She would attack so She could hardly hear her, "Always something ..."

It made Her wonder why the hell Margret had to beat Her up

like that because She didn't feel like anything but shit. No home, no money, lies catching up to Her, afraid of failing so avoiding working, and a lover who wouldn't fuck Her. For months the slide had been downhill, and fast. She had lost the apartment, worse, Her studio workspace within it. Equipment, books, sneakers, leftover plastic bags of marijuana shards, bottles with tiny specks of coke powder that She horded instead of throwing away…all of Her stuff had been spread to friends. She carried heavy stacks of books over to Martin's because it was close by on the Bowery. She took some clothes there, too. More clothes were out at Lesley's in Brooklyn, though. And She cursed it being too far to have to wrangle filled shopping bags on the R train.

Her possessions, Her life, scattered all over town now with various friends. Unable to work, to think, trying to get jobs, real paying jobs— She was failing at all of it. But being away from Margret was better for Her head than being with her. It hurt too much to hear those lectures.

"Don't be so upset all the time. So you're moving around, you should be able to be comfortable wherever you are."

Great. But Margret only moved twice, one time with Her, another with other friends. But then they found a place for Margret for at least two months with an acquaintance of Her's through another friend. Her name was Bitsy, but that was a contrast to everything about her. Not too tall, maybe that fit the name, but hulking, with greasy black hair, no chin and a pock-marked face. She was a bull dyke of the old school, wore awful, cheap suits for dress-up when she wasn't dressed like a construction worker—because that's what she was. Her personality, beyond everyone always saying she was "very nice," was pretty much zero. But of course this faultfinding picture was drawn through Her jaundiced eyes and Hers alone. Bitsy didn't know how she was being sniped at and it didn't matter—she would do them this favor. Bitsy would let Margret stay in her small apartment, the apartment She and Margret laughed about when they moved Margret in.

"Jesus, what a lack of aesthetic. Weird person, Bitsy."

"Shush. At least it's a place." Margret was firm. "And I'm glad to have it to use."

And She was glad, too, that Margret was settled. It was the protection She felt She had to provide for her, to do something to make up for Her fucking up every opportunity Margret got for Her— like not delivering all the prints for the *Shutters* piece. Now that Berlin show was screaming for an answer. How long could She avoid saying *no* to it? *Chicken shit!* How long could She hide it from Margret? So She put up with the nasty moving around and begging for places and looking for a permanent home for them. She was glad to be alone, though, to cut Herself off from everyone to live with Her depression, Her failure to be able to deliver anymore work, and the weakness She was sure that Margret hated in her. It was better she didn't see it. She hid Herself away.

Here in this fabulous loft in Williamsburg that belongs to Alan Saret. I find myself performing strange rituals, symmetric rituals, I don't know where they come from. I use my voice, my body. Is it because of the pyramid he has built here?

A week ago I was bitten in my sleep by something in the pyramid on the roof. One of the yellow jackets that live in a nest up there, or maybe it was a spider. There's a terrible bite on my right calf. Red round stinger spot, white circle and an inch wide black and blue bruise ringing the whole thing. It hurts so badly today I can hardly walk. Revenge of the pyramid. And nobody cares.

I do nothing but read, read Montaigne, read Agnes Martin interviews. Expression, getting yourself out. So I did that, some photographs are there, out, but no more. I can't work. And I feel like shit, alone.

I'm afraid. I feel so sick, the bite on my leg. The piece of extra flesh, the small wart-ish thing, under my arm has changed color all of a sudden. Ruby colored instead of beige. I'm afraid. I can't go on. I'm afraid.

Last night there was a blood red moon low in the sky. Part of me, like the piece of flesh under my arm. Half-moon, juicy, thick, red. It hit me when I walked out of the pyramid and stepped onto the roof. Took my breath away. Alone with it. The sweep of the skyline of the city glittering across the East River because I am in Brooklyn. Not a bad exile.

I find myself performing symmetric rituals to the sun. I need to go to a place where I can greet the sun every day. Lay with it. I will start a religion to the sun. Not the first, not the last. That's a decision to be content with. If I go to Vermont

will the sun follow me? In the Caribbean was it just too much? Both of them. The
sun as a playmate. I am through fooling around with meaningless affairs. I want
to work at my own work again. Expression. Be with the sun.
*   And I want to be with Margret, but not now.*

But there was Margret always Margret, the millstone She loved, around Her neck. She read about millstones, fucking heavy huge things, a ton or tons of rock. Big flat-sided circular stones with a hole in the middle so they could be turned to grind grain, with a hole in the middle so you can put a chain through it and wear it. She chose to do it. She loved her. Ever since She first met Margret She was obsessed by her. That gracefulness, those elegant hands.

"I don't want to lose her," was what She told Carla. Carla, who had lost Her to Margret.

From the beginning, fascination, that thrill fluttering over your skin when you're together, not touching at all. Still… Why could She not leave her alone, or just leave her? Sometimes She genuinely disliked her, or really knew she was not good for Her, for Her creativity. Lately She couldn't be Herself with Margret, not with all her lectures, the "shoulds," the disdain in her voice and movements. But She treated Margret badly as well—maybe. Maybe. She really could not admit it. Margret deserved to be ignored, to learn to be independent, to be cut off from Her affection until Margret showed some herself, *goddamnit*. Fucking judgmental for sure, and She hated Herself for it. And anyway, She loved her. Or needed her. Or something.

The beguilement began from the beginning. Wanting her, not wanting to lose her. And Margret knew how to play it. With her arcane sense of reality, a weird socialistic kind of 1960s mentality that said there was room for everything, anything one wanted to do or be. Fine. The problem was that she didn't act on that. Margret took over Her life and made it her own and then complained when She didn't live that life of Hers to Margret's expectations or needs. It was one of the things that kept Her captivated, kept Her trying to fulfill Margret's vague but stern view of life. She wanted to please her. Margret had a way of being a princess without ever daring to admit it, a way of making you want to do for her, be with her, keep running to accede to demands of which even she was not certain, although she bluffed a good game of knowing. She believed it, kept trying, because She didn't want to lose her. Obsessed. Possessed. Just another relationship dumbass fuck up.

When they were first seeing each other they would have terrible fights in the street. Shouting fights. If She didn't know exactly where they were going when they went out, what to do, or if they were just walking around Margret would start to pitch a fit.

"Where are we going?"

"I don't know, maybe the piers. Where you want to go?" She was usually mellow from smoking dope.

Margret would stop in the middle of the street. Gentle, elegant-looking Margret in downtown funky jeans, would start to berate Her. With rising volume.

"What's the matter with you, can't you ever decide anything?"

She ended up shouting at Her. But it was really Margret who could never decide anything, and She didn't see it. So She took the guilt on Herself, the challenge, and She got nervous and tried desperately to think of what to do to please her. She bought Margret's trip, was possessed by it. Maybe it was because of the mother-tone Margret had and could use so effectively on Her. Maybe She was susceptible to it because it was a tone Her own mother had never used, never had. Maybe She wished she did. Maybe She wanted that explicit domination, that distance from Her mother instead of the surface easiness there had been, that seeming equality, the apparent love She got—or wanted to think She got—got from Her mother without having to work for it. Acceptance, that's what it was. She never got it, although somehow She expected to be accepted, loved. So She fell into the obsession trap with Margret because she made Her work for it.

Me, the cat and the fly sit in front of the heater. The electric heater, quartz rods in the drafty loft like a castle. The cat watches the fly, flexes her fur when it gets too close, but does not attack. We know the fly is dangerous, a biting vampire only disguised with those transparent wings. It will grow. So we give it its place in our little line before the glow, in front of the heat. But when I arise everyone moves. The cat, the fly, the waiting souls who have been watching from their hovering places waiting, waiting to steal our bodies. They jostle aside as I go through them with thoughts of Sam, how I miss him, and my grandmother, how long I've missed her, and my Gramps too. The souls press aside like bubbles of air, watching. They wait to steal a body, but only for a time. I think perhaps they wait for the cat the most.

Anyway, they are not humming now. They sing no songs in the cold. In the silence I can concentrate. On what? When my grandmother was ill, the many times the death-hungry doctors used her, when she was ill I would try to distract her.

"A book, TV ... ? Grandma?"

"No. I have to concentrate," she would say, "on my pain."

Maybe that was the way to fight it. Without that maybe she would have died sooner. That would have been worse. Worse than the emptiness, the energy that went out of me sixteen years ago—a number I make up—it is longer. The same amount of time I was close to Sam. Now he's gone too. I can't believe it, don't want to. Time to be alone. To learn the lessons again. Fight, fight through the flying monsters, the spike-headed spirits who pierce my skin when they can. They hurt. I must protect myself. There, throw the radio at them and let it scream at them from its pieces that cling to the wall, each one singing a different tone. Songs of terror, shrieks of perfect pitch.

Perfect is what I seek. Perfect keeps me paralyzed. Perfect makes me small. Perfect, the razor at my throat. Dare not move. If I am not perfect the shiny edge will press slowly, slowly and rend my skin in the most perfect parting that makes two edges flowed over with shiny blue-red where there was un-seamed white-brown before. Perfect.

Perfect already and never knowing it. Trying to change and becoming imperfect. Can't accept. Why not? It is the demons. How they moan in my ears. How they swoop. My hair blows around my eyes from their force. They bite my fingers, wrap scaly tendrils around my legs, force me underwater. They hold my head in the tub, filled with ice, slowly the melting water fills my nose, and how they shriek.

Dead again. Dead still. I see myself dead. Dead every day. Keep away from the demons. Quiet now so they won't see, they'll forget about me. But I won't.

Perfect memory. That's the dragging chain. Links made of heavy soft lead that has been fashioned around each bit and strand of hair that has ever grown from my body. Self, the chains. Perfect. My self, my weight. Perfect.

The cat has not eaten the fly. The fly has hidden. All of us perfect. I pile the chain at my feet for a footrest, perfectly not moving, allowing each of us to be. No risk anything else will happen. And I hear the ghouls. The dead and undead packed tight in the air around me, humming.

Being alone now in Her friend Alan's loft in Brooklyn, because he left town for three weeks for a show, She reveled in it. She went to the girlie bars across the East River uptown where the model types hung out. Lots of heavy eye action around the room, look but don't touch. No pickups. But She didn't have the heart for it anyway. Too scattered, too anxious, the vibrations of nerves just below the surface. No home, no money, nothing but meanness from Margret on the phone. And Sam dead. She missed him, missed his head, his thoughts on Her work and Her lover no-lover. Her life.

She remembered how they talked about everything when they talked. About sex, about S&M. Carla, who he had always liked for her intensity about her art, her dance, had liked light bondage. She had screwed little hooks into the floor around their bed without telling Her. One day she came home with a bag filled with yards of velvet cord. Without a word she attached the cords to the hooks and told Her to get naked and lie down. She tied Her quickly, spread eagle, while she stayed dressed. Then she took a feather and a can of baby powder and set them next to the bed while she slowly, very slowly, took off her clothes one piece at a time, stopping to lean over Her, kiss Her, run her tongue around Her nipples, down Her stomach, teasing around Her down there, and over Her thighs. And She could not reach her, couldn't move enough to touch her. She could only beg with Her body, arch Her back to try to capture Carla's mouth, her breasts, nipples, the soft flesh on the inside of her thighs.

Jesus that's enough.

But Carla would not stop, took her time, tortured Her with slowness, softness. And the powder, suddenly she was turning the can on Her stomach, making a little mound of white before spreading it gently with her hands, then with her naked body. Like silk. Carla's skin moving over smooth talc, gliding on Her full length, gliding, undulating so effortlessly.

And *yes, yes.* She came to her without a touch.

Those had been fun times together. Carla's lithe dancer's body dominating Her, doing theater for Her. Different from now. Margret was passionate, could be passionate, but she would not learn so easily. Although she did, and she could come hard, head beating, arching, hands clutching at sheets. It was difficult to get her to give that intensity back, or to have the creativity to really blast Her with rolling *comes* in return. And now thinking about their fucking She wondered if She had given up too much, had let Margret get away with the sexual distance too much.

But that was bullshit of the purest sort, of course, because She wasn't into sex with Margret either—not now anyway, not most of the time, not really. But it was easier to blame her. Besides, she started it!—The argument that can't be argued with, as anyone who's ever been a child knows.

- It All Speeds Up. All of It. -
RUNNING

Weeks became months and She and Margret barely saw each other,
but they talked on the phone every day. They needed a hiatus, a break
from old patterns, ways of relating that were reflex actions to each
other. Both were more callous now, being apart. It was a bad patch,
they would get through it, work it out. They just needed some time
apart to feel like individuals. She started going to the bars again,
looking, and She assumed Margret would do the same, look for an
affair maybe. A quick fuck for a little fun. In fact, She hoped Margret
would get some experience, get out there on the streets and in the bars
and see what was around, then she'd appreciate Her more. Let her
learn what she had with Her, could have with Her. maybe she'd stop
being such a bitch.

But She was feeling pretty bitchy Herself. Sick of moving, no
money, and Margret being so comfortable at weird Bitsy's and still
lecturing Her on how She should calm down and "be comfortable
wherever you are."

Yeah, I don't see you moving around all over the city, bitch.

But so what, She wouldn't want to live at Bitsy's, not even to have
a decent place to stay. She would rather move around, crazy-making
as it was. She was lost, felt lost, felt strange without Margret, although
She liked being without her.

It was difficult to explain, even to feel those feelings. She didn't
know what she felt about anything: Herself, success, or Margret.

Sometimes things are so clear. Why is it sometimes things are so clear, and I don't want to admit it?

If I don't fight, it comes. I'm very lucky. I feel very fortunate, with an attuned-ness I won't admit, being alone.

Just last week I wanted every drug in the world to get by. Just yesterday, or the day before, I was ready to do anything for some "boy." To get that feeling of contentment, not perfect, but good, just so good. Drugs are no problem, cigarettes are. On "boy," the big H drug, you can be asleep and be aware of yourself sleeping. I've hardly felt better. Alone.

There was this inability of Hers to enjoy what She had at the moment. Always thinking it wasn't enough, wasn't cool enough, and feeling like She was being judged on it. She felt not only that She was being watched with whomever She was with, whatever She did, but that when She was with someone She was missing being with someone else. Interest waned when She got someone or something She had wanted. Constance Never Connie told Her She took Margret for granted. Did She? Or did She just not want to deal with her, or did She simply expect to be loved because She loved her? It was different—there was a difference.

Why is it that sometimes really magnificent people surround themselves with dullards? And people who really aren't worth much think they deserve admiration? Is everyone so afraid of the truth, their own truth, or at least another truth? There are so many.

I read Montaigne today: Affections that carry us beyond ourselves. Worrying over the future or past and not caring for ourselves in the present. We do not allow ourselves to feel the present. We want to conquer time. We tell people what to do with our bodies after our death.

Fuck it, go to the bars. She went with Kelly because she and Nance were on the outs the same way that She and Margret were. Both their girlfriends didn't really want to see them, were upset with their lack of attention to them. *Fuck it.* They left 8BC (on 8th Street between Avenue B and C) and headed for the West Village instead. They were going to a new bar they'd heard about. It was down a flight of tight stairs in some place on Christopher Street just west of Seventh Avenue, across from Village Cigars. No name but lots of cute girls.

"Bet you can't get one to go home with you right now."

Kelly was messing with Her, and laughed. But She didn't laugh in response, too busy taking four giant snorts from Her brown coke vial's little spoon. Quick slick, timed perfectly, a snort behind someone's back for just enough fleeting cover, or just turned away from a shoulder or someone jostling past to the bar... Coke and boast, the kind of *Truth or Dare* game She needed. Risk, but who cared—She was ready.

"Oh yeah? Pick one."

It was on. They got drinks and started to cruise the bar and dance floor, looking for prospects. Luckily the place was packed, dark, loud with Aretha Franklin's "Freeway of Love," smoky—typical. One girl caught Her eye. She looked like a miniature Brigitte Bardot. Very young, very much the girlie girl and apparently very much with a bulky dyke who never took her eyes off the girl. So She took another coke hit, and then never took Her eyes from young blonde either.

"That one," She shouted to Kelly over the music. The dark blare of "Shout" from Tears for Fears pounded its ominous bass-beat.

"Are you crazy? Her girlfriend would punch you through a wall."

"There's two of us. Just stay close and look tough if it gets weird."

"What?"

Kelly leaned in to have Her shout it in her ear again. She didn't look convinced, not until She smacked her on the arm.

"Ok ok. I'm right behind you."

The challenge was all She needed to feel powerful again. It erased all the control Margret took away from Her, the blows to Her self-concept from the "why can't you be" some way or another or "you should do this." All the talking and the taking, the swallowing, meant nothing when She was like this, on the prowl, lionhearted, lighthearted. Even flat rejection at times like these wouldn't daunt Her. She could always laugh it off in moods like these, powerful moods. Once a woman She had approached looked Her up and down, slowly, then just walked away. It made Her laugh out loud at her so openly that the woman stopped, turned around and wanted to talk to Her. But She had already turned away to regale Her friends with the apparent put-down that hadn't put Her down. Strong enough not to care, and it was the only way to be. Secure, willing to risk, letting rejection be the other woman's problem. In fact, not too much got to Her ego except for Margret pushing all the right buttons to make Her completely crazy when she wanted to do it to Her. But she would never admit that.

Now the chase was on. Kelly gave Her space and watched Her work. It seemed like there was no way She could pry the little blonde away from the big butch who guarded her like a bulldog, looked like one too in a stylish cutish-brutish way. That's what Kelly had to be thinking—or that's what She thought in Her coke-rushed, hurtling reality of Her own construction. She was dying to flaunt Her power at Kelly.

But She had already positioned Herself near the dance floor and started the game, already started to make eye contact. The Bardot-girl picked up on it immediately, subtlety. Quick glances, small looks when her big guarding girlfriend looked the other way. When she danced closer in the crowd, she made sure to head for where She was in the throng, made sure She was still watching her. And She was. She was glad She was wearing one of her well-cut jackets that was not butch but trendy over a black, silk, flowing sleeved blouse. She took off the jacket and showed off the nearly see-through fabric that hinted Her tits beneath. The girl noticed, She saw her notice, and pretended not to see. But she danced nearer to where She was, making sure her girlfriend's eyes would not catch the action by using the packed floor for cover.

She riveted the girl with Her eyes, no smiles. When the big guardian finally went to the bar to get a drink, looking back to her girl from farther away through the jostling, dancing crowd of women, that was when the girl danced right in front of Her, her breasts and hips moving, straining under cheap black leather. She didn't react to the show. The girl looked Bardot-pouty, Bardot-sultry at Her from under a Bardot-mop of hair. Still she did not move but kept staring, not smiling. She changed Her stance so Her hips glided toward the girl for a moment, then relaxed. The girl saw it, looked around for her dyke, double-checked ... and that was when She turned away so that the girl saw only Her back when her eyes sought Her again. It was a game, and She knew she would follow Her.

It was Kelly, though, who pushed through the crowd and thumped Her on the shoulder. She was freaking.

"What the hell are you doing? Her girlfriend knows what's going on over here. When you turned around she pushed through and grabbed the little blonde."

"Shit. Where are they?"

She said without daring to turn her head. She looked straight ahead while Kelly acted as Her eyes.

"Over on the other side, dancing together, kind of. You're lucky that she—... Wait a minute. Some friends or something are talking to her, the giant. Blondie's kind of just to the side, alone."

"Alone? Stay close."

She weaved through the crowd, heading for the girl like being locked onto a laser beam. Walked up to her where she diddy-bopped alone in the crowd to the music. Walked up to her, got close enough to touch and started to dance with her. Not a word, Her eyes on the girl's, they swayed together. Perfect attunement.

"Want to do something different tonight?"

And the Bardot-girl looked up from under fluttered lids, licked her sulky lips. She finally spoke so softly through the smoke and bodies and the beat from Madonna's "Like a Virgin" that She had the excuse to lean against her. In the warm press of bodies, drinks and cigarettes carefully navigated by, no one saw the intimacy.

"Like?"

She moved Her cheek next to hers. She breathed close in her ear.

"More than what's going on here."

"Call me."

That was all the girl could get out. Before anything went any further the girlfriend's hand snaked from between two women pressed nearby who were locked in a kiss. She grabbed the little Bardot-blonde by the arm, pulled her away. This was it.

She looked over Her shoulder for Kelly, first one backward look, craning through the pulsing sea of women, and then another. No Kelly. No fucking Kelly—and the large dyke glowering at Her. The woman advanced like only an angry, large woman can, her man-cut but tastefully blue streaked hair bristling like a stick-poked porcupine.

Jesus fucking Christ. This was not the way She imaged it in Her *everything's coming up roses at two hundred miles an hour* cocaine buzzed brain. She looked around, beyond the woman who was righteously advancing on Her, pushing women aside on her way. Then, finally, spotted Kelly through the crowd. She was sitting at the far end of the block long, packed bar, laughing, and making faces at Her. She wanted to kill Kelly. But the giant dyke looked like she would kill Her first. Bardot-busty-blondey had disappeared and She was left staring at the girlfriend who had carved a space in the throng. She fantasized there was steam coming out of the woman's ears.

Emergency Plan B: Most outwardly butch women were really creampuffs. Their bluster was usually all they had and didn't know it. Sometimes. In a flash, She smiled, flashed a flirtatious beam with welcoming eyes and stepped right in front of the woman: warm, sweet, flirting. The woman hesitated, and that was the signal. A hesitation, a slight deflation. Confusion made her falter: Was this a come-on? She could see her thinking it, or maybe she was thinking: She wants me. She could see it zinging through the woman's eyes, so She notched up the warmth with Her *take me to bed* look. She never thought about how Her reality was warped by cocaine's warp speed. Was She making up all this? These interpretations, the assumptions … She never bothered to question Her chemical world.

One sizzling, *come and fuck me* look, and She brushed past the woman with a hand placed skillfully, seductively on her arm. She kept going but moved slowly through the crowd, deliberately moving other women out of the way—the way you do when you meet a stranger's eye for a half-second and press them lightly aside, sexy but deniable, as you move past. When She glanced back with an audacious come-on look, She could feel Her eyelids flutter in the worst kind of obvious reflex that oozed sex, inviting the woman to follow. She did not, of course. But she didn't punch Her through a wall either.

"You're unbelievable! You fucking tart, you're unbelievable," Kelly was yelling at Her while She ordered a drink, safe at the bar.

"And where were you, friend?"

"I didn't think— Not that. I didn't think you'd do it, Jesus. You're unbelievable!"

"Living on the edge," She said. "Now just hang while I get her phone number. She told me to call her and they'll be leaving soon to fight with each other."

"Blondey girl? Her number, you're kidding? There's no way she's doing that. She'll get beat up. You'll get beat up. And I'm talking to you, so I'll get beat up!"

There were no fights. The little blonde was lurking around the bathrooms, waiting for Her. Their eyes picked up on each other's as they made the pass, neither faltering. The girl squeezed Her hand as she put the folded paper into Her palm. Her girlfriend was nowhere in sight, but She went into the restroom for a time anyway, took a few hits off a joint. When She returned to the bar, Kelly was frantic.

"She was here looking for you. She's going to kill you because you waltzed away from her like that and it finally hit her. She gets it, what you were trying to do with her girlfriend."

"Trying?" She said, and showed her the folded paper.

"Unbelievable. You're unbelievable."

Kelly was pissed off. She was envious.

"You made your point. You're not really going to call her."

"Why not?" She said it too fast then caught Herself. "No, of course not."

She didn't want Kelly to know anything She might do. And She knew Her relationship with Margret was too fragile for this. Besides, somehow She didn't have the heart for it. There were things they had to work out still. Somehow, for a change. She couldn't bring Herself to fuck around, not this time. Besides, the game, the challenge of getting that girl was all she'd wanted anyway, really.

She felt the same way for weeks. Opportunities with women threw themselves in Her path. Another night in another bar a woman She had been talking to for only a few minutes invited Her home.

"I probably can't come tonight," she had said. "But I can cuddle. And there's always the morning."

"Yeah, but there's still tonight too." She insisted a little too much, maybe, and the woman did not smile shyly enough. They stared into eyes bleary with drink and wafted toward each other, leaned together. It was as much for support as it was for potential sex.

"Let's see how you kiss." The woman pressed against Her to find out. "… Very good."

It was a swift, deep kiss, and too weird. So She left her suddenly and made Her precarious way into a freezing rain. She laughed out loud at Her freedom. She had the freedom to say no, or yes. All this grandeur—just by not being so close to Margret—and it was exhilarating. Alone, wind pelting rain on empty West Village streets. Not even a dog walker down Seventh Avenue, not even when She got to Christopher Street. All the more reason to hit the bar, The Duchess, one block down at Grove Street.

The Duchess was pure throwback hide-your-gayness-in-a-crummy-hole-in-the-wall that was guarded by an overweight Mob guy in a sport jacket with wide lapels and a gun-bulge. The decor was early Mafia rococo. Kathy was one of the six women in the dim, too-silent place of desperation there at the bar. She hadn't seen her in years, not since she'd tied Her up and fucked Her brains out. Heavy S&M, at least the heaviest She had experienced, and with a woman She had only met once before in Her life and never saw again until now.

Kathy was a big redhead, muscular and attractive, and she grabbed Her in a rib-crushing welcome as soon as she saw Her. That hit of pain was enough to remind Her of what She didn't want to feel again. The bruised wrists and ankles from tight rough ropes, frighteningly hurt nipples from clamps She didn't want put on but was powerless to avoid, a cunt sore from brutalization with a dildo, and although She protested enough to avoid a butt plug She felt the discomfort as if it had happened. Kathy had done enough and She wasn't about to give up that kind of control again, at least not with her. The only thing that had been good about it was feeling her solid body on Her, Her legs tied wide open, while she fucked Her with only her cunt with perfectly placed bone-shaking rhythm. She came so easily to her then, forgot about the pain from before it.

She was not into submitting to anyone, not tonight, not lately. Not with the mind-fuck submission She was getting from Margret anyway. So She refused Kathy, went out in to the wind and rain and felt free. She wondered what Margret was doing, but only for a second.

- No Time Like the Present for A Present -
SURPRISE

It finally happened. After four months She found an apartment big enough for both of them to live in where She could set up a darkroom for work. That was Her part, She found it. Now Margret would cover the money part—loan the portion of expenses that were Hers now because She had done Her part. All of this was unspoken, and expected.

The only problem was that the place wouldn't be ready for another month. There had been a fire in the building and the place had to be rebuilt. It was on Chrystie Street near Rivington on the Lower East Side: LOSAIDA. When She signed the lease the space was filled with charred rubble and construction debris. Too bad it was too destroyed to live in, but too good a place ultimately, to pass up. Too bad She had played out all of Her friends and was stretching them even further by borrowing money from them to come up with the first and last month's rent and a security deposit. She always pretended to not be completely dependent on Margret. Margret was still at Bitsy's and seemed comfortable. Why not? Margret was settled while She moved all over hell and back.

"You could come and stay there tonight, at Bitsy's."

She and Margret were having dinner at the DoJo on St. Marks. They had just looked at the new flame-scarred apartment together for the first time. It was kind of a celebration that proclaimed their being able to live together again.

"No thanks," She said. "It's cool she's let you stay, weird as she is, and I don't want to push it. We probably need at least a month before you can move into our new place."

She had Her overnight duffel with her, under the table, ready to stay anywhere She could for tonight or longer. With getting the new place and all She had misjudged where she was crashing, and when. She was only a little worried about figuring something out for tonight and knew She could probably impose on Nance again at the last minute. Nothing was going to ruin Her good mood. *Fucking A*, She had Her own place—soon.

"No, really, you could stay there," Margret said.

"I've got a better plan. Let's spend the night together but let's go to a hotel, that one over at Washington Square, toward Sixth. Cool, yes?"

"You have money?"

"Well, no, but—"

"I can give it to you."

"Me? –Us. It'll be fun."

"There's something I want to talk to you about first," Margret said as the check came. "I want to tell you ..."

She fiddled with the money for the check, not looking at Her. Finally, she raised her eyes.

"Jesus, what?"

"I have to tell you ... I'm having an affair with Bitsy."

It happened. She has left me. She says no. But it's a relationship, I know it. So disgusting. So disgusted. But was it so great before? Not really. Was she so great? I loved her, love her, I think.

She glared across the table at Margret. Her smile crumbled and She felt it, having the smile slapped off Her face. The noise in the restaurant was suddenly gone, shut off, then began again.

"I want to explain it to you," Margret was saying.

But She couldn't hear. Her stomach started to lurch and She felt She was going to throw up right on the table.

"I've got to go."

But Margret wanted Her to wait. *Wait for what?*

She grabbed her duffel from under the table and went outside, seeing nothing but a glare of lights, cabs going by. Margret caught up with Her.

"Don't walk so fast," she said it in the mother-tone. "I'm not going to follow you down the street like this."

"I don't give a shit what the fuck you do!"

She kept walking faster. And faster. Where? Nowhere to go, no money. What a great time to be told.

Thanks, Margret. Asshole!

Good Christ, Bitsy? No. Not her! A zero—at least in Her eyes. It didn't matter that She didn't even really know Bitsy—kind, apartment-sharing Bitsy. But to the jaundiced eye, everything is yellow.

Not just an affair, no guts to go to the bars and try to find a fuck. No, just go ahead and fuck with anything—and Bitsy was any *Thing*—fuck with any Thing that happened to be in reach. Living together, they were fucking living together—and evidently fucking. They had even met Her together, She remembered now. And now it all fell into focus. Bitsy's strange looks at Her from under those greasy bangs. And Margret's nervousness, short temper with Her over the last few weeks. Incredible, fucking incredible to be sleeping with that, a nothing. But Margret always took the easy way out, used whatever was at hand—and that was only the first insult She thought of.

Jesus fucking Christ.

She threw up in a trash bin on a corner near Tompkins Square Park. Margret was being touched by that ... that stupid dyke. Yes, lately judgmental but off the charts now.

Nowhere to go, no money. And told about Her lover's cheating in a restaurant.

Thanks, Margret. Asshole!

No guts, Ms. Politically Correct picked a great place to do violence to a woman she'd been with for five years. Great timing. She had bug-eyed Bitsy's place to go back to, and Bitsy's bed. They had laughed about that bed together when they moved her in—*too small, no action, ha ha*—and now Margret slept in it every night. Margret had that comfortable place to go back to and there She was, stuck. She was the one moving again, still. Nowhere to go while Margret was comfortable, really comfortable—if you've got no standards. Typical. *Motherfuckingsonofabitchmotherfuckingbastard! Goddamnit!*

Bitsy and Margret, Her delicate Margret? She threw up on the street.

Thanks, Margret. Asshole!

She had made sure the news would be extra hard to handle with nowhere to go, no money. *You bitch.* Nothing but a common bitch with a worse than common dyke.

She couldn't think, couldn't see. She just kept walking, shouldering Her bag. Two hours of walking, stopping to see where She was, where She found Herself, then walking some more. *Shit.*

She should have gone with the woman in the bar the other night and She might have had a place to go now. Incredible. She wasn't fucking around, had been turning down women and throwing away phone numbers so She could preserve a precarious relationship. *Devious, betraying bitch.* Solidly average, bland Bitsy would of course hang onto Margret for dear life because she knew she could never get a woman like that in a million years on her own. Who would look at that zero twice unless they had to, or found it convenient like Margret did. *Shit.* She wouldn't have touched Bitsy for a billion dollars a minute. And She vomited again.

There was no place else to go except to the new apartment. Since the fire the entire building was still unoccupied, no electricity or gas, but She shoved Herself in through the braced door She had seen. She picked Her way around the rubble and sat down. Then it all came out, all the pain, the hurt, humiliation, the loss. She couldn't believe it, could not believe it. Not to Her, this hadn't happened to Her before, not when She loved so much. *Lying bitch. Thanks for the pictures in my head!*

There were all those mind-fuck images of Margret fucking that fiend. Godzilla was cuter than Bitsy by a mile, and had a more interesting personality. *Oh god, them in bed together?* Margret coming under the Chinless Wonder. And She vomited and vomited again.

She spent the night that way, alone, throwing up turned to dry heaves, sobbing. All night like that in a dark abandoned building. Just Her and the mice.

Up all night, crazed all night. All She had were the hallucinations of them together, fucking. Dragged down so low, so low to Bitsy's level—by association. Margret with that, The Zero, in Her eyes. A surge of rage built in Her with the daylight. That's when She started to destroy whatever She could get Her hands on. Boards, bricks, hammers and saws flew out of Her hands against the pitted walls. She ripped down partially built partitions. The pain inside was unbearable. The pictures in Her head tortured Her. Them. Together. Her lover, the woman She cherished—she was in the same bed with the same woman every night, fucking.

- Forget Time. Die Now. -
DIRT

Margret came to find Her the next afternoon. Nance told her where She was because she had just left Her there in the new under-construction place. A real friend, Nance had been with Her all morning, horrified at the news.

"I don't even want to think about them together, makes me sick," Nance said.

The mention of the thought that came with those writhing images had consequences. It sent Her to the gutted bathroom to spit up and then dry heave again, a plastic bag at the ready. She shouldn't have had the coffee Nance brought. Why it was important for her to run to throw up in a no-walls, no-fixture bathroom? Must have been some inbred nod to civilization. It wouldn't have mattered where she hung her mouth into the plastic bag, but She ran to the roughed-out toilet every time. It had been the same all night and all morning.

"You can't stay here. This is a disaster, you're a disaster. Stay at my place. I've got a closet." Nance had said it, trying to get a laugh.

No way. She couldn't stay with Nance because She knew what Her mood would be like from now on, and wouldn't put a friend through it.

And then Margret showed up, wanting to talk.

"Always talk," She spit it out. "All I ever get is a mind fuck from you while you fuck with that pig-face. What's going on? Is this really it? Is it serious, or just a fling with The Thing? Which?"

Of course Margret in her usual indecisive way, didn't know. But she would not shut up. "I just hope I'm not using her to get out of a bad relationship with you."

"With me? You're fucking using each other, you asshole! You haven't got the guts to go out on your own and find someone, and she's too ugly and too much a zero to get anyone like you on her own so you both took the easiest, sleaziest way out. How fucking convenient! Jesus, who the fuck would have ever thought I'd have to worry about you living there with—What a fucking embarrassment. How the hell can you even admit it, to yourself, our friends?"

"I thought you would call me a whore," Margret barely whispered.

"You wish!" She screamed back. "You don't rise to that level, you're just a lazy asshole. You're sleeping with her because it's easy. But that's you, you like being taken care of and you're a user, an opportunist. That's what Sam said about you when he first met you. He was right! He said I should drop you and concentrate on my work because you're a fucking opportunist!"

Her anger skidded recklessly. She didn't care. She was too hurt to care. Margret saw there was no coping with Her and left—at first hesitant, a few steps through the rubble toward the door. Then as she reached it, suddenly spurred, and she rushed out. But She yelled after her.

"Fucking coward! Going back to the Chinless Wonder? Gutless and chinless, you two make a good couple. Asshole!"

She went and opened again and then slammed shut the door off its blackened hinges. She stomped into what might someday be Her studio to throw charred refuse around before She got that nauseous feeling again with nothing in her stomach to heave out. She hadn't eaten or slept for more than twenty-four hours but when She went out She went only to buy two packs of cigarettes to launch into another night and day of it. *Fucking bitch.* The pain doubled Her over.

Obsession was on Her like a closed claw. There was nothing She could think of, nothing She could do without thinking of them. And She could not at all bear thinking of them because sooner or later it made Her gag. It was a grim, painful fixation that colored everything with it, that stupid act, and this dumb, normal, ignorant attachment to someone else when a relationship becomes boring. It was still loving, She had thought. But it was certainly boring.

There was little that was rational She could admit to now. She didn't want to be understanding, refused to be in Her own mind. She didn't want to give up anything to understanding. Maybe She was afraid that if She didn't close off all the avenues Margret might come back. So Her rage continued, Her intransigence to Margret's offers increased, and Her taking shelter from being in any way forgiving was honed to a fine sneer.

It went on and on. An elegant smirk was all She had for Margret whenever She saw her. No, She would never take her back. She knew that from the beginning but admitted it only later. She did not really want her back but that admission was too painful, more honest than She had been with herself or Margret in years. And it was painful because of that.

Censorship is what I feel when I am not alone. Something stops me from disclosing, stops me from being in the freedom, from feeling free to be as I want, say what I want. Without long days of staying in my own head I lose the will to take risks.

Work that comes from me, not veiled, can only come by feeling I am not watched. Can only come by hearing my own voice, or some voice, in my head, uninterrupted. Uninterrupted by a breakfast presence, a check-in phone call, the knowledge that someone waits. Alone. The only expectations are mine. The only expectation is me. That is the work, being me. Knowing it. Saying it. But as soon as I feel too close, too hemmed in by expectations, what ought to be, I start to hide. I don't want to offend. Don't want to fight. Don't want to stand up to anyone. That's the way it feels. I need to hide so that I can uncover.

Got to feel free. Unwatched. Unwaited for. Alone. Otherwise it's only mediocre. It comes from somewhere and someone else, not me.

And of course She felt like a failure for some valid reasons and for some really paranoid ones. Like She thought it was valid to feel like a failure because She had fucked up in the relationship. She tortured Herself that it could have been—but obviously it could never have been—any different at all. More sensitive, more caring, more attentive ... She couldn't be, wasn't and fucking didn't want to be different, otherwise She would have been. Still, it was too bad but it was also ok to feel like shit about it.

It was all those paranoid reasons for feeling like a failure that became industrial strength delusions. Like when She absolutely knew that Margret thought She was stupid and ugly and a disgusting person to be with, and everyone knew it and were only nice to Her because they pitied her—the subhuman slime who got dumped. It was those paranoid reasons that buzz-bombed Her and stuck and burned like napalm when they hit Her head and set Her hair on fire. She hated meeting friends on the street.

"Jesus Christ, you look terrible," Nick stopped Her coming out of Pearl Paint on Canal. "What's wrong?"

"Nothing."

"Bullshit. Who died?"

She had to tell him—Nick was an abstract painter She had known for years. Everyone who hung around anywhere below Fourteenth Street, East or West Village or in SoHo, would find out. That kind of news, relationship dirt, travels fast.

"I want to be able to work this out just between us," Margret had told Her at one of the meetings—ambushes—that Margret engineered.

"Right. Just between us and the whole goddamn dyke scene and all our friends, you naïve asshole, and I mean really naïve, really asshole."

"Stop it."

Margret would always end up telling Her to "stop it" when She ranted at her. And She would always tell Margret to "get out."

She couldn't stand to look at her because all She could see was her with bulge-belly Bitsy. And She couldn't stand to look at her because she was beginning to look like Bitsy: wearing ugly sweatshirts, baggy jeans. Adjusting to the level of whomever she was with, Margret lost the artist look and took on a common dyke haircut and clothes because she was being taken care of by that Zero. She even started wearing those comfortable sensible shoes that English old ladies wear to hike in the heather or something. It felt like Her life was passing before Her eyes whenever She looked at Margret in her state of borrowed appearance. That hurt, her choice of "that Zero" and her accouterments instead of Her? Humiliating, disgusting. It would not leave Her head, the accusations, the ridicule, the pictures of them together ... It sent Her to Avenue C and 10th Street to buy drugs in the back of a fake bodega.

"Shit, girl," Constance Never Connie poked at Her, "those jeans used to be tight. How much weight you lost? Six hundred pounds, in what, like, couple weeks? I'm not getting you any more stuff, girl. Don't ask."

She argued with her. Since when was she, Constance Never Connie, the keeper of Her welfare? Nance must have already talked to her, told her not to support Her depression. She thought it was ridiculous. She needed something for Her black mood.

"Since when is coke bad for the downs?"

"When you come down, that's when, and you know it."

"That's why I'm getting two grams, I'll stay up. Come on for shit's sake, CNC."

She convinced her and they snorted up together. Then they went speeding through East Village bars, Alphabet City, starting at Avenue A. The WaWa Hut—King Tut's WaWa hut—and then the Pyramid, then to Sidewalk on the other corner that seemed straighter, from a society point of view, but wasn't because of all the bikers who hung there. But it was straighter from the gay point of view, and still ok. Anyway, it was there that Constance Never Connie scored two more bags in the bathroom. Just another day in the neighborhood.

She thanked the universe for Her friends. She was being held together by Nance, Kelly, Constance Never Connie, and the less close friends who She could seek out and who welcomed Her whenever She did: Nick the painter, Johnny and David, Mary Smith—not Mary the actress fuck—and Danny and the genius Koby, and there was Reno, the comedienne, just getting going then and playing the clubs. And there was Libby, a very old friend She hooked up with again. She needed them, close and distant, She needed all of them. The pressure of Her images that had to be released in words was too much for any one person to hear all the time. Poor Nance got the brunt, good friend that she was, but She knew that She had to spread Her grief around or She would burst with it. Like a ripe white pus pimple She had to squeeze out the poison of Margret every day, every hour.

Thank you, universe, for good friends, mostly for Nance. She would mutter it. Thankful for the downtown gang that was usually hanging out together, or not. But a gang who knew each other by feel, by ineffable bond of trying to make it—whatever that meant for each of them.

"You've got to eat," Nance told Her. "Eat anything."

"I can't. Can't keep it down when I think about them, you know, together. Can you see it? With that face—"

"Stop, don't talk about it anymore. I'll get sick."

It was Constance Never Connie who chimed in, but it was She who suddenly ran to the bathroom. Everyone could hear Her retching. When She returned, Constance had to make it lighter, clown around. She produced a dog bone from somewhere in her purse.

"I'll be ready. That thing comes near me I'll give her this. Say, honey, this yours, you dogggg."

But Bitsy never came around any of them, didn't travel in the same circles, never had. She didn't have enough style, was not interesting enough—that was Her story and She stuck to it, never admitting She might be wrong. Mary Smith, a sculptor, had pointed out, though, that it was unusual that Margret never went out with Bitsy in public. It seemed to her that she wasn't in any hurry to be parading around as a couple with her. She said she didn't "get it at all" that with all the wild girls around, why did Margret keep it up with Bitsy, the quiet woman? Mary did not give any negative description at the end of her musing, but She heard the worst in Her head anyway. She knew Margret kept on with Bitsy out of convenience and opportunity that was why. But once you do it, fuck, it means it turns into a relationship. It's a dyke law. Fuck a few times and you're in love, especially for women of the old school like Bitsy. And then of course Margret would get into it as well just to justify fucking her in the first place.

Margret told Her she loved Her "too much" and that was why she had to get away from Her to be on her own. On her "own" but supported and protected by her, a mortal, whose reward was to get to touch her? Right. That was real independence. *Whore!*

"You don't understand. That's what I had to do—me, I was the one who had to. I had to do what I did to try a life on my own."

"Fine, so use fat face. But don't think I'll ever touch you again after you've been touched by crud."

"You're disgusting."

Margret would leave Her after these encounters looking more crushed than disgusted. Or maybe it was only an act for Her benefit, or non-benefit, to give Her guilt. Or maybe it was because she had to go back to Bitsy.

Good, you bitch, go to your pet monster. Stay with her. So judgmental, more than usual. And it made Her ashamed, all the name-calling, the ugliness She spewed out.

But Margret kept coming back, wanting to talk, to be with Her. All She did in return was abuse her, berate her. Her wrath was intense even without seeing her, but confronted with the way Margret looked, the evidence of living with Bitsy, made Her wild. It didn't take much because Her mood was lousy anyway from being constantly exhausted by working to make Her new apartment habitable. Again, as always, Margret was no help with work, not that She wanted or needed her incompetence with real work. It was just another example of something for which Margret was totally useless.

Glad she's gone. But she wouldn't stay away.

"Quit coming around trying to get near me when your face has been in shit-cunt!"

"And you?" Margret finally screamed back. "How many have you been with? Who are you seeing?"

"Like you care, asshole."

And She suddenly realized that She wasn't seeing anyone. She had been working so hard and living so much in relation to Margret's revolting relationship that She hadn't been chasing women at all.

She thought of Carmen first, Saint Carmen of the Screams. She called her and "Yes, perfect," she would see Her that night.

Great. In the rubble of the apartment and in the only clean place, the bed, Carmen came and proved her purity to Her all over again. The girl was wonderful, better than Margret had ever been in bed— She needed to believe that—and She needed her. They fucked for hours, slept a little, fucked some more. Carmen left at four in the morning. Left Her with tender aches of satisfaction, of exertion, of being clung to... *Thank you, Carmen.*

The passion was rare, the languor exquisite, now of memories that made Her contract in a lovely spasm as She lay in the aromatic bed, thinking. *Thank you, Carmen.* It was the calmest She had felt in months. Then suddenly Margret was there—a firm knock—visiting again at nine in the morning.

Margret stalked, inspected the swept areas where She had calmed the rubble. Buckets filled with chunks of stuff, and dirt, and wire bits, and molding bits waited in a scarily overflowing collection by the door to be taken down and dumped. There was a slanted kitchen table and two chairs that were worse, boards on sawhorses She was using as tables for some books and photographs that She kept protected under paper and plastic. Margret stalked around the bed and eyed Her clothes, still balled up and thrown on the floor where She had flung them off the night before. She surveyed the scene of obviously heavy fucking and didn't way a word, although she looked pained. *Good.*

She had brought Her a fried egg and bacon sandwich from a good *bodega* and a Puerto Rican-made authentic coffee with milk, café con leche, two sugars. Delicious. She said she brought it because there was nothing to make anything with in the apartment and she wanted to eat with Her. But it turned it into a non-gift because She couldn't relax enough to enjoy it, couldn't choke anything down with her there—*cuntface.*

She hated Herself for it, the childish hurt She could not control, or really admit. So She drove Margret away again.

- Time Keeps Moving. But Where? -
SHAMBLES

The enchantment She always had for Margret intensified. Instead of being freed, She became more ensnared over the next months.

"I'm trying to move," Margret kept saying. "But I can't find a place, you know mine is rented. I want to be out of there."

"Yeah, right."

Finding a place, it wasn't ever easy in New York. But She had found one for them both, and now She was there alone. Alone after the debris, the filth She had hacked through every day for six weeks with the building's construction guys, with help from Her friends, good friends.

Now She was as settled as She could be with too much time to fixate on being dumped and no will to work, living on loans. She went out, sometimes alone, sometimes with Nance. Nance, who heard Her pain, frustration, rage. How often they went over and over the repugnant relationship. They talked on the phone, on the street, in restaurants, at openings, and in the bars in between cruising women. Everywhere. How much Nance put up with from Her, hearing the same stories, the agony and disbelief that it had happened, was continuing to happen.

"I can't believe it. I just can't fucking believe it."

"Hear that," Nance would say. "I know how it feels."

And she did. Nance had also been discarded, had her own heartache and bludgeoned ego. Unfortunately, She could not remember that girl's name, one of the ones who had hurt Nance. But that was all right because She knew how Nance felt even if She only vaguely remembered the girl's look. Only people who've been dumped really know the damage done and the ferocity suffered, the total disorientation that it explodes in your head, your life.

"You know this is really the best thing that could have happened to you, and you've got to remember it," Nance said. "You weren't happy. You never even acted like yourself around Margret. And she's been really nasty to you lately. But don't get me wrong, I like her, you two just got bad together. But this, it's fucked up. No excuse, it's horrible. You're right."

"Then I'm not crazy?"

"You are. You're totally nuts, like always. You feel like shit, and you're entitled to feel like shit now, that's all. It's a fucked up thing to have done to you, but it happens. You'll live."

She couldn't go to sleep without thinking of Margret, nor wake up without her on Her mind. And that was only the nights She didn't bolt upright in bed from a nightmare about her and The Thing. How could she have done it to Her?

How could you do it? Fucker.

"I didn't do it to you, to hurt you. I did it for myself, to get away from the relationship," Margret would say. "I love you. I loved you too much, it was bad for both of us, too constricting. You felt it too, be honest."

"I thought we were staying apart to work it out, we've done that before. But you lied, you, the great honesty asshole. You let me believe we were going to work it out, live together again."

They were in Her still under construction, but better, apartment. They were smoking cigarettes and circling each other around boxes and sawhorses, most of the time, yelling.

"We still can."

"Bullshit! You fucking left me!"

"But I didn't. I love you. I left the relationship, not you!"

"What the fuck? You and your fucking twisted shit. Semantics make the difference, never mind feelings, right? You're too much a coward to admit it and take the weight for what you've done."

"We did it to ourselves!" Margret screamed at Her. "And we can still work it out—us!"

"Right, bitch, not goddamn likely. Not like this!"

It would always end with Her shouting for Margret to "get out." And Margret always responded that she "loved" Her and the problem was that She didn't understand that it didn't have to be so bad between them. She thought that was crazy, and of course sought Her friends' support and opinions.

"Maybe you should try to talk without doing your wounded mad dog thing," Nance said it as they eyed the women around them in the bar. "You know, you're really not leaving her any way to get back to you, bitch-girl."

"Talk? I can't, goddamnit, because I look at her and know what she's been doing with Rotten Face and it makes me sick. I can't help it, it really makes me sick to my stomach still, and fucking enraged."

"No kidding, Miss Mad Dog." Nance tried not to laugh. "But you could try, you know. Wait, look at her, over there."

Nance was tired of talking about it, and so was She. She tried to look for women to fuck, the younger the better, although anyone halfway attractive would do.

The first one She picked up reminded Her of Ester, Ester of the Waldorf, the straight woman who couldn't come but who was so hot. Every time they were together—the affair lasted about six weeks— every time, Ester got closer to coming and discovered new ways of feeling, responding. And She found new ways to explore her. It was something Ester was more than willing to let Her do. That searching, that innocence of knowing another woman, was translated into moves She had really never felt in quite that way. Ester's straightness added a different flavor to fucking. She lived with her boyfriend and fucked him all the while they saw each other. That was with little information about AIDS then, and it was before Sam was sick—She would never fool around that way later. Being straight and servicing him primed Ester to give that same kind of openness to demands, or at least a practice for giving, servicing really, to Her. Ester sucked better than anyone She had ever had before or since. And she wanted to give rim jobs that made even Her hesitant. Ester insisted, but She couldn't get into it, not all the way. She let her do the lightest of it to Her, and it was the only time She ever got sheet burn on Her face and breasts.

She remembered how her muscles ached from resisting Ester, giving in only a little. But that was Ester.

The woman She picked up in the Strand Bookstore was different. She was an authentic new wave dyke. Penny, nearly as gamine-like as Ester, was a little older and not as bold as the straight Ester was. They had eye contact near the mysteries, stood next to each other in front of Fiction, and ended up looking at the same big spreads in the photography books. That was when She spoke to her about the pictures, good reproductions or bad ones in various books. It was Nan Goldin's work She could really talk to her about. Penny responded, friendly, in no hurry to leave and helped to keep the conversation going. Very encouraging.

"I'm going to the Cupping Room over on Broome for coffee. If you've got time ..."

"I love that place," she said.

And that was that. They had coffee, then Penny had to get back to work. She was an editor at Dutton and very cool, very interesting. They made a date for her to come the next night to see Her studio— ok it was Her apartment, but She had a real studio portion with Her darkroom, even if it was small. *Halle-fucking-lujah.* And now it looked like She was going to score a new girl on Her own. It wasn't that being with Carmen again wasn't great, it was. But She had known sweet Carmen before, and besides, she was still pretty much completely married to her long-time lover, so She was still able to see her only sporadically. But this Penny, raven haired, professional Penny was new talent, just what She needed to prove Herself, to prove She could get girls and was therefore a valuable human being on the planet.

She could prove it, needed to, and did. Penny was a little cool, not the most fervent fuck in giving but was into taking very well. Not a screamer, just intense, Penny laid back and took a lot, came a lot. She seemed like the kind of woman who was discriminating in whom she went to bed with and didn't do it often. She was, she said, "not interested" in a relationship because there was a woman she was hung up on, waiting for. Dyke drama again.

"Thank you for a lovely night, very lovely," she said and kissed Her, and left.

That she left was fine with Her. Still, She felt empty afterward.

There is no clock. It must be night, it's dark. KISS-FM never gives the time. Before Nance and I talked about our problems, loves. We are the hottest items at the bars, sometimes, so why do we not have who we want? The waitress at the Kiev who overheard us told us we're 'too cool.' Intimidating.

What time is it? What day? Not working takes me away. No clock, no TV, no lover, it all makes a difference. I am alone. I am so all right that it frightens me.

Next morning or afternoon, a little cool rain after intense heat. I sit in the roof door at Alan's. On the river a huge liner is pushed by small tugs, funny. I'm glad they did that for me, gave that image. The clouds hang down so close I can almost reach them, grey, cottony. The top of the Empire State Building is erased by them. The city puts on a great show.

I can't work. I'm so lonely. Why doesn't she call? Any she. Why don't any of them call? I know it's all for the best, to be alone. It has to be this way. But it hurts. Do I want to hurt back? No. Just show them what they're missing. I'll pick someone up, bring her back to this roof. But I know I shouldn't push. Don't push, it all comes.

I remember us at Cape Cod, at Wellfleet. We were great together. Whale watch, rain, hail sometimes, grey, cold but calm seas and fabulous whales. We saw twenty-seven Humpback and two Fin whales. But we, I, saw at least ten more. All over, close, feeding next to the boat, jumping out of the water to feed on krill. Green air bubble, gush of water from their huge mouths.

Whales, very black, blacker than I thought they'd be when I saw that first one, its side in the water. Black, in easy water. I spotted the first whale of the day. Like in Africa when I spotted game before anyone else. That was so long ago, long ago when I had money. The first thing I pointed out just outside of Arusha, were donkeys. Our driver Sa'Idi laughed at me. "Very good, mama," he said, "but these are Masai animals, not wild." After that I got better at it. I stayed up in the screeching sounds of the African nights and saw two Bongos, antelope-like chubby animals with beautiful while stripes and elegant horns. They are very rare, those Bongos, very shy. It's "good luck" to see them, Sa'Idi said. I thought so. Huge beautifully curved antlers, chunky body that was tan with delicate white stripes radiating from the underbelly. Bongo. I stayed up all night in Kenya to see them. There, you could feel the danger.

But Provincetown was different five years later. Different lover too. It all makes a difference. But really, what?

Her life was shit. Days spent zombied-out, not eating, sometimes seeking shelter in friends' company. Nance carried the weight of that as usual, helped Her through the worst. The disorientation was terrible. It was as if She didn't know how to live on Her own all of a sudden. Knowing Margret was there for Her, but not wanting Her around, made Her independent. Without her She felt helpless. She never unpacked cooking utensils, still didn't feed Herself. Between that and Her mood showing through in how She looked it was a wonder She ever got any women to go to bed with Her. But She did and was grateful for it. Lovely Carmen came around, and came, whenever she had time and that was always great. She never saw Penny again and that was all right too.

Concentration on a new affair or a new woman was impossible while She was immersed in Her own turmoil.

"Time helps, always does. Give it six months," Nance predicted. "You'll be human again. Maybe, knowing you."

Maybe. But would She make it until then without killing Herself? Not literally, not really, but She took every opportunity to take every drug that came Her way. That was in addition to those She sought out: coke, smack, crack and of course She smoked grass constantly. She also started to drink, not to excess, but more than She ever had before. From a few beers at a bar if She were out with friends She progressed to a few beers at home to make it through the day, and four or five Jack Daniels when She was out at night. It never made Her really drunk. She couldn't get drunk. No mercy anywhere.

And Margret's mood changed from conciliatory to *fuck you*. It helped Her, helped Her remember her bitchiness instead of her goodness.

Having those images of her in Her head helped when She went out and met new people. A little gentleness was what She needed, like She got from Carmen, always. And Nance helped the most by telling Her to "shut up and have a good time."

So She tried. Nance introduced Her to another circle of friends, wider than Her usual group, and She got used to going to more clubs with Nance and them. She got used to leaving the group late in the mornings, alone, after hanging out in after-hours clubs with new people. There was still that feeling of being weird, feeling empty, hating to go back to an empty apartment to thoughts of Margret that would not stop once She was alone. Loneliness was the killer that only coke could keep from twisting deeper.

She kept living Her life through Margret. She didn't know who She was without Margret there to nag Her. Damn, what a way to live. Women who approached Her in bars sometimes She didn't even notice.

"Shape up, asshole," Nance would say. "Life goes on."

"Yeah it do, it surely do ... one miserable day after another."

"Fucking nut job, period."

She agreed She was nuts, and totally negative about everything. She looked and felt haggard, slept little, forgot about food entirely. Living off the radio, K-ROCK, with songs She started to identify with stuff like "96 Tears" and, of course, tough and sad Joplin belting out that freedom really is free. Nothing left to lose. Ain't that the truth, Janis.

But fuck that. Freedom is fucking freedom, possibilities, new talent. Most of all a life, Her life, was in in Her hands now. No more worries about coordinating schedules, breakfast, going out with a lover who was a drag on Her. Very slowly She started to feel it, feel the fun of it all. Hanging out in dressing rooms of friends of friends who were playing at CBGB on the Bowery, sharing the drugs, meeting new crazies who She could be interested in for Herself. No extra baggage, no one who wanted to go home too soon, no one to be aware of, to protect, to see to. *Mother fuck.* It was starting to be fun for the first time in a long time.

She lived from party to club, from quick fuck to new friends. The worst was over, had to be—Sam was dead. Her photographs were kind of recognized in a small corner of the art world, getting a little riff off the old work that had been published. And no one really knew how She had fucked up the Berlin show Margret got for Her, how

She threw away the opportunity, cancelled it. Now She had a place to live, and somehow—She didn't know how—somehow She got by with enough borrowed and conjured cash, credit card shuffling, a little money from Her photographs now and then, a few.

Best of all She started to work on her work again, *Her* art. Make a life, figure it out. Start all over but not from zero. She wasn't trash to be tossed aside. She was just too much for the bitch to handle. *OK.* Margret could step down into a calm life with a construction worker, but She was heading for excitement with creatively bizarre people, people who let Her breathe new air.

- Overwind, Strip Those Gears! -
BREAK OUT

The parks were beautiful. Central Park, Washington Square and Tompkins Square, each in its own way. She enjoyed Herself, took care of business, errands, got stoned and shopped in between, bought a pair of boots, strolled back home. A gorgeous day, but missing Margret. It was one of the days with real sadness because She felt her absence, her affection not palpable, or had it been gone for a long time anyway? *Who cares?* They both fucked up. Disappointed each other, probably. She was much too stoned to think about it, though, only the feelings enveloped Her, made Her cry when She never thought She would. All of a sudden. Surprise.

Shit. She knew She had to be creative about these things, these sudden black lightning bolts. Be creative, that it leads to self-discovery was some kind of truism. Or maybe not. She was learning to both like and hate Herself better, different parts of Her, and different contexts. If She could only remember to accept that She was at times a judgmental fucker and insecure because of it, and sometimes was a compassionate, powerful human being ... as well as a hell of a lot of gradations of shit in between.

The worst times were feeling insecure. She was unattractive, clumsy at social things, awkward—all the things She thought when She hated Herself, and they weren't even all that original. In a book about women's diaries from the 1830s, She found the complaints were the same. Complaints? Isn't that what they always said about women, the way they label women's feelings? "Complaints."

She felt that way about Margret, She realized, felt that she

121

had been a nag. The unspoken label was there, a nagging wife, for Christ's sake. So what did that make Her? What a fucking discovery. Did they talk so little that they had taken on more of the trappings of conventional roles than they realized? Or did they take on those roles because they liked them, were somehow used to them in societal images, and what is endemic in those roles is not talking?

She had never admitted to any "role-ness" before. Too afraid, was that possible after all the years, twenty or so with women, still afraid, still hiding, still denying that some sort of yin and yang may be present? It completes nature, they say. But is nature really based on those strict kinds of power roles? No. Men pervert it—men's society perverts it. Besides, She always thought the yin and yang should reside in a complete person, the butch and the femme in one person, at different times, different places. But that had become an excuse for wanting them both without ever doing either really to extremes—or perfection. But that's what felt like freedom to Her, mind-freedom to compliment the physical freedom She got by being alone. And physical freedom to be a top and a bottom, too. It was fun. It was finally beginning to be fun after nearly half a year of a purgatory from which She wanted to emerge with the nerve to challenge dead Dante's experience. Challenges to dead men, easy for both reasons.

This is not the paper I wanted. I wanted graph paper with little squares. Lines. Filofax.

Perfection hinders creativity. Criticism is a block to it. So I force perfectionism on myself and don't feel right without the perfect paper, the perfect pen. I become intense in detail, extreme with details. I do it myself, then, I criticize myself. It's never good enough.

Not perfect. Why bother. It makes me not work. There's the answer: defeatism. The real answer is lazy. And afraid.

Why do I always forget philosophy?

The thing about successes and failures is that it seems the failures are always my fault, even when obvious assholes are obviously to blame. And the successes fade instantly as though unreal.

When I'm down I fantasize for the big hit, solve all my problems at once.

Work, just work, just depending on me is energy always so hard to muster.

Creativity—was it Freud where She read it? "Creativity is a response to the unbearable pain of loss and separation." Through art the artist repopulates the world. Art restores the split between the inner and outer world and we recreate what is most loved. Is that why the new pictures She shot and the hand-tinting She was trying were all about women? Everything about women.

It drew Her, the work and the content. She wanted to say something direct for the first time. No more subtle images of women that was once the hallmark of Her photographs. Women on women through hazy obscure techniques that produced gauzy, blurred effects. It was there, certainly, the sexuality just beneath the surface that some critics liked. But now, drawn into the new darkroom, Her hands worked of their own accord, sharpening, painting in red the intimacies She had laid just below the surface of the photographs before. Risk instead of subtlety drew Her, and She allowed Herself to work without censoring Herself. No one could see the new work yet, not yet. Always superstitious about unfinished work, this work, what She allowed Herself to show in it, made Her both afraid and exhilarated. She didn't know if She wanted the exposure of Herself the work would bring. But then again, so what? It was good work. She liked it and She held Her breath about it, not thinking about it too much, just doing it. Doing it.

When She wasn't working, there was the waiting. It was a waiting during which She could not pull in a deep breath, was restless, stared at the walls, did coke, didn't do enough coke ... How much She wanted to call—She missed Margret like a habit, like trying to quit smoking, you can't just stop. At least She couldn't. But She wouldn't call, wouldn't give her the satisfaction.

Should all this be easier? That's what a country song was asking. Saying goodbye, at least trying to leave, was Her answer. But She didn't really dare to question why it all made Her feel so shitty.

It was the radio's fault. Charley Pride's "Shouldn't It Be Easier Than This" was played nonstop. She had started listening to a country station in addition to rock and roll and reggae. Her life identified in folk poetry depressed Her a little, but not that much. She could experiment with and be whoever She wanted, whatever. *So fuck it.* She found She loved country music, a lot of it anyway. New interests or those never pursued lured Her now. It started when She met new friends, new girls.

She met more artists, musicians, photographers, dancers, students. Some were body builders, others were bikers. Bikers, magicians on the road, who, when they were men occupied a place of normal respect from Her. But when She met the women who rode, and rode so well, it was like falling in love for the first time. The competency, the skill they possessed was the same as what had first attracted Her to women. They might be teased as "dykes on bikes" but they were no stereotypical butch bruisers. Because of who they were in addition to being bikers they offered Her the latitude to fit in with them, connect with their heads. But it was more than that. They wore a raw sexiness with their leathers that was part of their mystique, the competence that extended to everything they did. If they could hold those roaring machines between their legs, what else they did there must be as vibrant, as pungent with courage. It was that, the courage, the risks they took with their bodies on the road and with their psyches all the time by just being who they were and living it large that zapped Her with a high voltage arc.

Cornelia, a leggy and laconic biker, saw it in Her first. She kept eyeing Her in the Pyramid and teased Her closer, closer to the aura of awesome engines with seats on them.

"You want to ride?" Cornelia yelled in Her ear over her friend's band that was jamming to bring down the walls. "You'd be good. I can tell by the way you move, handle yourself."

"No fucking way."

She said "no" but Her eyes were on fire and Cornelia caught them and held them with deep blues of her own. She couldn't look away. Tall, lithe, dirty blonde-brunette, clear-eyed Cornelia had a permanent stride that marked her a woman of means: herself. She was impressed, and She was also intimidated. She kept saying "no" through the loud sets, the coke in the cramped dressing room hall afterward, the drinking, and all the nights just like that.

"No."

No, She wouldn't ride. She kept saying it.

One day, though, Cornelia's friend Jean appeared unannounced with an extra helmet, insisting that She would ride, "or else." Young, strong, direct in what she did and said—and with a bad-puppy smirk—she tossed the helmet at Her.

"Come on outside. Get on, hang on. Lean the way I lean, got it?"

It was a big black Honda Shadow, a beautiful machine angled next to others there on Hudson Street. It was just outside of the Cubbyhole and women were hanging around on the sidewalk watching, and it was too cool to refuse, too quick to think about with the helmet in Her hands and all. Everyone was watching, urging her to not be a "wuss."

So She was suddenly on the seat, suddenly tucked intimately behind Jean's hips. The feel of Jean, of gripping those firm thighs with Her own was heady enough, but when the bike started everything went to an entirely different level. Vibrations. Pulsating sexiness, the rhythm of the engine, She was transported. The freedom and feeling of power laid over the real fact of the intimate closeness, the vibrations, blew Her away, took Her away, turned Her on. And Jean felt it but was a tease, played with Her.

"Take your hands out of my pockets or we're going to crash, you slut."

She said it almost like she meant it but she was moving her ass against Her crotch as she spoke. And She felt Herself falling in love. All at once, struck by lightning. She fell in love with Jean, with Cornelia, with tough and gentle Lizabeth, and with everything about them. She fell in love with what they rode and who they were.

It was sudden protection and support, a civilized gang. They were all comrades who shared the knowledge of risk and appreciated each other for it. Willa, who wasn't around much, was the pinnacle of that respect. Willa was thin, tall-ish, kinky haired, and as easily mild as the frayed jeans and t-shirts she wore. When she told stories about riding around the country, alone, sleeping at roadsides, the rest of them—city bikers—were disbelieving and awed. She said she and a 1965 BMW traveled together.

"I carry a cooler on the back," she said, "so I can have milk for coffee in the morning."

"Can you stand the luxury?" Jean was almost nasty, but it was lost on Willa. She was so straight arrow, so clean and honest that any negativity went through her or around her, bounced off her or something.

"It's nice to have something you like first thing when you get up and you don't know where you are, not exactly."

No bravado, no malice. Willa was in a world of her own design that consisted of nothing but her bike and highways and sometimes women. She was quiet and self-possessed and lived inimitably in a dangerous competence.

"Want to see it?" Willa said it to Her, but everyone moved as one to go along to see her bike, those who had seen it, and the sidewalk bar groupies who hadn't. It was parked just around the dark corner on Morton Street. It was huge and ancient with a kick-starter that looked like it would take three people to move it.

"Jesus Christ." It didn't matter who said it, it expressed the reverence they all felt. Everyone watched as Willa readied herself to ride.

"Hold this," Willa handed Her a battery she pulled from the pack that had been slung over one shoulder. "I've got to connect this. It takes a while."

They watched as she attached wires to the yellow sealed battery she said she had stolen from one of those blinking barriers at a construction site. She fed the wires from it to the spark plugs. Working calmly, quiet and steady around the bike, the group who watched her fell silent. Other women came out from the partying inside the bar. One of them was Janet with the shaved head, and she started ragging Willa.

"Fucking-A, you want some tape to hold that thing together?"

"No. Thanks, though," she said, focused on some connection. "It holds ok, once I do it right."

No malice to the wisecrack. No offense searched for in the tone. The watching group rippled a murmur of respect. They were staring at her, maybe kind of loving her.

Joints and Jack Daniels from inside-pocket-held pints were pulled out, passed around while they watched Willa work. It was the work of an odd genius, the Frankenstein of bikes. Everyone flowed with it into a party mood there on the street.

"Shit, this is huge. You ride this thing all over? How do you do that, ride so long, like to LA or something?"

"I like it." She was wrapping a wire around her finger, then looked up right at Her. "Try it."

Envious curses rattled around so She didn't think twice about being cool enough to climb up onto the seat, high enough to be on horseback. It eased Her forward, the tilt of the broad leather seat, until the front raised center peak stopped Her, caught Her clit and wedged hard against it.

"Jesus Christ ..."

"What?" Janet suspected something, handed off her flask. "Come on, what?"

"Jesus ..."

It was all She could manage. Willa watched a little shyly.

"Come on, let me try."

Janet was punching Her arm, breaking the spell. She yanked at Her to get off the bike, then plunked herself on it.

"Fuck that, man. No wonder you ride so much. Shit, you don't need any girls."

Everyone hooted at Janet but Willa didn't look up. She continued her connecting and fixing and tightening and priming and whatever else needed to be done to get the big Beemer to start. Gentle ragging on her popped from the women who were more stoned, having fun while they watched her, and more. They took turns climbing onto the seat to try it out, feel that ugly, wonderful seat they knew must be even more incredible when seven hundred pounds of machinery vibrated it against your clit with no escape.

"Here." Willa handed Her the newly wire-beset battery. "Can you hold it between your legs?

"Can she? Honey, after that seat I need something to hold between *my* legs."

Janet fought to climb on ahead of Her, elbowed Her. But She was already cradling the bound up S&M looking battery, yanked it closer, so She won.

Joints, flasks went around again while Willa mounted up and asked them to watch for her brake light when she tested a final connection.

"Yeah it works, was it broken?"

"Sometimes it doesn't do it."

She held up her finger to show them a long wire from the battery wrapped around it. The brake light was operated by that wire on her finger. It lit up when Willa made the connection by touching the exposed end to the metal brake lever on her right handlebar.

"Goddamn," everyone seemed to say at once.

"You ride like that?" Janet said, then turned to Her. "And you're going to ride with her?"

It wasn't worth answering. She didn't bother to think. Her, the neophyte and sudden bike slut would take any ride just to ride, especially to feel that seat. She took another gulp from someone's flask, climbed on and hung on, the battery edges digging into her thighs. Willa kicked the big stiff starter, and *oh God* the bike bellowed and quaked to life. Cheers went up, applause. Willa revved the engine to a deafening thunder, pushed it upright with one leg and *wham* they were off on a bullet that was really a giant vibrator. *Son of a bitch!*

I am alive again, being alone. Alone with friends is the way I live my life. Go to parties alone, leave alone, sometimes come home alone. The rushing sound in my ears has stopped, except for sometimes. Sometimes, the worst times. Sometimes I want her. But mostly I can't forgive her. Sometimes the old terror chews, hard grinding teeth on my heart. I can feel it. Incisors tear into my chest, molars grind slowly the bitten flesh. Sticky blood drools over my breasts, cakes on my nipples.

Eat my heart out, eat your heart out. Someday, sometimes, eat your heart out too, bitch.

How many times have I shaved my legs to go out only to come home alone, or, with a girl who doesn't shave?

She needed people around Her, friends. In fact, when She thought about the times She was in threesomes, the friendship had been what made them good. She thought about an earlier one only because She was surprised with a sudden threesome now. Before, it was when She was with crazy Ann and She got into it with Ann's old friend. Cheryl Ann, another addicting Southern belle. The other woman who got into it was a singer, drug dealer and all around strange person. She couldn't remember how She came to know her at all. She barely remembered the threesome.

She had brought them all together accidentally and it turned into sex somehow. She was almost living with Ann then in her penthouse and Cheryl Ann came to visit her from somewhere in the South. For some reason, one day She was there in Ann's place, alone with Cheryl Ann and waiting for Dori, the singer, to go to dinner. When Dori got there they all smoked, got very high and very nuts, and somehow got into telling stories about their experiences with women. They were sitting on the floor, backs propped against the couch that faced the fireplace with no fire.

"Have you ever done it with three?"

It was the inevitable questions asked by one of them. There were two "no's" and one "yes" in response. And it was Cheryl Ann who was the honest one who admitted it so readily.

"So you're not as shy as you look," Dori said.

"Yes I am. It just depends."

"Well, if it depends on us," Dori passed another joint, "what do we do to convince you? Want to watch us?"

"Us?"

She tried not to act surprised so She wouldn't look uncool. She could barely recall the few times She had slept with Dori and wasn't sure She wanted to do it now.

"Why not?" Dori said.

"I don't know why not." Cheryl Ann was slowly leaning against Her. "All you want me to do is watch? That's all?"

And no, that wasn't all. Talking about it, laughing, throwing aside awkwardness, they somehow began. Cheryl Ann was kissing Her, and Dori was caressing Her breasts as well as Cheryl Ann's. Then they changed, somehow, and Cheryl Ann was pulling off their clothes while Dori went at Her crotch. They were suddenly naked on the twisted discarded clothes, naked on the elegant Persian rug that was one of Ann's treasures.

Christ. The feel of it on Her bare back reminded Her: *Christ, what about Ann?*

"Hey," She pulled her lips from someone's, "Ann's going to be home—"

"Shhh, we can hear the elevator. Don't worry, baby."

And Cheryl Ann moved a gloriously velvet body on Hers. She forgot about Ann, accepted the stupid reassurance that any of them were going to be in any condition to hear a gunshot in the room much less the elevator in the hall.

"Oh honey, that's so nice."

Cheryl Ann started to really move, rubbed her breasts over Her like a cat. Tongued Her nipples, and then moved down on Her, and this was while Dori worked on Cheryl Ann from behind. Every plunge she made into her from the back made Cheryl Ann press against Her, grab her, take Her with her in rhythm with the feel of every heave, every sound. Every cry Dori made because of Cheryl Ann was echoed by Her, feeling the sensation magnified through Cheryl Ann's body that was moving on Hers. And when She came, it didn't stop them, they just rearranged their bodies in some silent understanding. Dori and She were kissing then, hungry and hard. Cheryl Ann came between them, pried their hips apart. Her tongue went into Dori, and two fingers into Her. They sighed together, threw their legs around each other. Their bodies tangled, moving, rubbing sweaty flesh over sweating flesh. Surrounded by softness, no one left out, drowned in wetness, moving creamy woman-flesh and opening up, so open. Trusting.

Now and then a finger slipped out too soon, "Oh no." Or an elbow was stuck into someone's ribs, "Ow." It made them laugh, reorganize, explore each other in a hundred new ways. And they must have come a hundred times, all of them together, or two together with one watching and offering a slap here, fingers probing there. No one was left out. It was free, vivid fun. And by some miracle Ann did not walk in on them.

But that had been then, years before. She hadn't had another *ménage* until now, last week. It was so strange that Nance wouldn't believe Her.

"That doesn't happen to anyone, you're fucking lying."

"Ok, I won't tell you the rest then."

"Come on, let's have it, bitch. What's the dish? I'll decide if it's true or not."

She told her about the girl, Amanda, She met in St. Marks Books. Not like Penny the editor she met in the Strand, this was different. The good news was Her luck in bookstores was better than in bars.

Amanda was young, twenty-three or –four, a brown-haired cutie with contrasting too-white skin. They talked about a film sound book She was re-shelving, as she was kind of working, helping a friend who worked there, she said, covering their shift.

"You make films?" Amanda said.

"Thinking about it, getting into it with some friends."

It was true, Janet from the biker girls wanted to make a film and wanted Her, with Her photographer's eye, to help her with it.

"Yeah that's what I want to do. Maybe you can use me for a sound person. I've worked on sync in class already."

"What class?"

"In Boston ..."

They talked easily, flirting. But Amanda had to leave, was meeting friends for a performance, then a reading, and then rock and roll. But she wanted to see Her.

"Tomorrow?"

"Great. Eight. Here."

That felt good, done and done. So She went and had a good time hanging out, doing drugs, sitting in the Pyramid's basement dressing room before and after the gig from the cool band that was so hot, the Bush Tetras. Home at four in the morning, high and suddenly realizing only then that the date She made with Amanda conflicted with the date She already had for that night. *Damnit.* She couldn't break it, didn't want to, because it was Alice of the sex toys again— She was finally going to connect with her again for the first time after years. No number for Amanda and not wanting to blow it with her,

She called the bookstore when She got up in the afternoon.

"Who?" someone said. "She doesn't work here. You mean the one who was helping Frederick? I know who you mean."

"Can you give her this number?"

And all She could do was hope. She couldn't think of a way to see two women together who were strangers to each other, or maybe if She had more time She could figure out some story to make it happen with two dates at the same time. But there wasn't enough time in the universe for that. Was there?

She ended up spending the night with Alice, and it was wonderful. Like old times, the easy fucking they fell into was like they had known each other's bodies for years. And they had, but not consistently. There was some kind of connection, comfortable excitement that made it a joy for them every time they fucked. They made up for their lost time. And there was no call from Amanda. Too bad, but there was nothing She could do about it. She was happy to have found Alice again and Saint Carmen and Penny from the Strand. *Can't have them all* ... But She was trying.

She had enough women and new friends to keep the obsession with Margret from paralyzing Her. It was as if the sulfur colored sky of tornado weather, that heavy constricting atmosphere, was finally passing. Slowly. Slowly, but starting to break to clearness at least. If Amanda never called it wouldn't matter. But she did.

It was three days later and She had spent the evening with Alice again at Her place. Alice left early to go home and an hour later, at one in the morning, Amanda called.

"I'm on Twelfth Street, can I come over?"

Are you kidding? She was there in twenty minutes, and in another fifteen she was in Her bed. No coyness, no wasted time. They started making out and then they were in bed fucking. Amanda wasn't very expert but that didn't matter. She was cute and had skin that was truly flawless, everywhere. They had a good time and she left to return to Boston at about four or five. Like a dream, like a fucking dream, and that's what Nance thought.

"You've lost it this time, you crazy fuck. That doesn't happen to anybody."

They laughed about it and Nance ragged on Her about it for a week, disbelieving. But the next weekend Amanda called again in the early morning.

"Can I bring a friend?"

They drank a beer, smoked a joint and got silly, then Amanda said that "she told Sally" about Her. And Sally, the freckled redhead who was slumped at one end of Her ratty couch, looked directly into Her eyes. No shyness. *Oh really?* She looked right back at her without blinking. She and Amanda were on the couch facing Her in the low rocker, close but not close enough. She extended Her leg and pressed against Sally's. Amanda got up and kneeled next to Her, turned up her face to be kissed. As She did, She reached for Sally without looking, put an inviting hand out toward her. And Sally took it, came to Her and felt Her breasts while She kissed Amanda. Somebody sighed, and they adjusted their positions. She turned and searched for Sally's lips. As they kissed Amanda straddled one of Her legs and began to move lavishly, teasing her own cunt.

Soon they were on the floor and Sally was naked. She couldn't remember how or even if there had been a process. She was just naked all of a sudden, as if by magic. Amanda was pulling off Her shirt, unzipping Her jeans. *Jesus-fucking-A, who are these girls?* She wasn't so turned on, or so high, that She couldn't tell what felt strange and a little bizarre. But She didn't protest and Her head zoomed along to catch up, even though She was a little apprehensive, just a little. It almost felt like too much, of course not really, but She thought it was all too fast. The feeling didn't last long, though, because soon it was too much to stop.

They were both on Her, Amanda sucking Her tits, Sally eating Her out, slowly, her tongue doing whirls and trips that made Her stop breathing. She reached for them both with Her hands, made them move nearer so She could find their soaking sex and play with them, into them, pinching their clits. And they loved it. Experience, that must have been what these youngies were looking for, or else they did this all the time, but She didn't think so. They were a little clumsy, a little too excited, too blown away by what they were doing. They only wanted Her, weren't interested in each other and wanted Her to do them, fuck them together. Then later, after they had moved into bed, they wanted Her to fuck them in turn while the other watched, or played with herself.

"I don't fucking believe it," Nance said. "It's your fucking fantasy."

"Definitely fucking. Next time I'll take pictures so you'll believe it."

"Do that, bitch liar."

Nance wouldn't leave it alone and ragged Her mercilessly until they ended up laughing about it. These things just don't happen in real life but Nance had to concede that Her life was hardly real anyway. And She could hardly believe it Herself.

They had left early in the morning just like Amanda had done the first time to return to Boston. She said she was a student at B.U. but She never found out anything about Sally. They came—and came—and then they were gone. Like a dream for sure. She never heard from them again. That was fine with Her. She felt that it, they, were Her mystical prizes for months of suffering. Her objective rewards. She began to care less about who was fucking Her Margret.

- Does Time Pass in Hell? -
HASSLE

The streets are stained with trails of piss. I walk carefully, not stepping on the sticky lines with new handmade boots. I think about the girl who flirts with me, the come on and stay away. I laugh out loud. Nobody notices. Everyone on these streets is talking to themselves, to the air. I think about her, the chase. She broke down and asked me out and I said, not tonight. She was surprised. I'm not easy anymore. Been fucked and have fucked, no more desperation. Must get rid of one, don't like who she is anymore. Good in bed but her head's not right. Same age, but too old.

She had not been careful with Her body. It was either a yeast infection or herpes from what She could figure out with Nance and Kelly. They yelled at Her for not being careful, for jumping into bed with strange women. Kelly tried to convince Her to use dental dams. Nance gave Her rubber finger cots that looked like rubbers, real rubbers. Distasteful. They argued about how easy or difficult it was for women to transmit AIDS to women. Was it only hysteria or real fear? There was so little information about AIDS in general, no one knew. No one really knew anything, still. And this was all after Her Sam had been sick. After he was gone.

All She knew was that there was something weird going on with Her body, and Nance told Her it wasn't surprising considering the way She didn't eat regularly, partied until daylight and beyond, and took all kinds of drugs that lowered Her resistance: coke, smack, grass and hard liquor. But She didn't want to think about it. New work, new friends, rampant fucking was all She could deal with for now. Keep the crazies away, call it living alone not loneliness.

"I saw Margret with someone. Are you two still together?" Pat called only to get the dirt because she hadn't spoken to Her in a year.

"We're split."

"Wow yeah, it looked that way. Sorry. Hey, you want to have dinner?"

What had Pat seen? She was tantalizing, "it looked that way." What did that mean, Margret was fucking The Thing in public? It was on Her lips to ask but She didn't, wouldn't. She accepted the dinner invite and fantasized She might go ahead and fuck Pat just to let the word spread, since gossip was what she seemed to do best. Anyway, She could not resist finding out more so She met her at Vaselka for kasha and blintzes because She couldn't talk her into going to the similarly lacking in romantic atmosphere at B&H. Both places were without ambiance, or rather they had Eastern European linearity, but B&H had better kasha varniskes and absolutely fabulous challah.

"So is Margret with this other person?" Pat couldn't wait until they sat down. "I mean she looked like—"

"Not her type?"

"Yeah!"

She laughed it off, told Pat they each had lives of their own now. She didn't want to hear about what Margret was doing—but that was a lie, of course She did. Just from Pat's tone She could tell she had seen her with her new lover, and was surprised by what she saw. She pumped Pat a little for some dish. She said she couldn't ever remember names, but stories reached her. Pat was only one of the larger circle of acquaintances like Nick, Mary Smith, Johnny, Koby, or anyone who started asking about it, the demise of the long relationship. They started to blindside Her with questions and innuendo. They were not friends but dish dealers, gossips, or else they were women who were willing to capitalize on the big split, like Pat was doing. It made Her wonder what offers Margret was getting from the relationship vultures. But she probably wasn't being sniffed out because after all she was already in a relationship with her, Bitsy.

Then one day it happened: They met. One day on the street there was Margret, alone, looking tired, dragged out. All of a sudden, She wanted to hold her, take her in Her arms and rock her like She used to.

What's the matter, baby? I'll make it better. She wanted to say it but would not dare. And Margret's eyes were soft, smiling, as she moved to kiss Her in greeting but stopped when she saw Her hold back.

"Hey, good to see you," She said, and surprised Herself with the feeling in Her voice.

"Me too. You look great," Margret responded with equal emotion.

"What, these old rags?"

"They are not. I don't remember them."

Margret touched Her lightly on the collar of the leather jacket, the white Vanson. She melted just like before, the delicate fleeting touch, those tapering fingers just brushing over Her. They stared at each other, blue eyes on brown, saying nothing. Then looking away before they could speak again.

"How have you been?" Margret whispered.

"Ok, really ok. You?"

"Busy. Working a lot and ... Just busy."

"Yeah."

And they were staring again, without words again. She wanted to hold her and feel her against Her once more, just once more. The break had been too sudden, an amputation. Margret must have felt it too because she reached for Her, let her fingertips run like blown leaves down the sleeve of Her jacket. A testing, asking gesture that she repeated. She was asking with her hand and her eyes, tenderly.

"Maybe, maybe we could have lunch," Margret said.

"Now?"

"Of course now."

She didn't know what to say because She was on Her way to meet Janet, the shaved-headed biker. But Janet had already missed two dates they had made, she might not even show.

"But if you have plans."

"I ..." She obviously needed time to think. "I do or did have something, but it's ok."

And She was suddenly walking along Third Avenue with Margret for the first time in months. Walking the Village streets like they had so many times before, so many, but never quite like this. Anxiety blinded Her and She nearly stepped in front of speeding cabs, used four matches to light a cigarette and was brain-numb for blocks. No conversation sprang, or even limped, to Her lips. They walked silently, each feeling the strangeness that was hard but also honeyed. Sweet strangeness, silent strangers now. When they accidentally bumped together at a corner She said "sorry," and Margret said, "don't be." *What does that mean? What the fuck does anything mean now?*

They went to Leshkos on Seventh and Avenue A like they had so many times before for cheap Eastern European food, bad lighting. Good times, fights, strained times had gone down at those plain square, worn-out tables where others were eating alone or reading or having relationship relations of their own. But their new drama wasn't as visible as it had been. The difference was in them now, deeper. She was nervous, but She didn't feel as badly as other times when they had still been lovers. She didn't care, She realized. She didn't care what Margret thought of Her, not as much anyway, not in the same way. The only thing that was almost the same as it had been early in their relationship was the warmth, how She was suddenly feeling toward Margret.

"It's good to see you," Margret said. "You're really all right?"

"Fine."

"I've been hearing you're having a good time."

"What? Who told you that?"

She tried to look innocent. But She knew any number of women at the bars probably reported back about who they had seen Her with on any number of nights.

"Never mind. Are you working? New prints?"

"Some." She said it with more enthusiasm than She intended and Margret looked pained. She hadn't wanted to hurt her, and knew Margret had a right to be angry. After all, She had thrown away that Berlin show. But She didn't want to give away anything about Her work now, not anything.

"What about your writing?" She asked it to deflect the focus from Herself, and hoped She sounded normal. "Doing any poetry?"

"No. It's hard. I can't write."

"Sorry."

"It's all right. You can't do anything about it."

Was that a challenge? Margret looked away. Did she really not want to talk about her writing any more than She wanted to talk about Her photographs? Or did it only look that way? A challenge, that's what it was. One of Margret's veiled challenges, something that could always get under Her skin, get Her to react. She didn't realize it until now, when it was almost too late.

She felt compassion for Margret first, then resolution, the phase that made Her want to change things for her. After that came the power trip culmination that would impel Her tell Margret what she "should" do. At the end of this *sub rosa* interaction was guilt. And She followed the script, again. Dutifully, She felt guilty now when Margret ended up critiquing the suggestion she had lured Her into giving.

"Why are you telling me to do that? It's impossible, I couldn't. I don't have the money to take a studio."

And Margret made it sound like it was somehow Her fault that this was true, that this was Margret's situation—never mind that she owned an apartment that was bringing her sublet money every month. Never mind anything: She had bought the trip. Again. Seeing Margret like that, having felt so nostalgic and warm and being strong enough to let Herself even sit with her again led right into the "be the savior" head-trap that made Her feel responsible for Margret's life, responsible somehow for her work, her happiness.

"I can help you find a—"

"Never mind." Margret made a motion to the waitress for the check. "I'll pay for this too. Stay, eat."

"Come on, wait a minute. I'll look for something for you. I know I owe you ... I can help."

And it was the power of it, the power of feeling that She should, and therefore somehow could, protect Margret and change Margret's life. That was the real hook. Her ego-hook was Margret giving Her the power, or tempting Her with it, of being able to help her so dramatically. She never questioned why Margret needed such basic assistance in living in the first place. Worse, She never turned down the temptation, the bait, to prove omnipotence, prove Herself. Who wouldn't want to be someone's savior, the ultimate fixer?

Margret stood up, crumpled the check in her hand. "You don't owe me anything. There's nothing you have to give." She turned away, then turned back. "Thanks for the suggestion. I need a work space? Thank you, I didn't know."

Margret rejected Her solution, mocked any solution. Again. And again, She was shocked and hurt at Her failure, at failing Margret. The worst consequence of living this head trip was the inability to see the absurdity of the position She was in from the beginning. She never asked when they were living together why the hell Margret's inability to work at her own art could possibly be Her fucking fault? Not Her fault in the way that always flowed in the undercurrent of Margret's complaints. Complaint. It sounded like a complaint when Margret said it, not like an artist worried about her work but like someone whining about it being too noisy to think in New York. *So complain to the mayor or move or just shut up and work.* What could a lover do about that? Getting blamed for it was guilt-flinging taken to a high art. Guilt-flinging at a hundred paces, and Margret was a national champion, always on the mark.

"At least you have a place of your own where you can be alone and do your work."

The waitress came with the food they had already ordered. Margret hesitated, and never wanting to create a scene, sat down. Silence hummed between them over the snatches of conversation and clink of plates and cups around them. Guilt. There it was, so readily called up in Her even now after so much time. Silence. They each concentrated on trying to eat, buttered the challah. Smiled at the waitress refilling their water. In the holding back between them, all the thoughts of compassion, power and guilt caromed in Her head. It was true, She did have a place where She could work and enjoy being alone, theoretically. She was lucky. Maybe She was obligated help find a place for Margret. Could She do it? Go with her, look at apartments ...

"Hey wait a minute. You don't have a place," She found Herself saying it, and pushed away Her plate. "Whose fault is that?"

It was what Sam had always said in his Superman kind of way. "Well, whose fault is it?" He said it whenever anyone fucked themselves up.

"What are you saying?" Margret was angry. "It's because of us, our relationship that I'm almost on the street, goddamnit. It's because I had to leave the relationship that I don't have a place of my own but you do."

She pushed away any glass or plate in Her reach like She was readying to leap from the booth. But She only leaned in to meet Margret's rage instead.

"After seven months you still don't have a place because of us? What about you fucking Bitsy-bitch?"

"God damn it, I don't know why you always have to be so nasty. If you didn't react so badly to everything I might be able to work in your studio too! The one I'm helping you pay for!"

"I'm trading you my work! I'm paying with the pieces I give you."

"Will I live long enough for them to be worth anything?"

She could only stare at Margret. Her head was exploding, but She only stared. When She finally did find words to arrange, there was calmness in Her voice. Never mind the silent detonations that preceded it, She sounded calm.

"I get it. It's my fault. It's my hurt about what you did, presumably are still doing, that keeps you away from your work. It's not that you're living the way you are because you want to? Right?"

"Want to?" Margret snarled. "Who wants to live in someone's living room?"

"Oh? You're not sleeping in her bed anymore?"

Margret muttered a curse under her breath and looked away. She waited for a second to see if Margret might say something else, then She pushed back Her chair, stood up.

"I guess that answers that, doesn't it? See you around, Margret."

She turned, headed for the door. Didn't hesitate, didn't bother about stopping to pay Her half of the bill. She was too lightheaded.

Without thinking, She found Herself buying a pair of biker gloves for Jean. It was only afterward that She realized it would help the flirtation with her. The images of Margret, her soft eyes, elegant hands, didn't bother Her at all, not until She was at home alone. The old pressure of speech came back then and She had to talk about it suddenly. Tell Nance, get her opinion. What did it mean, that business about using Her studio? Did Margret want to get back with Her? The old feelings of warmth crept back, then flooded back. And She knew She needed help, so She ran to Nance's apartment.

"What the fuck does it mean?"

"Do you want to get back with her?" Nance was bored.

"I don't know." And it was horrible that She didn't know. Confusion flooded over the clarity She had before. The high of walking away was gone now, like She had never felt it.

"Look, you have a date tonight with somebody, don't you?"

"Killer cute Jean, the biker girl."

"So go have a good time. Forget about this shit. You let her get to your head again, asshole, that's all. Forget it. Go out and see what happens."

Right. See what happens. She repeated it to Herself like a mantra, struggling to not drown in sticky feelings from the past that weighed Her down. Her flash of courage and lightness was only a memory.

"By the way," Nance said. "Try not to fuck her until you figure out what you've got, you know? Won't hurt you to pass up one girl for one night until you see a doctor."

"Yeah, yeah, yeah ..."

- Keep Twirling Backwards.
Crash All the Clocks -
BACKTRACK

"Feel better now, lady?"

The cab driver was a sweetheart, a long-haired gentleman. When She told him to pull over, that She was going to be sick, he didn't flinch. He made an expert stop in a discrete spot next to parked cars. It allowed Her to open the door and vomit without being seen.

"Thanks. Sorry, man."

"Don't worry about it. We all got troubles."

"What, it shows?"

They both laughed. The kindness of strangers washed over Her.

"I see it all sooner or later. You're not one of the good drunks." He glanced at Her in the rear view mirror as he sped down Second Avenue. "You got nice eyes but you got trouble."

"Just around the edges."

They laughed again. It surprised Her, but not that much.

"It sounds like a country song when you talk about it."

"You like country? That, I didn't figure."

"Lately, man, that stuff's just too true."

He pounded the steering wheel, cracked up. Then he fiddled with the radio until he found 97, the country station.

"*... too gone for too long ...*"

It could have been any country song. She found all of them, without distinction, bolstered Her depression, gave it a rhythm to torture Her more easily. From Randy Travis twanging out heartbreak to Shelley West salving the pain with Jose Cuervo, all of it was directed at Her.

"Oh shit," She muttered.

"Your old man split?"

"Something like that."

She almost said, "No, it was my old lady" but who knew what he might do with that? She felt so much better after throwing up but She didn't feel like fighting Her way out of a cab if he turned out to be a gay basher.

"Hey, forget him, lady, you're beautiful."

"Thanks," She laughed. "I'm doing ok. It's just now and then, you know?"

He knew. And he had a suggestion. She listened, and decided *why the fuck not?* She was too wired, too miserable to go home alone. She had completely blown the date with Jean, acted like an ass, got too drunk, couldn't get anything fucking right. She was left with the oppressive weight of failure. Failure with Jean, failure with Margret. So many things She had done wrong rushed back to Her, so many thrown away good times, or maybe they were times that could have been good if She hadn't been so passive, so weak and thrown them away. She could have made the relationship better, not been so afraid about Her work, about deadlines, and so terrified of failure. Maybe if She could have resisted deifying Margret so much that it made Her avoid any shows or exposure so that She wouldn't be proven to Margret to be the failure She was sure She was. Maybe if She had been honest with Margret about all that—all that awe and fear that made Her too afraid to lose her. Would that have meant She valued Margret and the relationship more like Margret was always insisting that She didn't? It was Her fault. She had thrown away too much already in too short a life. The circular obsessions wouldn't stop.

"So what you think, lady? Need a little help tonight?"

"Sure. Let's go."

"Cool."

He took off from where they had been sitting in front of Her building. It didn't take long to get to the Christopher Street piers but it seemed like forever to Her.

"A little one on one?" he asked before he got out, parked a respectful distance from knots of men doing deals of one kind or another.

"If you can, great."

He came back with the tightly-folded packets, two for Her and two for him of coke and smack, one each. Then he moved the cab away from there, the scene of the buy, to a spot further down by the trucks under the elevated West Side Highway. He stayed in the front seat and did his. They really didn't talk, falling into that unwritten New York law of being perfectly comfortable with a stranger, respectful of space and silence. Respectful until there was something that engaged both people.

"... *whatcha gonna do ...*"

Twang twang, oh woe oh woe. They sang, not together, but with Reba McEntire on the radio and it felt good. A little weird, but good. She couldn't decide, couldn't think about it. The drug dealers who hung in the shadows stayed invisible, but the gay boys who cruised and fucked in the shadows or in the trucks didn't care who saw them. She wondered if this was dangerous, in general for all of them, and for Her in particular. She was the only woman there at the edge of the Hudson in the middle of the night. She was burying Herself, living on the edge of the grave. Was that what She tested now, how much She could tempt danger, death, anything darkness brings?

"*Noted Photographer*" —No, make it "avant garde" *because they'll find the new work. "Avant Garde Photographer's Body Found in River"* would be the headline. "*Autopsy shows evidence of cocaine and heroin in large quantities ...*"

"Let's get some more," She said to the cabbie.

He said "ok" and, both of them being high, didn't notice that she got out and headed through the shadows with him. It was a mistake they didn't notice until it was too late. Dealers eyed Her, Her relatively small stature, and they seemed to label her as fish bait. That's what She thought—but She was very high. *Fuck it.* She sat a little ways away from the cabbie in the shadows at the edge of the pier, snorted up what he brought and mesmerized Herself watching the black water undulate below. How would it feel to be down there, in it? She nodded toward it, squinted down at it. Not so far away, not too far.

There was something She had read in Montaigne that She couldn't quite remember. Something about dying, when life is not worth living anymore be glad for a reason to die. But what was the reason—failure? A better reason was simply wanting to, wanting to die.

Sam. How I miss him. Why do I nurse sick people, like him, and things like the neighbor's cats? Sick creatures. Does it mean anything that I got into it, get into it? The giving takes over, then it gets to be too much and I must flee.

Again the disease. Visiting the disease, ineffable AIDS. Armageddon. Armageddon. I am nothing. I feel like nothing new, good, compared to what? Just raw. Raw.

The cops made a sweep, hassling the hookers who had come around. Seeing that, the cops a block away, the cabbie straightened up, opened the rear door for Her while he leaned on it to hold himself up. Then he pulled away slowly. After only a few blocks after turning onto Washington Street he stopped.

"That's it. I'm done."

He slumped comfortably behind the wheel. Great. She got out and started to walk. Fucked up, definitely fucked up. What the hell was She doing here, doing drugs with strangers? She could have been dead by now. That was probably too dramatic. Could have been dead, that's what She wanted, the *could have been*, the challenge, the flirtation. Back to the river, head back around the corner to Christopher and head for the Hudson again. Try again, see what it feels like on the edge, the real edge beyond Her fantasies.

By the time She passed the last of the still occupied heavy-duty men's bars just east of the Highway, different night people were around. The street wasn't deserted. This is New York, there's always someone around—usually anyway, in meat racks like this. Some men eyed Her, some prostitutes made sounds, but She walked past them right to the edge of the black river without anyone really caring. She stood with Her feet hanging half over the edge of the wooden pier. She was a lousy swimmer and would probably sink like a stone, plop, right to the bottom, the very dirty bottom. It made Her laugh. She laughed out loud. To be stopped from jumping because the water was too dirty was so bourgeoisie that it was funny. There must be raw shit down there. Disgusting. And She laughed, almost lost Her shaky balance.

She remembered this happened before. Skiing in Canada on a trail too advanced for Her. She remembered telling Sam the story and how he laughed, small, with his small wry grin. Anyway, there was a sharp drop at the edge of that very narrow track, at least a hundred feet or so. She had laughed then too when She realized the seductive danger. She laughed when one ski hit an icy patch and deflected Her toward the edge. It forced Her to recover quickly. As She tried to do that, and it took some doing, She thought She might be thrown over the steep edge. But She laughed at the fantasy, and the laughter made Her ski slip again. It caught an edge on a frozen root near the precipice and tore out part of it. She lost control, was thrown off balance. *Wham.* She hit a small bush-like tree with many low branches just at the brink of the drop off, luckily, and was stopped. So she was hanging there, ski tips waving in mid-air over the cliff and laughing like a fool.

"You be a foo' girl." She could hear Constance never Connie saying it as if She were there. And She stepped backward off the edge of the pier before She might not be so lucky in Her recklessness this time. The water was too odious for Her middle class sensibility—the need for suicidal release be damned.

She had things to live for like Nance, Her work and Kelly too. So much. Even Margret, because She had to live in spite of her, and in the opposite way, for the women She had yet to meet of course. Another hit of coke and She started to walk.

"Yo, baby, yo come'ere," a definite pimp, but unsure of Her look, was half-hearted. "You got nowhere to go?"

"Yeah, I do, thanks."

He spit and faded away. She had to stifle stupid laughter because it would be more than stupid to let him hear. She was a fool playing in a world She didn't know. Ignorant. She beat it, really beat it out of danger, again. So She wrote another headline in Her head: *Amazon Defies Death, Junkies, Pimps and Terminal Comedy.*

It had been light for some time before She realized it. Traffic got heavy before She really thought about where She was. She had been enjoying walking, singing, crying. Crying was what She did last, crying about Margret, about what She couldn't keep, all the time wasted in worry, uptightness. And there She was, all the way up in Central Park, sitting by the lake and discreetly doing still more of the coke and smack the cabbie scored for Her. How She got up there was a series of brightly jetting images. Did their order really matter? She had walked, walked a hell of a lot and now She was tired, wired, fucked up but in control somehow. A lot had happened to Her, continued to happen, but mostly in Her head.

"Shouldn't it be easier … La la, something …"

Song lyrics describing Her life was bad enough, but She couldn't even keep them straight. The sadness, that's all that counted. It kept Her company all day. When She finally got back downtown to Her place it was nearly dark. There were five calls on the answering machine from Nance alone, each one more pissed-off, interspersed with calls from girls.

"Where've you been?"

"Not really sure. Around. I'm pretty wasted."

"Dumb bitch, not buying that. What the hell happened to you?"

She was too embarrassed to tell her. Suddenly it all seemed too ridiculous to admit to, literally, too wasted. She ended up wailing like a baby over the phone. About Margret, about the good times She had thrown away with her, about all the wasted time. It was a cleansing cry, a druggie cry from a cleansing night and day. Nance listened; she was a rock.

"It'll stop hurting. Just don't see her again, dumbass. Don't bother, you're all right on your own."

It was true. If there were any truths still hanging around that was one of them. She was all right, more than all right, alone. How many times would She have to learn it, fight it, learn it again.

"Weird it's not like riding a bicycle," She told Nance. "Physical stuff is different. You learn something and that's it, you've got it down forever. But head shit, emotional shit is like learning the same things fucking over and over. You get it, figure it all out, and goddamn if a few years or a fucking few days, for me, it happens again. Anyway later you're stepping in the same damn streams again, dealing with the same bullshit."

"Got that right."

Another truth hanging over Her like a shiny guillotine blade. She had to remember to look up.

Walked in the park with squirrels and ducks. A baby duck swam under water for so long it scared me. I walked straight, not on paths. Walking the hypotenuse, something I rarely do. When I do it is only physically, walk the hypotenuse with my body, not with my life.

Why do I hide? I'm afraid. Bored by knowing people too well, anxious at knowing them too well. Afraid to speak my mind. What will I lose? Who will I lose? Will I lose me? Or them? Why do I care so much?

I get afraid when someone asks me if I'm angry. Of what? My anger, or their reaction? My murderous rage. My fear that I don't have a right to be angry? Don't have the right to be angry. I always rationalize, see the other and others' points of view. But I am self-righteous, that's because that's the only way I won't cave in. I can get my truth out if I'm a maniac, but I can't just say it. Fear is too great. Fear of what? Them, me, losing them, losing me? But I could only gain. Is that the right answer I'm so afraid of, winning?

A baby duck ducks under water and is gone for a very long time out of sight. Swimming, I guess. But maybe it's hiding, just below the ripples.

- Keep Ignoring Time Until It Goes Away -
RETURN

She needed Saint Carmen of the Screams again. She was Her dose
of trust and pure hotness. But the girl couldn't make it. Living with
a lover was a definite drag. And She remembered it well. Being
single on the streets was more fun but had its own problems. She had
become an activity junkie, some weeks being out every night Monday
through Sunday, running to performances, openings, parties, staying
out, hanging out at the Aztec, Downtown Beirut, The World, the Cat
Club and the Clit Club over on the west side or wherever the floating
party might be ... and picking up women, doing drugs. Just regular
fun—ok, maybe a little manic.

When there was a lull for a few days She got restless. That's when
memories of Margret would get to Her. That's when it felt and looked
like every dyke in the world was in a couple. It took courage to be out
on nights like that, and real resilience to go home alone.

Margret called. She shouldn't even talk to her, but She did.

"I'm sorry you had to leave the restaurant like that. I didn't want
to fight."

"Me either. That's why I left."

Silence. Two people on the phone and nobody talking.

"There's something I want to tell you," Margret said and paused.
Jesus, what now? She was holding Her breath.

"I found a place for a while, a year sublet," Margret said. "I
wanted to give you the number. I'm there now."

"What does that mean?" She hated that She let it slip out. It was
a question She had not yet found an answer for in country music
lyrics. It made Her vulnerable, exposed.

"It means I'm finally alone until I find a real place of my own."

"Good for you," She said it and thought She sounded honestly pleased.

"Maybe you'd like to come by and see it, on Friday?"

The invitation was like a buzz saw in Her brain. It paralyzed Her. "Hello?"

"Yeah, I'm here," She said, then lied. "I was just checking my book." But She was doing nothing but staring stupidly at a wall. If She had an appointment book to check She couldn't get Herself together to look at it anyway.

"What time are you thinking?"

"Whenever you want," Margret said.

More responsibility. She tried to think fast, to calculate what was the most strategic thing to do, when to get there. Somehow She did not think to say, "No."

"How about early? Five?"

"Good, then we can have dinner later maybe."

What just happened? She hung up and felt weird and numb. Weak. Her hand was on the phone to call Nance immediately but She hesitated. *Not this time.* This time She would figure it out for Herself. There was something She wanted to do.

I read about Julius Caesar's clemency. Suetonius said he was "mild in his revenges." There were these pirates he condemned to the cross but had them strangled first, merciful. And he punished his secretary, Philemon, for trying to poison him, with "mere death." What a guy.

"So this is it."

She said it to Margret after She lit a cigarette. It didn't matter that She was still breathless from the obligatory East Village sixth floor tenement climb. She needed the time to collect Herself.

"Come sit down."

It was a typical railroad flat in layout, but small. She didn't take off Her jacket and sat on the new couch in front of milk crates loaded with feminist journals and books. She saw copies of *Trivia*, the intellectual journal of "voices of feminism," neatly stacked. Margret poured some wine and then set to rummaging in an ugly new backpack "for joints I got for you." From the look of that pack She surmised that Bitsy had given it to her. It had no style and that was her style, none. *Stop it!* Her jaw tightened with the memories, the pictures of them together came welling up like another bout of the throw ups She hadn't had in a long time. She was beyond that, took Her eyes away from the symbol the backpack was, the intrusion of someone who had touched her goddess. And She forced a smile at Margret as She accepted a joint.

There was small talk then: the grass, the apartment, the stingy views from dirty windows that looked out onto another building's side. Cordial. Margret sat diagonally from Her on a chair, close enough to pass a joint but not too close. Now and then Margret's fingers would brush Hers, send shock waves through Her, then flutter away. She took deep breaths when that happened to help Her remain witty and charming. She made up Her mind to never miss a beat in the conversation.

"I forgot." Margret stood up. "I have some cheeses too."

She went down the hall to the kitchen and left Her alone. Like a junkie left alone with money, Her eyes snapped to that ugly backpack. She had a jones for pain, for the reminder of what had happened, what had been done to Her. She hadn't deserved it, not like that, the way it was done. The fucking bitch. But She stopped Herself, took a breath and thought instead of Margret's eyes, her hands, her elegance. By the time she returned with a tray She was composed again, smiled. Margret sat near Her on the couch, shy, a little nervous.

"Good brie."

She reached past her nonchalantly before leaning back. Margret nibbled, sat back next to Her. A rampant feeling, something, leapt between them. It made them both silent.

"We should talk," Margret said.

"I'm not so sure about that, but you know I've always felt that way."

They both laughed. As warm and familiar as old times, the good times.

"Maybe you're right."

"No kidding? Damn, I thought I'd never hear you agree about that."

"Things change all the time," Margret smiled softly, openly.

She took her hand, and Margret did not pull away this time. More silence, then She moved toward her, and Margret turned her face to Her, offered her lips like she hadn't done for so long. It was like kissing a new girl. Gentle, probing, tender. Margret's lips were so soft. They were so very fine that She was afraid to ravage her— something she always felt before, not wanting to take her hard. Like before, Margret opened to Her slowly, slowly as her tongue tasted her lips, her tongue that was offered between Her lips. And She took it with care, gracefully. Margret's fingers found Her neck, caressed exquisitely over skin that burned. They held each other tightly and then hungrily, their bodies together as She leaned her back, lay on top of her.

She pulled up Margret's top, felt her smoothness, moved up to her breasts and caressed them softly at first, then harder. Margret opened her mouth wider, took in Her tongue. It was like the first time they were together, Margret responsive, wanting Her. She kissed her neck, moved on her so Her thigh pressed up into her crotch, jeans against jeans, hard. Margret made a little sound in her throat and She pressed harder, thrust against her. Margret clung to Her, breathed hot in Her ear, moved under Her. She wanted Her, wanted Her again like she had so long ago. And She moved again, unsnapped and unzipped Margret's jeans, put Her hand inside. Her underwear was sopping. She thrust up to Her in a spasm of wanting when she felt Her touch. Her hand caressed her cunt through the underwear, and She knew Margret could come soon this way, only a light touch on her clit and she moved her hips up, held tightly to Her.

"Are you there, babe? Ready?"

"Yes."

"Then we're even."

She yanked Her hand from Margret and pushed off her, stood up. Margret was stunned.

"What are you doing?!"

"We're even now. See you around."

"Goddamn you! Goddamn you! Why are you doing this?"

Margret was screaming at Her back as She headed for the door. And She was so polluted by Her own meanness now She couldn't resist the last shot at her. She stopped and turned.

"Next time buy your own damn backpack."

She slammed the door behind Her and She went, clattering and running, down the steps like She was afraid Margret would come after Her. Hysteria prickled at Her, made Her laugh in a wild, spastic way. She had done it. She had gotten to her, done it to her but good. Damn, how She loved it. *Fucking bitch.* Let her try to jerk Her chain again. Now She was ready because now it was on Her terms. She loved it, oh god how She loved having done it to her. She ran down those six flights, hit the street in a rush and took off like She knew where She was going. But She was totally zoned out. Laughter broke from Her sporadically like another one of the street maniacs lost in their own heads. Only words rang in Her head.

Got her. I got her ...

She was wild, crazed, striding hard along the streets, hair flying and grinning like an idiot. The only thing was that She realized something slowly—She realized She was crying. Tears came inexplicably from Her eyes and would not stop. Crying but laughing, or laughing but crying in spite of it. It confused Her, made Her angry. *Fuck it.* Margret would survive. It wasn't such a terrible thing, not compared to what she had done to Her.

Fuck this, She said it to Herself. Then said it out loud too.

"Fuck this shit."

She headed for the nearest bar, one of Her favorites, Mars Bar on Second Avenue and First Street. It was a funky looking place where strange people never thought She was strange. Some bikers hung out there, men bikers, but that was fine. Tough, that's what She wanted around Her. Toughness was what She felt, or wanted desperately to reflect who She was suddenly, or wanted to pretend to be. *Fuck this.*

"Jack, please. Up."

The spikey haired bartender didn't nod, blink or look like he was breathing. He turned away to get Her drink. She glanced around at the big guys in leathers, the only kind of people there. They glanced at Her as She drank without wincing, throwing back the whiskey. She was red-eyed from crying and had a dumb determined smirk on Her face. She finished the first drink with Her first cigarette and ordered another. The leather men nearest Her shot a look, with approval. By the third drink one of them was buying it for Her. And She started having fun on her own.

She could be anything She wanted, say anything she wanted. Nothing left to lose, free. She talked to the guys and began to fly, lighter. They talked about bikes. Harleys, Nortons, Triumphs. Triumphs, for sure.

- Oh Hell, Just Go Faster! -
TAKE OFF

My mouth burns from yesterday's cigarettes. I want to be alone, left alone. In my skin I can feel this. Just leave me alone.

My life rushes by, out of control. I need myself, help me.

A bony finger pokes around her eye. Her hands are helpless, tied down like that. She does not struggle, although she could move her head. Why? The hard finger, damp, will only pursue. She had not even the will of normal reflexes anymore. The finger probes, pushing against the tender skin at the corner of her eyes, and she does not flinch. Soon it will poke straight through her eye. She knows that, can feel that, senses that, has predestined it, conjured it, awaits it. She sees it and wants it finished.

And she feels the demon's fingernail against the white of her eye. It presses in very slowly. In her memory the tune of a calliope she heard once somewhere in Amsterdam plays again.

She had nightmares about what She did to Margret. She dared not tell Nance, She was so ashamed of it. Why did She need Margret to be an image come to life? Why did She need to validate Herself by owning Margret, needing to keep her like a rare photograph? It was fucked up and She couldn't admit it to anyone. There would be retribution but it would not come from Margret and certainly not Nance, who might be shocked for a second but who would end up laughing about it after yelling at Her. The payback would come somewhere in Her life. Someone would do it to Her, sooner or later. Or it would be something just as hurtful if not exactly the same.

One night She dreamed about Sam—Sam alive again. And they were talking on the beach at The Pines on Fire Island. He was talking about stars and seashells, the commonalities they shared in feeling and shape. Shells that would be polished as brilliant as the stars, their radiating lines always from a core, a heart, that was like the light lines of stars.

"You know there are others we can't see," he said. "Invisible stars. Or shells that get broken but the light is still there and we're just too damn blind to see. And whose fault is that?"

He was tough. It was our fault if we lost out on anything that was there in front of us to use, beauty, that we couldn't see. *Whose fault?* Ours. Sam always thought people got what they deserved, made their own fate. He was old school WASP about it. He was goddamn tough.

Thank you, Sammy.

It made Her feel better because Margret was her own fault and, of course, so was She. Fine, so the power was Her's and so were the consequences, that was why She had a hard time taking control. Cowardice, being afraid of the certain consequences for Her own mistakes. *Coward.* Without mistakes and taking the weight for them, would She ever learn anything? Forget trying to be perfect that kept her paralyzed, she should just fuck up and take the weight. Go ahead, fuck up and go directly to jail, then advance two squares. Take a risk, take the weight. Take the knowledge and run even if it's not like riding a bike and you've got to learn it again and again and again. Whose fault is that?

Maybe She wouldn't die or be maimed in a motorcycle crash for what She had done. There was no excuse for not living Her life as She started to do again, on her own.

"Aren't you ever going to get a bike?" Nance taunted Her.

"As soon as I can beg, borrow and steal the money for shots of my work that magazine is thinking about using. Maybe the publicity will make someone want to buy. Maybe. Then I'm getting a bike. Have to."

"About time. But I thought you'd work it to be carried around on those cute girls' bikes forever."

"Jealous? It's cool, but I can't pick up any girls on my own without my own."

"How much do you need?"

"You offering? No shit?"

"I'll loan you the money if you take me around with you, bitch, and share the girls."

"No problem, *mon.*"

"And you can't do that. No fake Rasta talk, it's part of the deal."

They had a deal. Biker girl summer glittered in the distance after nearly a year of purgatory on earth. She would take the risk.

She went back to serious hanging out and being a ride slut, sliding on behind any woman biker who offered. Whoever asked turned out to be any number of attractive women. The only problem She had, when the usual memories of Margret didn't plague Her, was trying to decide which girl to focus Her flirtation on that would lead to bed, a brief affair. There had been a lull in Her fooling around because of the aftershock of having been, almost, with Margret. Probably She had been unconsciously punishing Herself for what She did by not allowing Herself to fuck with the girls She could have in the weeks after the incident, Her meanness.

Now She had choices and She had to make the effort to focus on one woman for a hot minute, otherwise She would get no one by seeing them all. There was the awesome and elusive Willa with her gigantic old BMW. And there was little Jean of the teases who was always around with her new bike after she traded the Shadow for a CB700 Nighthawk, black of course. Janet with the shaved head was nuts and fun and rode a crotch rocket, a red Kawasaki 750 Turbo. Kathryn was like Willa, a self-sufficient strongly attractive woman with a black Harley FXR Cruiser. And there was that cute groupie, Elisia, who did not ride but who was intense and completely always around, always. Choices. Life was definitely not bad.

But then again, She was paying dues along the way. As She was leaving for an afternoon ride with Jean, She made the mistake of ruffling through the mail before she left and picking out the letter addressed in Margret's handwriting. Worse, in a fit of masochism, She actually put aside Her excitement to ride with Jean and read it. A stupid thing to do. When Jean saw Her she had to say something. She was late, and there was something else.

"You ok? You look all pale and shit."

"Just hungry. Let's go."

And She put it out of Her mind. The accusations She had just read, the brutal shots about Her pettiness, cruelty and aggressiveness. Margret called Her a hypocrite, that She was not the person She presented Herself to be. She was a fraud. Margret wrote that she was a fraud unworthy of love and loyalty. But was that true? Was it really who She was? If She was, it was because She was like that only under the conditions of Margret-ism. Was it possible that She was like that all the time, with everyone? Same old shit. Accusations and guilt giving. Forget it. Have fun with her new friends. Let Her hands play over Jean, fooling around, as She hung on. *Enjoy the ride, goddamnit.*

She had to remember that being stoned meant having a good time. It always had before Margret, when smoking joints became rote and not something to do to get silly. *That's why they call it getting high for chrissakes.* She had always told Margret that when She tried to get her to have fun without including her usual boring analyses.

"Faster!" She yelled it through their helmets now and Jean twisted the throttle before She'd finished the word. She had to turn partway around to grab Her arm to keep Her from flipping off the back of the bike. She laughed at Her.

"You asked for it."

"Jesus, a little warning next time!"

"Can't hear you ..."

"Liar!"

She smacked Jean on the back and the bike shot forward again. This time She was hanging on tight around her waist. The bike zigged around manhole covers, zagged through breaks in the painted lanes. Just to give them a little kick Jean slalomed up Sixth Avenue, heading for 25th Street way over by Tenth Avenue to score some grass. She skidded to a fancy one-foot-down bike-arcing stop when they got there.

"You asked, you got it. Got you where you wanted to go," Jean said, rapping on the top of Her helmet.

"Will you give me anything I ask for so fast?"

"You really are a slut. Fuck that, I'm not doing anything else. You can walk home, bitch."

"I love it when you treat me bad."

"Now who's a liar? Big talk, little toughie."

Jean snatched the helmet from Her and bounced Her on the ass with it to hurry Her toward to the deserted-looking building to score. She stuck both helmets on the bike and lit a cigarette to wait for Her. When She got back with the ounce they were splitting, they rolled a joint, took a couple of hits, then hit the streets. They laughed, fooled around, rode around the city. They went from Battery Park to check out the water and roar through Wall Street canyons to flying up the East Side Highway. Jean finally cut across 14th Street to get back to familiar haunts from Avenue C to Third Avenue beyond where it became the Bowery, and from East 12th or so, around Tompkins Square Park and beyond Houston. All the while they talked about art and who was having a show where that they knew, and feminism and whatever was interesting in the latest edition of the *Village Voice*. They argued; they flirted. It was all light and fun. Good times, never heavy. She always had a good time with Jean.

Jean with her perennial just-out-of-bed hair, flattened in places, sticking up in others, was slender and puppy-like in action and general cadence. Lovely, young, feisty and fearless, she didn't take shit from anyone. But at the same time she was girlish, lacking in knowledge and experience about life things like jobs and leases and being wary of trusting everyone. Maybe those traits were just from youth, maybe unimportant, but they were noticeable. All of it was completely charming on her, this buoyant consequence of innocence that was so alluring. She could teach the girl a lot about sophistication, experience and taste and Jean could grow with it, with Her, and go beyond whatever She gave her.

That was really it, giving her what She had the desire to do, give to the kid so she could do it. She found Herself calling Jean "the kid," the "cutie"—and she was. Jean hated it, said that she hated it, but not really. She knew it was affectionate and respectful, no matter what the narrow politico correcto types might insist about it.

Jean was special to Her, fun. They clicked together. But of course Jean was involved with someone and at the same time was carrying a torch for another woman as well. She calculated Her chances were not great, not at the moment anyway. It wasn't important this time, though, the need to fuck and move on. Maybe it was because She didn't want to move past this one so quickly.

"Besides," Nance said, "that's the way relationships usually start, bitch, for normal people. Getting to know somebody and liking them instead of leaping into bed first thing, like you do."

Right. She had forgotten how real relationships worked. Either married or fucking every woman in sight constituted Her conception of relating lately. *Slow down.* Time to slow down, to prove Margret wrong. She needed to find out what kind of person She was with women without having to prove Herself or be so afraid of criticism. Who was She without having to figure out a standard to adhere to, without being afraid of rejection? That was the hardest to get rid of, Her fear of being pushed away like Margret had done so many times. She carried it silently like a hidden knife to be flashed and stuck in Her own back when She was insecure. It was used to prove She deserved to be insecure. She was nothing.

Lighten up.

Maybe this was all part of paying dues. Maybe it was just part of warding off the curse from Margret by not being able to have too much fun without her. But the letter she wrote had unnerved Her. It made Her work to get back to the feeling of freedom She thought She had already achieved and reveled in for too short a time. *Fuck it*, She wanted to live, prove She was worthy of living, already back from the brink but still living on the edge. So much fun still to have, and Jean was vibrant with it. Could She wait for any kind of normal progression with her? Or maybe She didn't want to, and that was all right too. Still, *slow down.* See what happens.

Don't decide your life before you live it.

- Is There Ever Sideways Time? -
ELISIA

Elisia was the worst woman She could have taken up with in Her flimsy fledgling state of maturity—if having broken totally with Margret the way She had could be called mature. Elisia was darkly quiet and unfortunately not so much adorably shy as she was just plain awkward around people. Her sense of humor ranged from nonexistent to peculiar. She didn't laugh at punch lines, but at inappropriate times. When she did laugh, though, she had a glorious smile. She showed a real beauty those few times when something—whatever weird thing it might be—pleased her, then she smiled. The problem was that She could never really figure out what would please Elisia and so She ended up trying too hard and being too nervous around her.

"Are you blind?" Nance said. "She's just like being with Margret. You're acting the same way. Do you like feeling like shit, or what? I can't believe you. Why not go out with your other girls? You're allowed to have fun, you know."

A challenge, or maybe masochism, had drawn Her to Elisia. And She was curious. She wanted to know what could get to her, what would make this gloomy woman loosen up, cry out? Elisia was gloomy, dark in mood and look—like an introverted intellectual with short black hair and big black glasses. Like a snobbish private school girl with a mean streak, she had that feel. And she was quiet, very quiet, unimpressed and unresponsive. Maybe it was just Her own sick fantasy, to find out if this woman became suddenly, mysteriously, magnificent in bed. She was driven to find out, to test Her fantasy no matter how uncomfortable it was to be around Elisia. Another conquest, but a very challenging conquest, was what She wanted.

"You're fucking nuts, but we knew that. You're going to get fucked up. Open your eyes, she's Margret! Only weirder."

Of course She didn't listen to Nance. It was too intriguing to see Elisia warming up, the introverted woman She caught looking at Her. She would look away when their eyes met, but she always stood very near to Her at the bars or anyplace they met. It was a possessive gesture, although she could rarely make conversation—awkward. There was something in the air between them, though, an unspoken attraction that made the distance between them smaller and smaller. This was a woman She did not have to wait for before falling into bed with her, like Jean. Elisia would be a quicker, less important challenge.

She would try to do it, to relate outside of a relationship. It was for Her own education, that was the excuse She used. She could learn from and enjoy women without depending on the old roles of lover, simple fuck, or buddy. The in-between relating that involved both sex and closeness was newer, kind of. Carmen was like that, although She had forged that relationship before. She could do it again, even as fucked up as She still was after Margret, although intermittently better and worse.

"Learn, goddamnit," Sam would say. "There's always something to learn."

And She remembered that's what Her grandmother would say, too. *Go ahead and try. See, you learn something.* But that was so long ago.

She couldn't remember what act or actions went with it. With Sam it had always been easier, because he ranted so regularly his displeasure with people who didn't work for what they wanted. He hated laziness, never was lazy himself, and he worked so hard at anything he did that it looked easy. He should have been compared to the really great collectors, ones who made a difference in style and paradigm shift in addition to excellence.

And when he got sick ... When he got AIDS. When the disease laid him so low—he kept reading when he couldn't walk anymore. He kept collecting, studying the newly discovered old silver he wanted to buy—his shift from collecting photographs. He did it from his bed until the day he died.

"Always something there, goddamnit. You've got to have eyes, that's all. And when you think there's nothing left to learn you might as well die."

But he went ahead and died anyway, even though he knew he had so much to learn. It wasn't fair. Fucking AIDS. She remembered again how She had lost more than Margret in all this. Sam, and so many more, so many. Too many. All with the stinging weight of purple Kaposi marks. In comparison, Her problems relating to women were bullshit. But what's anyone to do? Everyone seemed to have their own unique shit to deal with no matter who and how many died. Sickening.

So why was Elisia so difficult? She should figure it out because the woman obviously didn't want to give Her a hard time, obviously liked Her enough. They ran into each other at a party at Bonnie and Aloma's down on Lispenard Street—but that was a lie. Of course they knew the other would be there because it was one of those not-to-be-missed things. The women who were throwing it were an artsy power dyke couple with a great loft on the top floor in the building where *Printed Matter* was on the first floor. One was an *Art News* editor, the other a food cosmetician who prepped dishes to be photographed so they looked fabulously appetizing, never mind they might be slathered with glue to make them shine tantalizingly for the shot.

They'd said, "Maybe I'll see you there" to each other, as if they might not be there—part of the game. Of course they both passed the test: they showed up.

There would be plenty of action up at the party after the relative quiet of Church Street at that time of night. The motorcycles lined up on Lispenard proclaimed the biker girls were already there. Lucky for Her, though, Jean wasn't, which She discovered after cruising the place when She got upstairs. She was free to flirt, except for dour, silent Elisia always watching Her—even though whatever might be crackling between them wasn't serious. There were some cool women to drink with, smoke a joint with. There were performance artists, wannabe Laurie Andersons or Ann Magnusson types, some of the Guerilla Girls were there, but a few activists from ACT UP made sure there was a serious halo of gravity that arced out from wherever they were standing.

It was a great party and She started drinking Jose Cuervo early. She was pleasantly surprised to find Elisia was carrying a pint of scotch in the inside pocket of her motorcycle jacket, and wearing not much else in there. Maybe she wasn't so strange after all—although she only hung around the edges of the party, spoke only to those who approached her, and plenty did because she was cute. She was keeping an eye on Elisia, but She wasn't one to stand around at a party. She kept moving, zipped from one group to another, got a little drunk and did more coke and grass to take the edge off the tequila. There was a blonde, Susan, who was really drunk and kept following Her, trying to make out with her in corners, in the hall, in the bathroom, wherever she could grab Her. It was mildly obnoxious, but also flattering because she was blonde after all. She noticed too late that Elisia was staying close behind this silly scene and she would appear when Susan got too handsy, suddenly offering Her a drink from her pint. She popped up out of nowhere once when the blonde had Her pressed up against a wall.

Cornelia, of the ancient BMW arrived, saw what was happening with these women and took Her aside to rag on Her. One gesture from her brought sweet Lizabeth to ask Her to dance so She could catch a break from Her pursuers. But while they were bumping in a dance Elisia appeared to stand too near, not dancing. This brought Cornelia and shaved-head Janet and another bottle of Cuervo. Some guy who had his dick hanging out of his pants danced by and they applauded him, then appraised him—commenting without much interest—when he was gone. They camped up flirting with each other, grinding together in various combinations to whatever was playing: Madonna's "Like a Virgin" or "Material Girl," or Tina Turner's "Addicted to Love," or the "Conga." Of course there was Tears for Fears, "Shout," which could depress Her in such a virtuous way. It didn't get better than this, that's what She felt then. She didn't even care that Stevie Wonder's "Part Time Lover" was too prophetic.

With nearly everybody bouncing, singing to that, Elisia quietly and determinedly pried Her away from the biker girl group with Janet, Lizabeth and Cornelia by moving in between them, pinning Her with her eyes. Sexy, darkly seductive, not masking her moves, Elisia turned her usual uneasiness into a murky magnetism. The change was lost on no one, and Cornelia shot a one-up move that surprised Her.

"If you don't take your girlfriend home, I will."

"No way," She said with a half-laugh, half-growl.

"Think so?"

The challenge was enough, not that it was needed given the way Elisia was acting. Those eyes, the serious intensity of her sweltering, mean, come take the snob-girl if you can, looks were too much to ignore. But She had to play the game, not make it look too easy. She broke away from Elisia's sexy tractor-beam and turned to flirt with the heavy-handed Susan. It forced Elisia to move with Her, and move between them.

"Don't you want to come home?" Elisia said in Her ear, under the music.

"Now?"

Elisia took Her by the hand and led Her away. They went down five flights to the street and caught the first cab they saw. There, in the cozy back seat something changed. Elisia moved away and was leaning way over against the door. She wouldn't look at Her anymore.

"What the hell? What now?" She was high enough to let the words burst out.

"We're going to my place," Elisia said.

And they rode in silence. Uncomfortable. Nance was right, this was like being with Margret all over again. The come-on and the go-away routine. *Terrific. What now?*

Elisia's place was at the edge of the East River, almost under the Manhattan Bridge. It was a huge empty loft occupied by only a table, two chairs and a small bed in the farthest corner. There were boxes all over. Two bare 30-watt or so bulbs hung from fourteen-foot ceilings on long cords and kept the space in dim, grim shadow.

"Sit," Elisia said, indicating nothing and not looking at Her.

She sat on a wheeled stool at the table that was littered with cameras from 35 millimeters to medium formats, two of them beautiful Rolleis—vintage Rolleiflex that made Her envious—and papers, books and more books stacked on the floor all around. And after a minute, not far away in the gloom She started to make out the boxes, and there were equipment cases. Zero Halliburtons and their silver latches with black camera lenses and black barn door lights piled on and around them.

"You do film, right? You shoot in here?"

"Sometimes."

She didn't look up as she rolled a joint, standing at the side of the table. She was rolling from stuff she took out of three different plastic bags, making a concoction joint. She focused her eyes enough to follow Elisia's taking a pinch of herb from one bag another from the next and suddenly thought of her as a silently mad scientist, adding arsenic and MDA, the original love drug Ecstasy, to the mixture. She'd find out soon enough, took the joint from Elisia after she had already drawn long and slow on it. Their fingers touched and made them hesitate, their hands suspended in mid-air like Michelangelo's image in the Sistine Chapel, only female and real. They seemed caught in time like that, fingers touching on a joint with a cavernous, humming darkness for background instead of heavenly jumbled sky.

The dope, whatever the mixture was, hit Her like a ton of bricks. She felt like She was submerged in warm water all of a sudden, languorously, like slow submersion in a tub. Her eyes clouded then cleared. Her heart pounded. Elisia watched Her, those heavy-duty eyes on Her, so She smiled and then looked away. Silence. No music, not even the sound of traffic outside. There were only long draws on the mystery joint.

"What's in this?"

"This and that. Do you like it? It should be killer."

"Yeah."

So much for conversation. She was stoned beyond being able to put together thoughts and then actually verbalize them. She couldn't think of another damned thing to say. She began to feel like they should just hop into bed to quit being uncomfortable, like having sex would change everything and make everything all right with sun, rainbows and unicorns. *Fucked up.* It was insane to think. "If you can't talk, how can you fuck?" She could almost hear Nance saying it, but still, She had done it before. Sometimes it worked— sometimes it was a disaster. *What the hell, why not?*

She got up and went around the table with the nearly finished joint, handed it to Elisia from behind. She let Her hands rest lightly on her shoulders, and caressed them gently. Elisia froze, then leaned forward and slipped away.

"Where's your bathroom?"

She hid Her irritation. And Elisia indicated a general direction with her head.

The bathroom was an adventure. Getting there was a long, dark walk down what felt like an abandoned high school corridor. There was only the padding sound of Her sneakers as She went a little cautiously, searching for a door that looked different from all the others that opened to dark, spooky classrooms. But after what seemed like hours, She found an arched opening, dark and spooky, but She had a lighter and matches and used them with shaky, halting, success. When She left the stall in the line of them hidden only by those partial institutional doors She felt disoriented, stoned, with a weird sense of secrecy in this echoing once-public facility, all alone. And She still had to navigate the long, dark, bare corridor back to Elisia's loft.

She made it, entered the darkness from the hallway that now seemed bright by comparison. She scanned for Elisia who was no longer at the table. A few moments, and then She could just discern her form there in the shadows, lying on the bed.

"Well hello ..."

She said it as She sat near her, put an arm on either side of her and leaned lightly on her to kiss her. Elisia did not move, did not respond at all with lips, pressure, movement of any part of her body. She was either dead or passed out. She listened for breathing.

"Elisia?"

She didn't budge, but she was breathing. *That was that.* She took her jacket from the back of a chair and left, thinking a little guiltily about not being able to lock the Fox lock on the door. *Tough, goddamnit.*

She made Her way into deserted streets there at the East edge of the island, etched with dark buildings—forget finding a cab. A little unsteady but glad for the fresh air, She headed home and kept an eye over Her shoulder. But the only threatening thing that happened was a police car prowled behind Her for a block, evidently deciding if they should follow Her to a dope score or arrest Her for trolling for "johns." This neighborhood was too sketchy and abandoned for pretty much anything, though.

"Thanks, gentlemen, for the fucking escort!"

She yelled it at the cops as they cruised past in their silent car, turned and slid away without disturbing the menace in the night. She was in the middle of a very long, very dark, very creepy block. The worst. Having had excellent scare-training from Her growing-up days in gritty Detroit, She knew one of the things to do to protect yourself in an intimidating situation is act crazy. She started to sing.

"Jose Cuervo you're a friend of mine ... Did I dance on the bar ... did I start any fights ... ?"

The contagious song was part of Her new country legacy. She mangled the lyrics all the way home. *Fuck it all,* She blurted out now and then to fill in where She couldn't remember the words.

"Fuck it all. "

And the walk made Her wish She had a bike. No more 4 a.m. walks alone, *goddamnit.* A motorcycle of one's own, yes, Virginia ...

- Sometimes Time Really Can Stand Still.
Or It Seems That Way, Or Not -
RETHINK

Elisia rang Her bell at ten the next morning, apologetic and more animated, more normal and interactive, than usual. She lit up a joint and passed it.

"I can stay for a while. If you're not busy."

Girls. It was enough to make Her go back to men just for the simplicity of it, the ease of sex with no drama. Well, less drama.

"I have to work in the darkroom. Deadline. A magazine wants some work, means money."

"I'll come back tonight," she said and was gone.

Jesus fucking Christ. Was this the normal development of a relationship that She was supposed to try out, learn from? Leaping into bed without all this preamble was easier. She went back to bed and tried to sleep, ignoring calls the machine picked-up until She heard Kathryn's voice. It was Kathryn with the Harley. Her call, She took.

"So I thought you'd want to come along," Kathryn ended up. "If you don't mind hanging onto me for three hours."

"I only get to hang onto you while we're riding?"

"You really are bad. I wasn't going to tell you this now, but I can only carry one sleeping bag, and you're kind of small, so—"

"So you asked whoever would take up least room on your bike. Thanks." She said it with mock hurt. They both laughed.

"Hey come on, maybe I can tempt you with something else?"

"I'm tempted already."

A beautiful Harley and sleeping with that handsome woman—strong featured, clear-eyed—was more than enough enticement. All that and a weekend in the country up near Woodstock was exactly what She needed to clear Her head of Elisia. The only hitch was that She had to break a Friday date with Jean the cutie tease, although it might be the best thing for the girl to miss Her a little. Just thinking about Jean gave Her a nice knotty stomach, an excitement stomach. She was special, seeing her or not seeing her didn't matter because that girl was usually not far from Her mind anyway.

And when She went over to Nance's apartment and told her, she said, "Sounds like fun. But are you even into this woman, cuz she sounds a little butch for you."

"So what? Do I have to have a type? I wouldn't mind being taken care of for a change. Why can't I swing both ways instead of fitting into the goddamn dyke slots, butch or femme? Fuck that."

"What about your infection?"

"Seems cool."

"Really, doctor? You're fucking crazy. And what about Margret?" Nance pinned Her with a squinty look. "I saw her yesterday. She ended up crying while we were talking, wouldn't tell me why though. What'd you do this time?"

Oh shit. She had to tell her about leading Margret on and leaving her hot, begging. It was time to take the weight for that. So She told Nance what She had done to Margret, finally.

"You're insane, you fucking bitch! I don't believe you did that. No wonder she looks so bad. Asshole!"

"Come on, Nance—"

"No, that's really cold. You just had to get back at her. Now I know why you didn't tell me about it, the way you fucking tell me everything, for fucking hours."

"Come on—"

"It's fucked up. *You're* fucked up. Fucked up thing to do ..."

And She had to hear it from Nance, the terrible things She had only been telling Herself. She had to hear all the recriminations She ran in Her own head. They hurt more coming from Nance, her rock, her touchstone to reality. After Nance vented, and it took a long time, after that they could talk. Nance ended up listening again to the pain that made Her do it, but she didn't forgive Her. Acceptance, not forgiveness.

"You're fucking mean and it's fucking scary." Nance threw a joint at Her head. "Looks like you're not done with her yet. You want her back."

"No way!" She yelled it too loudly and shot up from Nance's ratty couch to keep the joint from burning anything.

"Give me a break, try being honest just once, asshole," Nance said, deadly serious. "And she wants you back too."

I can't stand it. There is a cloud around me, a heavy fist enclosing me. I walk around and smile, talk on the phone and everyone says they're glad to hear I'm doing better. I'm not. I can't even tell my friends the pain anymore. I cover up. And it's killing me.

I'm reading Gert Hofmann and Gerald Kersh, Prelude to a Certain Midnight*—haunting. Nice and depressing, so oblique but so direct. I feel like I'm going to die. I must work, be alone, leave the world.*

"Did she tell you that, that she wants me back?" She blurted it out. Nance's voice had snapped Her back from crazy thoughts.

She thought Her voice was echoing—it wasn't—so She got up and sat on the edge of the window, farther from Nance who stayed on the couch. "Farther" from anything in an apartment like Nance's on Avenue C meant maybe two feet. But She suddenly needed any space, and air at the window, and the feel of the metal fire escape She could lean out and touch to feel grounded.

"I'm not telling you anything word for word because I'm her friend too," Nance snapped. "But you should cut the hurt bullshit and get real. She'd move back in with you in a minute. So would you, asshole."

"Fuck that, I've got girls to mess with." And She vamped, striking a pose at the window to lighten the mood.

"So predictable. Let's see." Nance lit a cigarette and threw the match at Her. "You've got totally zoned out, weird-ass Elisia who you should never even think about being with. And there's this butch biker girl who'll probably want to marry you, and you'll hate that. Then there's Carmen who seems the best of them but won't leave the marriage she's in and needs to be in and who would want that from you if you ever really got together. Let's see, who else? I can't fucking keep track and really don't fucking care."

They were sharing Jack from Her pocket-bottle by then. Lucky, because it tempered Nance's "I've had it with you" tirade. After the outburst that cleared the air in the tiny, overfilled room, they both relaxed. Nance had a right to slam on Her.

"Wait a minute, there's that Boston girls thing I still don't believe," she said. "And there's whoever else I forget that you've been fucking your brains out with."

"Jean. You forgot her, the killer cutie."

"*P* fucking *U*! That girl is full of it, full of herself. She's a player, into seeing who will go for her, follow her around like you. She's got a couple of jerks like you she's leading around. How can you even fall for her girlie come-on shit?"

"But she's so hot."

"Bullshit. She's not that hot, not even that cute. It's the biker thing, that's all. I wouldn't get involved with her."

"How about I stay away after I fuck her?"

"Fucking crazy. These women aren't even in your league. Why don't you find a nice professional woman?"

"Fuck it, *mon*. What fun is that?"

"No Rasta talk!"

Too much to think about. Back with Margret, being with Margret again? She couldn't feel it. It scared Her. How could She see Her girls, have two of them one after the other like last night? Elisia came back, got into bed with Her finally, awkward but willing. She made up for passing out at her place. Her body was linear, no padding, not easy to fit into and feel. No embellishments of breasts or hips—linear. But she was responsive, more responsive than She had expected. Elisia gave her lips hungrily, opened to Her hands willingly. She explored her, entered her, made her cling to Her, bite Her shoulder, and come.

173

But She didn't come Herself. There was not enough time, not enough passion in Her because She concentrated on giving to Elisia, giving her a good fucking, the coming that did not make her call out but gasp and dig short nails into Her arms. After that, she gave no thought to Her satisfaction—She could tell. Elisia laid with Her until they both knew it was time for her to leave. A mutual, silent decision. It was strange but all right, although it left Her horny. The choice was to do Herself or call another girl for pussy delivery.

She went through Her address book. It was only ten thirty, someone would come—and come. Jean was who She wanted but it wasn't time yet. She wasn't finished teasing Her yet, and She knew it. Carmen, of course, it was Saint Carmen who She had been missing. And now She wanted her.

"Right now?"

"Take a cab," She told her.

"All right."

Perfect, just perfect. She hadn't been with Carmen in too long, and She was excited by the thought of her. She rushed around to clean up the evidence of her first date tonight. Fluffed up the always-heavier-than-you-think futon, took the coke cans and beer bottles and snack remnants from around the bed. Re-perfumed the sheets to cover the fragrance of sex. Put Her t-shirt and jeans back on without underwear.

She was in the middle of rolling a joint when the buzzer rang and jolted Her into dropping grass all over the table. It didn't matter—she was there. Finally, sweet Carmen of the Screams.

- When You Die, Does Time Go Away?
Who to Ask ... ? -
MERCY

Margret called. *Damnit.* This was not what She needed after a night in bed with Carmen. It was Her own fault for forgetting to turn on the answering machine and, worse, like an idiot picking up the phone in a reflex move when She and Carmen were having breakfast—her lover was away and it was a treat to be spending real time together. This was rare, special, and they had already decided to spend the day in bed together.

"Difficult" did not nearly cover what that call and the crashing sensations were like. There She was with the feel of Carmen's nakedness pressing against Her. A turn-on over coffee. And there on the phone was Margret, seductive. It all made Her head clang and all She wanted to do was get off the phone.

"I need to see you. We have to talk," she said.

"Sure anytime," She said with obvious fake normalcy.

She tried to stop Carmen's hands from reaching between Her legs. And She tried to focus, concentrated on sounding natural.

"We have to start again, don't you think?" Margret was sincere, pained. "We can start fresh."

"Yeah sure, we'll talk."

"You sound funny. You don't want to talk?"

"I'm not, I don't ... Look, I just got up, let me call you back."

Carmen was on her knees, her lips at Her down there and her tongue beginning to play over Her. All this while She tried to talk to Margret.

"There's someone with you, isn't there."

"No no! Let me call you back, ok? I've got to wake up."

Carmen was working it now. Her tongue was moving into Her.

"Bye." She threw the phone down, grabbed for Carmen. "Jesus!"

She had been holding back forever it seemed, but it had only been a few minutes. Still, She grabbed for Carmen and pressed her head between Her legs and came, came loudly. It was a good, odd orgasm there on a straight-backed chair at the table with breakfast coffee not even finished.

But there was more. She slid off the chair and kneeled with Carmen in a deep make out. Then they rolled under the table. They fucked again and She made Saint Carmen of the Screams, scream. Finally, they stopped, right there where they were: on the floor half under the table and panting like fighters. They got up slowly, sat back down in the chairs just the way they had started.

"Coffee's cold."

They said it at the same time and laughed. Easy. It was always easy and good with Carmen. But when She got up to go make more coffee She noticed something that made Her stop. The phone receiver She had thrown down had missed the base. The phone had been off the hook all this time. *Oh fuck no.* She hoped Margret had hung up and hadn't heard all that. She felt horrible suddenly. The pull of Margret tugged on Her heart again and She tried to fight it, to forget it. She didn't want Margret anymore, She hoped.

"Was that the 'other' woman or 'another' woman?" Carmen said.

"Where?"

"Very funny. On the phone before. I'm not the only one you see, and I've never even asked you for that. I'm just curious."

Her big eyes were soft and her pouty mouth smiled. It flared up the closeness between them, the real affection.

"There's no one like you, Carm'. That's really true."

She said it with the ring of truth, and it was. She felt different, wonderful and accepted with Carmen and by Carmen. And it seemed that she felt the same way about Her too. The mutuality was precious, prized and resilient because of a real friendship and real affection that took everything to a bedrock level, mutual respect.

"I wish we could be together more," Carmen whispered it.

"You're the one with the lover."

"Maybe not for long." Carmen watched for a reaction.

At first She felt joy, then panic. Then deep panic. She remembered suddenly what Nance said about being "careful with Carmen" because she was the "marrying kind."

"Things can't be that bad, there's always ups and downs," She said.

"She might not come back this time."

"You don't seem too upset."

"Because of this? Very funny," Carmen mock slapped Her, then kissed Her. "It's the roller coaster, I'm tired of it. You know how it goes. But you're free now."

Right. She was free, at least ostensibly if not in Her own mind, and Carmen "had enough" of her relationship, she said. So they went back to bed together. This time the answering machine was on with the volume turned down low. But as they made love She could sometimes still hear messages that came in, depending on Carmen's sound level. Twice it was Jean the tease. And Margret again. Then Janet. Finally, there was Kathryn with a departure time for their motorcycle trip the next day ... or had She fucked away a night? Was it supposed to be today? Later?

- Time Is What You Make It. Really?
Sounds Like Bullshit. -
THE STREETS

There was a calmness after the heroin. There on that blanket under a tree at the edge of a stream. It was after four hours on the back of the Harley, hanging onto Kathryn. The intimacy of those hours, pressing leather over the vibration of the bike, was like naked hurtling over asphalt. After that rush, the downward spiral of snorting smack washed Her smooth. A calm that gauzed the world like taking acid had done before with its prisms of color instead. She could remember being different, thinking differently than She did now.

This was afterward, after She rode alone for the first time. The vibration between Her legs had thrown a smile on Her lips. First time riding alone through the wind, with the wind. Laughing, loving it, She tried to slalom the bike without success, made a wide leaning turn at the country intersection and headed back toward Kathryn who was waiting at the spot in the road from where she had instructed Her and sent Her off.

Fuck first gear, try second.

A Rush. Kick up to third, twist the throttle toward you with your right hand. Fourth, fifth, and gone. Her head snapped back, then down.

"Look up! Look where you're going!" Kathryn yelled.

She kept going, kept riding and zapped past her. But after She slowed at the intersection into that wobbly, arcing turn She knew it was enough. She hit the brakes, rear brake right foot, front brake right hand—and the wheels locked and shuddered the bike under Her.

Kathryn, running, grabbed the bike from behind just as it was heeling over, buckling Her left leg beneath it. And She let go the clutch lever with Her left hand and stalled the bike, lurched it, but didn't drop it.

Kathryn knocked on the top of her helmet for Her to take it off. She thought she would be angry, but Kathryn leaned down and kissed Her instead. Country silence, birds' soft songs, and a strong, reserved, promising kiss held in the handsome woman's arms, leather on leather. The strength, the serene and silent country after the roaring awakening on the big Harley equaled raw excitement. Unbare fleshiness.

"You don't have to stop."

Kathryn smiled and gently pushed away from Her. Without a word she got on the bike and She slid on behind her, pushed Her crotch against her ass and pressed tightly with the insides of Her thighs against the outsides of Kathryn's. Kathryn reached back and ran her hand along Her leg now and then as they rode. And as they rode She let Her hands trail down to Kathryn's crotch. More intimate than sex, more powerful for the promise, the thrill ran through the bike, and because of the bike.

It felt like salvation, or certain death. Both were the same. Riding motorcycles, doing drugs—*Never at the same time*. Kathryn was cautionary, but her touch was exciting. She wanted more but She couldn't move a finger because of the heaviness of the smack, their reward after the ride, so She thought She'd have to wait. But Kathryn moved, and caressed Her. Reserved, direct, ardent. No tease, a secure woman who wanted Her was taking Her little by little into a slow whirlpool, sucked in by centimeters. Her hands, the pressure of her lips, her body on Hers all moved inexorably toward certain longing held back only by the strength of its inevitability.

It was painful, the slowness, then real pain as Kathryn started to bite at Her breasts through Her shirt. She grabbed Her hard, slowly, and sucked Her fingers deep into her mouth. Something She had never felt before in instant intimacy, a determined drawn-out lovemaking that took too long, made Her want too much. Kathryn didn't undress Her for a long time, not until she had caressed Her fully with that strength, that silence. And it was so quiet, like falling asleep—but that was the smack, too. The smack and Kathryn's deep sleep-fuck seduction.

When she finally did it, there was little to do. She was ready for her, so fucking ready. She came fast, but long. She clung to Kathryn before, during and after, and She wanted more, couldn't let go. But Kathryn wanted, too, and somehow that surprised Her, at least so soon. She pulled Herself out of Her molten, leaden world and touched her, smooth and unhurried. A lean, long-limbed body unashamedly opened to Her. And she was beyond open and she wanted more, more than just Her outside of her. Kathryn said "more" and She went deeper. She pushed and slid, feeling Her way, feeling the tightness open up. All the way in, out. In, then a fist, make a fist. And deeper. Kathryn was lost in it, sighed. She moved in her, deliberate, in and in. She hadn't done it like this, never so deep, so hard, so much. She felt everything, all the wet, the smooth, the spasms. When it was finally finished and Kathryn came, She had to stop, but slowly. And even though She stopped, Her body or spirit or something, went on and out somewhere.

And they did more—drugs, not sex. The fucking had been profound enough to allow them to relax in each other, with each other. Now they were on the nod from the heroin, touching sometimes, but more lost each in her own thickly silent world than wanting the other. Their communication was on another level. They watched the stars together, listened to leaves on the trees, the grasses, sounds of small animals. They lay together not sleeping but being asleep in the nod, in that languorous nether-state of smack. Her mind dragged over the shards of Her life in images or non-images of women, fucking, drugs, motorcycles—but very little of Her photographs, the work that frightened Her with fear of failing, being exposed in it.

After moderate success with Her work in that journal She had begun new work but was not continuing it. Too wrapped up in proving Herself in other ways like being sought after in bed, being tough, exploring more risks, more drugs, more women. More of everything.

Sitting on an escarpment top, this time in Quebec Province. The earth is the same, people are the same. Nature recapitulates nature. The terror of nothing new, and worse, not mastering the old.

What have I learned in these months? Death. And success voodoo. The land is everywhere so sweet. But I always know who's behind me, creeping up. Need to do that everywhere too.

Climbed a very rough trail. "Steep and Hard" a sign had said, and I should have read it first instead of when I finally got back down—it was right. Little caterpillars stuck to me because the trail straight up was massed over with trees and growth. Sweat, bugs, crackles in the bushes near and far. Hard climb. Finally reach the hawks soaring over the cliffs. They look at me like prey. But they decide even I am too big, although I think they would be tough, attacking.

Later a bee will be in and out of the car. Now, I should have brought the water I wanted to. Go alone, be alone, get stoned—no one to correct mistakes. I took pictures, drew little pictures. With the bugs, the chipmunks, butterflies, dragonflies, birds—gigantic robins, little hopping brown-feathered whatevers, hawks, maybe a hummingbird—and a rat, maybe it was a mole. A leaf fell right in my lap. Thank you.

Yesterday I saw a northern lands hewn-wood cathedral. The graffiti on the wall said "Stray the Course," that must be in Canadian. Good for them to do it like that. I love Canadians.

What have I learned, these months? I know. Can I tell, and tell? The wind in the trees, all the way up the escarpment. Change of elevation, the sign said is 70 meters. Did I climb almost a half-mile? It felt like ten. Annapurna in the Himalayas it was not, and that's fine. I like to live at the top of mountains but they frighten me. There it is. Success in a sentence, or lack of it. Thoughts of success, being there, not wanting to get there.

I go and sit near the edge of the escarpment and feel the sun on my face, feel the wind, hear the insects, the birds. And some guy who is parked far away below wafts the can-can and "Eroica" at me on the wind.

"You want to ride more?"

Kathryn asked Her when the sun was high and hot and they had had their coffee and sex but no more heavy drugs. Another lesson? The Harley was heavy for Her but low enough to almost get flat-footed on either side.

181

"Just take it easy," Kathryn said. "No running it out through the gears. Practice some turns like I showed you. Practice stopping, but slow. Hear that? Use just the front brake, then just the rear. Feel the difference. Then do both, but slow."

It was great, and it was scary. She learned how to lean with the bike, to feel the power, how to cling to the tank with Her knees, how to know the vibrations and what they meant. She couldn't help grinning stupidly. The competence and the freedom She had felt only on the back of Jean's bike was nothing compared to this. The real stuff was beginning to be Hers. Kathryn kept cautioning Her that a motorcycle was no toy—it wasn't just a sexy accessory. And she felt that, was learning it. Learned when She inadvertently over-revved the engine when She stopped, or misjudged the power and felt the difference in the vibration and the sudden surge beneath Her that almost threw Her off time after time. But leathered and helmeted She felt invincible straddling the engine, and free. Free and competent, the symbols She needed for Her life, for success. No Margret here, no spillover from a life with her.

A new obsession, no longer Margret but motorcycles. She made Kathryn stop at bike shops whenever they passed any in small towns all the way back from the country. She wanted to sample bikes, helmets, leather jackets, gloves. Fuck Margret, and fuck her narrow life. She wanted to slash through space on a bike, feel a girl behind Her the way She clung to Kathryn with pressure against Her ass, along Her thighs. A long ride home was time to flirt, and the rest of the smack and a little coke to finish once they got there. Dreamy lovemaking, but lean Kathryn told Her she had no more to give her.

"This is it, all of it. That all right with you?"

She told Her she wanted no involvement, no emotion. Was that "all right?" It was fucking perfect. Perfect from the Harley rider. No bullshit, only drugs and good sex, shared honesty—no more or less. *Thank you, universe.*

It reminded Her, in its thorough opposition, to the affair She had had with that doctor before. Carol was a successful obstetrician, African-American and very middle class. Fucking in her well-appointed office was a kick at first but the emotional ups and downs for a simple fuck was soon not worth it. Expensive man-tailored suits and handmade pipes—some of them antique Meerschaum she smoked only at home or in exclusive clubs, dinner out where she snapped her fingers at waiters. All of that should have told Her that Carol was too tight for Her. Some money spent and some too-straight fucking with Her always on the bottom was loaded with "do you love me" and "who else are you fucking, bitch?" that it wasn't worth it after a few weeks. She would rather have this biker's honesty than that physician's control and head games. No relationship was exactly what She wanted, and hardly any had any relating. Couldn't take it, didn't want it.

Smack was better than coke, less depression afterward, more control, more fabulous feeling. But She didn't have enough money for all She wanted to do. Friends started telling Her to cool it, She was doing too much. *Bullshit.*

She could do anything and not get caught. She wanted drugs. She wanted to ride. Hopping from one woman's bike to the next, She tied to practice, pick up the finer points.

"That's how it sounds when you've got to switch to the reserve tank. It kind of sputters, loses power," Jean said. "Feel it? It's the lever down there. See?"

And She listened and watched and learned. Took it all in. Looked at carburetors that meant nothing to Her, flexed brake levers just to get the feel. After that, She rode whenever She could beg a bike for a few blocks. And She started looking for cheap used bikes without having any money—except for Nance's offer that She couldn't forget.

- Time Is What You Fill It With? -
FLIRTING

Looking for bikes, looking for women. Women were easier to find
than the motorcycle She wanted. RoTina and her lover were friends
of Nance but RoTina flirted with Her brazenly when her lover
couldn't see it, couldn't catch her doing it. Purely sexual, no pretense
of anything else, the woman wanted Her in bed, wanted a fling from
a long-term relationship and She was the wildcard—now the single
woman at any gathering of couples.

A gathering of couples—that was the usual dyke scene. Couples.
The only thing holding Her back was seeing a copy of Her own failed
relationship in those pairs. That was why She couldn't quite bring
Herself to fuck RoTina. She knew and liked her lover. So She held
back, ran with Jean who She couldn't shake anyway. No sex, but there
was a closeness, a wanting to be with each other that would not go
away. They had great times, did drugs together, stayed together for
days, chastely but so close.

Nance told Her she was nuts, of course. "What is this anyway,
some kind of weird mother-daughter thing you're doing? Give it up."

But She only laughed at Nance. She couldn't give it up, and neither
could Jean. They liked each other and no one else could understand,
because everyone else saw the sexual undercurrent between them. Just
being close, though, seemed to satisfy them more intimately than sex.
Nope, She wouldn't give up Jean or the specialness that relationship
was beyond any others She had.

Elisia dropped away after the one night of sex, although they
still talked. They even went out together sometimes. Kathryn came

around with her Harley now and then for drugs and silent sex, then went away again. Mostly the bike obsession took Her mind off Margret, although Kelly and Nance kept bringing it back to Her.

"You should talk," Kelly said. "Don't you want to know what went wrong?"

"She wants to get back with you, but you didn't hear that from me," Nance said.

"Doesn't matter." She said it with indifference, pleased it came out that way.

"Isn't there anything she can do? Think about it."

It had taken nearly a year to feel human again, to not feel like a piece of trash. So, "no," She really didn't want to explore the reasons they broke up, no matter how much it all still rattled in Her head. She was fighting it, ignoring it, filling Her life with new obsessions. Riding, fucking, partying. Running away ...

I dreamed that a man, big, was trying to ride two small ponies stacked one on top of the other. The larger bottom one bucked and kicked. But he kept putting the smaller one on top of it and kept insisting on riding them both that way. I told him to stop but he told me he'd do what he wanted—real mean.

I stood there sweating, shaking, watching. Paralyzed. Then I ran.

Olivia wouldn't put up with the partying, girls, or Her beloved drugs. On top of all that, she didn't want Her to ride a motorcycle. Olivia was a lawyer, worse than a lawyer, an assistant district attorney. She was in the public eye, prosecuted big cases, an established woman and tough. She wouldn't take any bullshit but she offered Her the world. They met at a toney cocktail party She hadn't wanted to go to but did anyway. She had to. She was on the guest list because *Shutters* magazine had published two of Her photographs.

Olivia was average height, streaked silver hair and dressed with corporate care. They talked easily after being introduced by Judy, the editor She had once been so attracted to but never went anywhere with it. But Olivia, She suspected immediately: she couldn't be straight. She looked into Her eyes too directly, kept the conversation going too pointedly and leaned too close.

"It's been some time since your work with Judy and I've heard some rumors about *ArtSpeak*. You must have new photographs," she said out of nowhere.

"Not as much as I should."

"And what's the reason for that?"

A demand for an answer in a genteel tone, but it felt like a slap. It stung because it reminded her of what Sam would always say: *And whose fault is that?* The cadence was the same but that was all. Now pale grey eyes watched Her and She felt uncomfortable. It was a prosecutor's gaze and it made Her wonder if she had already seen a file on Her or something.

The city power holders were always doing stupid drug sweeps, maybe this was a setup. This woman knew, had seen pictures of Her buying stuff on Avenue C, smoking joints on the streets. Maybe it was the last "t" of heroin She bought from that heavy-duty dealer, the tenth of a gram for eighty dollars—and She was planning on getting another. But, oh no, this was it—this woman knew about her. This big deal Assistant D.A. was going to bust the middle class, the artists, musicians and students instead of the poor street people for a change. That's why Judy left them alone to talk—Her mind raced with it—Judy must know about the planned bust!

Damn, what am I holding?

Two or three joints were in Her cigarette pack as usual, and they might make a big deal of it. *Oh shit!* She had forgotten the small coke bottle that was still in Her jacket pocket, left with a few good hits in it. This was it. She was cooked.

"I suppose there must be a more complicated reason than those of us who aren't artists would expect. I didn't mean to stop the conversation." Olivia was smiling at Her silence.

"Sorry. I mean, you're right. It's complicated just to work sometimes, too much living in between."

She kept the jumble of Her last months at bay in Her head and willed Herself to stay in the moment. She flashed a smile and tried to act cute. When all else fails, flirt. Olivia laughed.

"You know I always find it odd to learn that artists are not prone to easy answers. But that's what's so interesting."

"Interesting? I don't know about how great it is to be distracted by life, just living in this city."

"But isn't that what you use in your work? Doesn't art imitate life, like they say?"

Very sharp, this lawyer, and she was definitely flirting with Her. Maybe She wasn't being set up to be busted. Maybe She could relax.

"Yeah, sometimes my work rehashes my life, like laziness turning into not working."

"You're hard on yourself," Olivia said and laughed. "Or is it that you want some strokes? What you're doing is hard, otherwise everyone would be doing it. And you want some sympathy. That's right, isn't it?

The prosecutor was waiting for an answer. *Fuck that.* Her natural aversion to control kicked in like a reflex. Olivia was waiting: yes or no?

"I don't know."

"Evasive?"

She pinned Her with a defoliating look. Normally that look would have kept Her from saying anything even if She weren't paralyzed already.

Evasive? Fuck you.

But Olivia started to smile, erasing her accusation with a "gotcha" wink that showed she had been messing with Her head. That was a total surprise. And just as She was beginning to relax with her they were interrupted by "suits" who wanted to meet her, right then, the celebrated D.A. But She didn't care.

She was glad for the break, and glad for the waitress with the tray of drinks who was suddenly there. Very cute. They smiled at each other. Familiar? A quick hesitation held them. The girl adjusted her little bow tie with her free hand.

"Must be something, working these things," She said.

"Bizarre. But I know you from somewhere."

"Maybe."

"No, really," the chestnut-haired girl gave Her a napkin for Her drink. "You hang out at the Pyramid. I saw you once going down to the dressing room, Mad Orphan was there."

"Right. They're The Lovelies now."

"I know. They're pretty great."

"Want to meet them?"

"That would be incredible!" The girl nearly dropped her tray, excited and all smiles before she had to pry herself away to pass more drinks. And She smiled after her cute ass outlined by the tight black skirt as she moved through the crowd. But when She looked away She was caught by Olivia, watching Her.

"I assume you're going downtown," Olivia said. "I'll give you a ride."

"Thanks."

She tucked away the napkin with the phone number on it that the waitress had stuck in her hand on the way out. Without missing a beat, She pocketed it and kept following Olivia's elegant cape. Outside, a tasteful dark blue Mercedes sat just down the block on 58th Street, and they were enfolded in it too quickly, the street sounds gone. It made Her nervous. The dope in Her pockets, the attractive older woman who was so no-nonsense. What the hell was She doing with her? Was she or wasn't she gay, with that big public profile and all?

"You know I do like your photographs and I'm a little surprised to hear you say you haven't been working."

There was opera on the tape deck, Madama Butterfly being summoned by her uncle, the accusatory *bonze*. "*Cho-Cho san!*" It was chilling, one of Her favorite parts.

"I mean, I've got some new work. You're an opera fan?"

"If you don't like it I can—"

"No leave it. I was raised on it."

"That's surprising." Olivia didn't hide well that she really meant she was impressed. "But I won't be sidetracked from asking you about your work. Well?"

Damn tough woman, this one. And She was jonesing to light one of the joints hidden among her cigarettes—just because She couldn't. It wasn't about need—it was about freedom.

"It's too new to talk about, that's all."

"I assume that means I can't see it?"

Christ. She lit a cigarette. Made sure She tapped out a real one instead of a joint from the loaded soft pack of Camel Lights. This woman just didn't let up. She wouldn't quit. It made Her angry, combative.

"No one sees it yet. But if you really want to come up for a minute you can see some of my other stuff." Throw the challenge back. Fuck feeling intimidated. She wanted to see what this woman was really into.

The place was, of course, a mess. A pair of jeans and a crumpled shirt were on the floor, the dining table was stacked with contact sheets, cups were ringed with old coffee stains. Stacked, red milk crates with those woven plastic sides had been lined up to make an L-shaped bookshelf. The see-through cubes, set on their sides, allowed glimpses of photographs, lenses, magazines, small sculptures, and books inside. This construction made the barrier that defined a bedroom on the other side. Five feet high and porous, it kept the bedroom alive with an in-the-corner-of-your-eye invitation.

Wine-stained glasses, ashtrays filled with cigarette butts and mostly-smoked joints littered the rest of the apartment and especially Her worktable. It stood in the farthest corner announcing and anchoring the territory that was Her "studio space" with its tucked-away darkroom.

This is it. She fantasized the cops breaking in within seconds to slap Her in handcuffs. Nothing, none of it was lost on Olivia's practiced eyes.

"How heavily are you involved with drugs?"

This was it for sure. It really had been a plot. Get an attractive woman to trap the dumb dope fiend, that's all it takes. What the hell could She say? What should She say? Olivia could wait out Her silence and was watching Her. When She glanced over at her, though, She thought She saw maybe a half-smile, maybe a tight-ass little smile?

"Ok, I smoke a little."

"You smoke marijuana a lot, not a little, from the evidence," she said. "I can't see this. Can we sit over there?"

Olivia turned and headed for the couch at the living end of the space, not the studio. Surprisingly the visible ashtrays there were only filled with cigarette butts. How could she have scoped out everything so fast? There was nothing incriminating from the couch point of view except for the general mess.

"You want something to drink?"

"No thank you. I only drink socially when I have to."

"How about some coke? —Ca-cola?"

Olivia laughed and told Her to "relax" because she wasn't accusing Her of anything. Certainly not "that." And She breathed a little but knew if Olivia even guessed She was also a total coke-head instead of some minor little grass smoker, there could be serious trouble.

"This time you had no warning, didn't expect a visitor. Next time you'll be able to prepare for me."

"Yes, ma'am, Ms. D.A. extraordinaire."

She drilled Olivia with a smile, absurdly flirtatious. Use anything to keep the cuffs off, She thought. And besides, She kind of liked her. She liked her toughness. Nance had told Her to find a professional woman, stop fooling around with airheads. This woman was exciting, interesting, smart, and challenged Her. She liked that. She could flirt with her but She also liked Olivia's self-control in the face of it. No pushover, she. She was serious but She could make her laugh and that was kind of fun. It seemed like she didn't get the opportunity to laugh much usually. Who could, prosecuting murderers and rapists? And she was good at doing it, got plenty of good press. An established well-bred, Smith-educated woman who talked to Her about art, opera and books was a change.

She found Herself sharing quotes from Montaigne and talking about the creative process—with partially formed concepts, but trying to talk about it at least. She learned a little from her and taught Her a little as well. They talked. By the time Olivia left, She was high on nothing but the conversation, the ideas. Then She lit a joint.

Live a life this way, without a lover, and I am me. Too many women, a little self-destruction. Work a little and worry about money.

What was so different about Olivia, beyond the obvious? Depth, seriousness, scathing perception. But was that so different from the individual special traits of Her regular women once She got to know them and go into their heads in addition to their beds? Everyone is valuable. Is that true? Or did She want it to be true? Too egalitarian, too wimp-shit. Of course there were differences, to say there weren't was old hippie bullshit or nauseating Christian pretense, all equal. Olivia was different on the other level that frightened Her, the trappings, the dazzle. At Her age She should be as successful as Olivia, should be getting commissions for her work instead of battling Her way through new wave art forms, communicating on obscure levels in weird ways. And always talking about women, shooting women for Her work, wanting women.

What was wrong with Her? Did the proof of Her existence come so starkly, so singularly through attraction, desire, cunts? Wombs and creativity, was that the fucking connection? Not fucking connection literally, only an expletive. Or was it? Her life was a fucking expletive. Energy sucked out by diversion. More, it was energy given away, given up out of fear. Fear of success; success is responsibility. That was it about Olivia, the courage to seek and make and accept success. That was why she was different, not from other women, but from Her.

Courage was the attraction, toughness, just as surely as Her attraction to the biker girls was their courage and competence on those dangerous engines with wheels. And a calm covered Her like that old time bullshit calm of religion that makes stupid people happy because it gives them answers. The answer for her was courage and striving, but it was really one thing. The calm that flowed over Her was an answer, an answer for Herself, something about Herself. Olivia was different, different from Her. It was that difference She wanted and that was an answer.

"Go for it," Nance told Her. "She sounds like the best thing to happen to you in a long time."

"I don't know if I'm ready. I want to have a summer of fun on my own bike first."

"Shit, if you have any more fun I'm going to puke!"

And there was something true in that, the excess of fun. It wasn't that She wasn't have fun running around and learning, because She was learning. But learning what, exactly? What did it all mean? It meant She was putting Her real work on hold, although She was still shooting, still developing rolls of film, still searching for images. Kind of. Living is art, too, or should be. It meant She was exploring new adventures, meeting new people, finding and fucking new women. It meant She was finding a life alone without Margret. And it meant She was finally, hopefully, forgetting Margret, no longer living through her, or in spite of her. But that wasn't true: She was still living in spite of her. All the running around was that, and it was also a running to Herself, trying to sift and shuffle Herself out of what attracted Her, what She ran toward. And then there was what She hated. And there was who gave to Her, and who didn't.

Goodness, that feeling in your soul, in your stomach that is sweet and calm. The people whose nearness you seek, and when they are close fortify you, ease you. If She only would listen to Her heart, no, to Her self, it would always tell Her, in knots in Her stomach or in shaky nerves, or the calm of a long exhale.

Olivia seemed to offer calm. But so did Jean the tease in another way. They were the alpha and omega in Her life, the women in between did not matter so much not at the moment, and She lived Her life in moments trying not to make connections to days, weeks, a lifetime. Was that it? But the connection, the symbolism was there. Jean would come and stay with Her like a puppy loping in the door, already in the middle of a story she wanted Her to hear. No hello-kiss until she had dropped her bag, saw Her smiling at her, then she would give Her a quick one, and continue her story. The girl made herself at home, took baths, cooked meals for them, and accepted Her doting welcome. No pressure, although She had wanted her once, maybe still did on some level. She valued Jean's presence more.

The easiness, a little dykeling's endearing silliness that made Her laugh—that was part of her, too. The girl demanded nothing but that welcome, and She was comfortable giving it. They were affectionate company and She couldn't bear to lose the girl. Little chance of that, given her continual visits and long stays as if the apartment were Jean's second home.

If that was either alpha or omega then Olivia was the other, the opposite. She would make demands, would never understand puppyness or love a puppy-girl, whatever it was with Jean. Maybe that wouldn't be so bad, not understanding a need that might dissipate with her kind of courage. Was She age-ist, needing the youth and afraid of the older one? That's what the politico-correctos would charge Her with, among so many other transgressions. That was what She was, though, it was true. It was what She knew in Herself, that need for eternal youth. She feared maturity. Maturity meant death.

- Sometime, Just Forget Time.
There Are Worse Things -
RELATING

Adaptation from deep country to Tompkins Square Park where pigeons flutter dirt around broken bottle shards. Adapt but remember. Forced to endure open sky, massive trees, a scream of overgrowth, torrents of green. Forced to endure the sun and pure gentle rain, the silence and the birds. There are birds here, too, with the pigeons. One now with a worm in its beak hopping near the poor, dirty tree nailed with the rat poison sign and the rat under it skulking into its hole in daylight. The bird eyes me through the slats of a bench. The germs from the pigeon shit are eating through my jeans as I sit. I'll get a disease from all the human spit too, but not like the boys, not like what they've got, goddamnit. My Sam is gone with so many others, every day.

The clop of the cop's horse on Avenue B. I found a bottle of crack before I sat down. It's a find, or poison. A plant by the drug police who are sitting on the upper floor of one of the buildings that strangle the park. They watch everything—me picking up the clear vile with the blue plastic cap with the chunks of white stuff inside—watch with big binoculars or telescopes. They watch and see everything, write it down.

I sit and smoke, accosted by pigeons. Constant city sounds, not noise. It's only different from the country, not worse. The junkies on the nod wobble from their bench. The cop's horse is clomping too close, in the park now. They quaver off in slow motion. Junkie slo-mo.

The pull of another person. Always so strong. It makes me feel so obligated. It's only change. Be aware of changes. Different, that's all. Experience. Is anyone right?

They flew to her house in Maine. Rangely, Maine and Moose Lake

Meguntic in a rugged outback almost too primal for Olivia's fineness. They had been out together for dinner, walking in the park, having drinks—just three times together—and then to Maine. Immediate closeness, intellectual connection beyond flirting.

"I don't believe it," Nance passed the joint. "You two haven't even been to bed together and it's like you're negotiating some kind of prenup agreement. I mean, shit, what do you give in exchange for the country palace and the city penthouse?"

"That's the fucking problem, what to give," She said.

Olivia paid for everything, never asked for anything, only Her company. She made her laugh, and Olivia made Her think, reevaluate Her life. Their closeness was being built on realities that somehow needed to be there before the romance. They held hands walking in the woods, leaned against each other preparing dinner.

"What did you learn from being with your last lover?" Olivia wanted to know, seriously, while they made dinner together in her place. And She told her, maybe getting it clear for Herself for the first time. She had to tell it to someone who didn't know, someone for whom that historical reality was important—but not really because she wasn't there. She could have told her anything. So She told her about how things, possessions, Her time, Her privacy, were not so precious anymore since She wasn't with Margret. Without mentioning Jean, She explained how friends could be in Her space now, lie around on her bed, borrow things, use Her towels, makeup, books, without Her feeling possessive of them, too protective like She was before. She had always been a nervous lender, of possessions not money, but now She didn't worry at all. Before no one could have dared to lie on Her good, white wool Scotland blanket with street jeans, now She did it with them.

Eating, watching TV, or anything. It was as if losing the precious goddess image that was Margret for Her, a photograph come to life— what a stupid wuss, or mental defective, or whiner, trying to cling to the brilliance She lost with Sam's loss—anyway, it made Her give up. She gave up the fight to keep control, pristine control of everything else. She was looser, easier. Nothing left to protect. And that was good because of the freedom it brought Her.

"And do you feel this freedom in everything? Lovers too?"

She looked away from Olivia's question, her prosecutor's look. Her first instinct wasn't to be honest but to hide, although that seemed to have changed as well.

"I see a lot of women."

Olivia got up from the Adirondack chair near the sundeck railing from where you could see miles of pines and the mountains. She came to Her and kissed Her lightly on the lips. The pressure of her hands, though, hard on Her shoulders was more powerful than the kiss.

"That will have to change with me."

"I know."

She said it too fast, but only She made a note of it. They embraced, caressing lightly with that intense green and humbling north woods for a backdrop. Then Olivia led Her past the sundeck's glass doors, through the two-story vaulted ceiling living room with the stone walls, and up to a windowed bedroom. What happened there was upsetting. But She tried to convince Herself that it didn't matter, that it shouldn't matter. But it was worse than bad sex—it was dishonest sex.

There was the relationship to be worked on, real relating. Olivia was the symbol of what She wanted, of what She should strive for in Her life to be a success instead of running away from it. Should do, should be.

Nance kept telling Her that Olivia was "the best thing to happen" to Her. And She would say *yeah*, but She really wasn't so sure. Olivia started calling Her whenever she wanted to, insensitive to Her need for time, Her own time. She started to feel like She was on call, there was an undercurrent, an assumption that Her life wasn't as important because Her schedule was loose. Her own. After a month Olivia began asking questions that were too meticulous, too probing. She wanted to know where She had been, with whom, and why She had been out at all. She wanted to be able to reach Her at any time so She needed to be near a phone.

Like a leash tightening at Her neck, even if only a string of control, it tugged at Her. Olivia didn't get to where she was by being compromising or doing things halfway. She was accustomed to success, to owning things—and She started to feel like one of those things, owned. She was a thing to be there for her like her car or country house. But still, she was good and intelligent and could be fun. But the power differential made a difference. She tried to talk to Olivia about it but she didn't see it, would not admit it. She was "willing to discuss it" with Her but ended up deciding it wasn't true. *Wham.* The gavel pounded, decision made.

"Besides, you have all the power in bed." Olivia patted Her hand.

She was too much the coward to argue, to tell her that it proved Her point. She performed for Olivia. It was not supremacy in bed. She performed. There was no other way to say it—She performed. She had to, and it was so weird.

They stayed together on weekends and during the week Olivia would sometimes send the city's limousines to pick Her up and take Her to the penthouse for the night. Those trappings, that bit of luxury was only that, and barely even that. The sense of playfulness that would have made something like that so much fun was missing. It wasn't that She would have minded being kept. Maybe She'd be able to pay back Margret, or make some credit card payments. But She did mind. Was it that Olivia kept Her in bad style, a kind of blunted style, instead of flamboyance? When they were together they cooked dinner. More precisely She watched while Olivia cooked and they talked about events politics, philosophy, but never really with lightness. She felt restrained, tired of hearing about the law and the minutiae of Olivia's day.

She started to miss Her life. The drugs, being available to the string of girls coming in and out of her place. She liked being high but couldn't be around Olivia that way. She liked flirting and ended up realizing that this step had been bypassed in their relating and She was suddenly in a relationship again. Worse, She was suddenly married after barely a month. She started to feel the anger and hide it, and that made Her angrier.

"I don't think I'll go to the country this time."

"Why? Do have something to do, photographs you didn't finish during the week? All right then, we won't go. We can have a weekend in the city."

And She found it hard to breathe all of a sudden. She couldn't look at her, and She started to pace. Rage drove Her faster as She listened to Olivia lay out plans, specific things they would do together, always together *goddamnit.*

"No," She told her. "I need to be alone."

"You're alone all week and so am I. I need to be with you."

"No." She said it quietly, and was aware of controlling a primal fury, a need to bite and claw like a trapped animal. *What the hell is the matter with me?*

"But why?"

"I told you, I want to be alone."

Olivia burst out crying. *Oh fuck, a noose! A trap! A trick!* It had gone too far, way too far.

"I've got to be free," She gasped it out, but strong somehow— irreversible. As soon as it was out, She felt stupid. Wasn't that a song lyric, for chrissake? From a thousand and one songs?

"I know," Olivia snuffled. "I've seen you not wanting to be close, but I thought you'd get used to it. I thought you'd like being with me more."

That did it. If she knew, then why had she held on so tight? But it was Her own fault, as fucking usual. She allowed Herself to be controlled and the woman took advantage, took Her, kept Her like a possession. *Fuck this.*

She ran out and headed for her therapist. That was Nance, of course, Her tolerant and open "ear." She had leaned on the door buzzer and run up the four slights to Nance's place. And, right at her door, Nance wanted to know how She got away. Sarcastic, blowing smoke circles with a joint into the hallway, she asked about the D.A.'s handcuffs and if they were monogrammed or not.

"I had to run, man, literally run out the door."

"Did you leave anything there? You must have."

"Nothing important. Jeans, tops."

"She'll probably have them bronzed or keep them under her pillow and sniff them."

"Fucking worse, she'll take them to the police lab, find dope grains or some shit and have me busted. It's all your fault, you're the one who pushed me with all that 'best thing that ever happened to you' crap."

"You didn't have to listen, asshole."

They drank, smoked and finally laughed when they were high enough. But for Her there was still an edge of nervous laughter. She worried about retribution, always retribution. She always feared it when She did something so clearly correct for Herself. It was the curse of what She had done to Margret that day, leading her on then leaving her begging. She almost ducked, expecting a well-deserved lightning bolt.

Coke helped. Nance dragged out a gram and they sucked it up, Nance almost more than Her. The woman liked her blow, could actually snort Her under the table when she wanted to. They did it all and flew off. They discussed the oddities of their lives, laughed like loony, evil kids.

"Back to square one. What are you going to do about Margret?"

"Shit, nothing!" She wailed it comically, and punched Nance on the arm.

"Come on, you can't hide. She wants you back."

"Did she tell you that?" She was monotone, quiet. Like a sudden IV wash of an antidote spread in Her veins—She felt almost straight all of a sudden. And She desperately needed to be high, stay high.

"You didn't hear it from me, but…" Nance paused to blow two perfect smoke rings. "She's pretty miserable, doesn't see why you can't forgive her and have a relationship again, but at a better place. You know her, she says it's all process, women marching on, learning together, blah-blah, shit like that. It's what they do in her circle, you know that."

Margret wanted Her? Her, the failure, the fuck up? Those exquisite fingers, her elegant body could be Her's again?

"Stop, goddamnit!"

It's what they do in her circle. She could not face that evaluation again, Margret's disappointment—real or not, She *knew* it was there. Politically, fucking painfully correct, that would always be Margret. That was the distilled truth and it made Her cry from laughing about it. Nance the rock, the seer; she hadn't been wrong yet about Margret or any of Her relationships—except the Olivia disaster.

"Ok, you know that Margret's fucking politically correct. What does that mean—she's got standards? So what? Maybe you could learn something instead of vamping your juvenile delinquent shit all the time. Just see her and then both of you can leave me alone."

"What? You hate me now? I should see her and get more pain, feel like a piece of shit again?"

"Assholes can take it."

They burst out laughing. Idiots. The coke made everything easier.

But not quite everything. She found that it wasn't over yet with Olivia. Maybe it came because She had slowed down Her life with her, not running as fast. Figure out the relationship, see what happened for a change. She did not have to run so hard, so fast, to get away once the paranoia left Her.

But Her paranoia was adaptive, usually—and eventually proved to be correct, sometimes. Olivia wanted her on a leash, Margret wanted Her to hold a leash and walk her, walk for her or carry her. What did Jean the tease want? Maybe only a buddy, maybe a mentor— but at least the girl was fun, didn't sap Her energy, yet. Comfortable paranoia. Forget them all, go to Carmen again, find a bike to ride. Slice through the air, cut through the bullshit, give it full throttle and run away. Why didn't Olivia buy Her a bike? If that woman had been sensitive at all to Her needs instead of keeping Her like an object, she would have tried to please Her, help Her stay free or at least feeling free. But she didn't approve of motorcycles.

Fuck you.

Fuck them all. Find a bike, run away.

- Running to Save Time, Takes Time.
And Money -
ELLEN

Gleaming black with a red pinstripe, chrome fenders, a 1982 Kawasaki 454 LTD was Hers. A little heavy, a little high, but She would get used to it. She didn't tell anyone about it, not even Nance who had given Her the money a while ago that She had been hanging onto. She bought it, didn't say a word, went and bought a helmet and a lock then cabbed it back uptown and got on the thing.

"Good luck," the guy She bought it from had said.

She rode off slowly, very slowly. She kept to side streets, barely got out of second gear, but She got it home. It took Her some time to obsess over the best and safest place to park it on the street so it wouldn't get knocked over or stolen. She circled the Chrystie Street block just below Houston twice before She was satisfied with a spot. She was drenched with nervous sweat. Arms and back aching from tension and the death-grip She had kept on the handlebars. She undressed and soaked in a hot tub. Her new black helmet shone where She could see it on the bathroom floor. A bike of one's own, Virginia, She had done it.

She sneaked early morning and late night rides every day for a week and at the end of it was ready to fight real city traffic. She would go across Houston to the Cubbyhole in the West Village. She had her shiny black bike, black helmet, white leather jacket, jeans, tasteful black cowboy boots, and a sapphire bracelet. Tough and invulnerable.

"You have a motorcycle?" a small, dark woman came up to her at the bar. "Can I have a ride?"

"Maybe." She grinned like a jerk. "Want a drink first?"

The woman smiled back in a teasing, hungry way. There was no one in the place who She knew, fortunately, so She didn't have to explain the newness of Her riding skills. It would be a problem to take home the woman, Ellen, because She had no experience riding with the weight of passenger. Hell, She was barely experienced in riding at all. But She wasn't thinking of that.

The romance of the bike had begun. The woman's deep brown eyes seduced Her, and her hands were not shy. Just having the bike did this, it was obvious—it was magic. Sitting close in the bar, the Cubby Hole again, and touching Her, the woman worked at drawing Her in. It's something that wouldn't have happened, She was positive, without Her cool leathers, the gleaming helmet prominently next to Her on the bar. Ellen drew Her in with her body but also with her conversation, a serious intelligence despite her sexy come-on routine. She hadn't expected so lofty a catch so quickly with Her bike bait.

"The problem with art history is that it's men's history. And it's also narrow because whatever got chosen to be photographed, archived, was *chosen*. That's the point. It's only what we've been taught to think of as art, but it's not all that was 'art' in the world."

"Exactly. So you're an art history major or something?"

"Just because I'm divorced doesn't mean I'm brain dead from being around men. And, yes, I did study art history."

What the hell kind of statement was that? What a way to let information drop.

"You mean you fuck men, is that what you're telling me?" She said it evenly, no big deal, no judgment. She just wanted to know, in these times. In these times.

"I used to. I guess I need to know if it makes a difference."

"It makes a difference for health reasons for sure. I don't trust married men to be honest about who they're hitting up besides their wives, know what I mean?"

"I know. But since everything, AIDS, I've had safe sex with men if that's all that bothers you."

"All?" She blurted it out with a sarcastic edge.

"I mean, would you not want to even talk to me for other reasons, political reasons?"

"Shit no. I'm the least politically correct dyke you'll meet, probably."

"Good," Ellen said, "so am I. I don't like their narrowness any more than I like the narrowness of art historians."

"Dogma is dogma, right or left. Whether it's churches or feminists, I hate it."

Ellen put her arms around Her neck and kissed Her. And she surprised Her even more than that.

"No politics. All I want to do is have fun. Let's go."

She took her out to Her beautiful bike, and Ellen was properly impressed. While she gushed over it, She was silently worrying about how to handle the extra passenger weight. Being able to ride with a passenger was something Kathryn told Her came far down the line when a rider had experience. She could barely ride Herself, how was she going to take this woman? Ellen climbed on the seat but She suddenly realized She was saved: no helmet.

"Can't ride you without a helmet. The cops'll stop us in a second."

So Ellen got a cab and She putt-putted away on Her sexy bike. It worked out perfectly because Ellen didn't witness Her shaky moves before they met at Her place.

It had been two years since Ellen had been with a woman and now she was as fresh and appreciative as a virgin. She was also shy and insisted on safe sex, which was fine with Her. No tonguing kisses, no going down on each other. Weirder, though, was that Ellen did not take off her underwear. No problem, the sex was intense. And Ellen had a nervous giggle that was sweet and freeing in a way. They spent the night together, all night, without ever really resting. In the early morning Ellen left, unable to sleep because she felt "too good" she said. When she was gone She fell back again onto the crumpled sheets, but not really resting either.

Her head was too active. She played the memories, city memories, of those just finished and those already reminisced. She did it by instinct, adaptation to the pace proven too quickly with the early-hour ring of the phone. It was Olivia on the machine and She felt that She had to pick up. Had to, and She felt another notch tighten on the collar She thought was gone.

"Did I wake you?"

"Yes."

"I thought it was late enough, nine ... I want to see you. I'm on your block with breakfast for us."

Jesus fucking Christ! She didn't want to believe it, but did when She couldn't catch a breath again. How could she do this to Her? *How dare she, how fucking dare she?*

They had talked, before, when She left Olivia. She had called and smoothed things over, on Nance's urging. So she knew, Olivia already knew. She knew that She wanted and needed space. Olivia had agreed. It was done, over. This was too much, She didn't want to be married, *goddamnit.*

"It's getting cold. You'll buzz me in?"

"I'm not awake ..."

"I don't mind."

What the fuck if I *do?* I *fucking mind!* She should scream it at her. But what the fuck if She did mind, because it obviously didn't matter. So She didn't say anything and caved in. Why did She feel She owed her something? Not just something, kindness.

It was horrible to see her, to choke down bad eggs and ham from a bad restaurant, not even a good *bodega,* when Olivia could have had eggs benedict or eggs Sardou delivered from someplace really cool. There it was, the sign of being kept, but only like a low maintenance bauble.

"This can't go on," She told Olivia again. "It's too close. I can't do it, honest."

And again tears from the tough District Attorney, and a desperation She could not solve—didn't want to. Now there was a morning that was going be wasted on it. It would sap Her energy, to have to seal over Her rage like this, to keep it from erupting out in ugly ways at Olivia. Manipulated by tears, but only outwardly, Her mind was set, the outward trappings and expression didn't matter. This woman would never be anywhere near Her heart again. And when she finally left, all She could do was go back to Her hastily smoothed bed. She wanted to capture the fragrance of Ellen and Her that might still be there.

How my life dribbles by. I complain too much. Is this the only experience I capture in its quintessence? What about the cool breeze that comes in from the fire escape? And the nearness of a stray furry cat who stays close to protect herself in a primeval way. Stay with the larger animal. But, poor cat, the human animal is treacherous and will turn on you. It was a cruel accident that we developed speech and so much power. We should all put gun barrels in our mouths. One, two, pull, bye. Left to the other animals, the planet would be a better place. One, two, all together now. An awesome global bang.

No one will commentate. No live pictures of the dead. The revolution will not be televised nor talked about, except maybe by the chimps we've polluted with sign language. The animals after us will survive. No overlay, no torture, from us. Only survival.

Hauser said that survival, the Marxist approach, the assurance of survival is at the base of all experience, all art. The totality of life and art. The overriding totality of survival.

I look at Chinese landscape paintings. Rice paddies look like drawings I did compulsively as a child.

She took the bike for a ride although She was too tired, too angry about Olivia. And She fell going around a corner. Distracted, not looking where She was going, She dumped, slid, felt the burn on Her thigh through Her jeans. It wasn't bad, but lifting the bike was a bitch. Gas seeped out of the tank; She didn't dare light the cigarette She needed. She rode back home slowly and got some towels to wipe down the poor bike. Not today, She almost said it out loud. She knew She couldn't ride anymore with a body aching from fucking and then sliding on asphalt. Get stoned, take a soak, worry about money, think about Ellen, forget Olivia, long for Jean—and surprise, She decided to return a call to RoTina. She had left Her a message saying that she was "free now." But RoTina would have to be later. Not wanting to be alone She called Jean, and she came in an instant, happy to be back in her second home after staying away because of the stifling affair with Olivia.

She spent the afternoon with Jean, just being with her. Laughing with her, maybe loving her a little, She got out of Her funk. Then finally, She called RoTina back, and they met at Cafe Mogador on Saint Marks Place. Down a few steps, gloomy and intimate inside. Perfect for their first real date, legs pressing under the restaurant table, grabbing hands, not really eating the colorfully spiced food, then heading for Her place.

Passion, sudden passion from RoTina, and from Her in spite of Her aches. She found Herself moving with her slowly, feeling something inside of Her and making love instead of just fucking for the first time in a long time. Passion translated into that intense slowness, the deep coming. Surprise. She looked at her finally as She hadn't before. Dyed blonde short wiry hair, deep brown eyes and skin. Her body was nearly perfect, compact, smooth, unblemished except for some freckles, her breasts small and taut.

They made amazing love together, rough love and gentle love, for hours. It was eight hours until they were finally exhausted. She was more exhausted than RoTina. The riding, Her dump on the bike, two ultra-long fucks in two days got to Her and She had to send RoTina home gently but absolutely. The next day Her leg and hip throbbed with pain, growing bruises from the bike mistake. But both sides were sore—all of Her was sore—from heavy lovemaking. She had to admit She felt terrible.

Nance had no sympathy. "You don't know when to fucking quit fucking. Take a break or your girls will kill you."

She didn't tell her about the bike. Her life was too public already. Nance told Her that Margret had been asking her about Jean, had heard about Her and the girl through the downtown gossip grid. Even Her neighbors knew whenever Kathryn with the Harley spent the night with Her because the bike was so damn noisy when she left in the mornings. And almost everyone knew about the long-standing sporadic affair She had with Saint Carmen because they shared overlapping friendship groups who dished to Carmen's lover about her running around on her. The biker girls had seen Her too often with Elisia. Even though the affair was definitely over with her, everyone still talked. And it turned out that Ellen knew the politicos who were Margret's friends and told them that she was getting a divorce and, more importantly, she proudly told them all that she was seeing a woman: Her.

Word spread. Even RoTina told Her she had heard about most of Her involvements from the bars. She laughed and said she "wouldn't mind" getting involved herself. Too much, too open. She had to hide. It was going to be Her and Her bike, alone, from now on. And so She did it. Alone. She went and got the bike, wired on the license plate Kathryn had given Her (taken from who knew where) and rode across Houston Street, heading west.

The river spread out between Her and Jersey. High white clouds hung exposed to Her like never before. No car gave the openness, no bicycle the speed. She was trying out the highway on Her own. Scared, staying in the right lane, tense but able to enjoy when She let Herself look and be awed by it all. The pavement rolled just inches below Her feet, blurred past.

Don't look down at that, look where you're riding, stupid. The highway is no place to dump.

She tensed, breathed, focused. She watched the monoliths of machinery ahead, eyed them coming up behind Her in both mirrors. Trucks, She hated them. Slow down, downshift, clutch in and throttle off, kick down, clutch in and throttle on, slow down. And again the hunks of metal slowed, again She had to kick down, repeated the process and moved Her lips to speak it like learning a new language— or praying. Another time, maybe twice more.

Shit, what gear was She in now? Did it matter? Yes. Wait, She could tell by the feel, the sound of the engine ... There She heard it, got it. Now into fourth gear. Then the trucks ahead receded from the vulnerable bike. Speed UP, kick UP through the gears, glance at the RPMs— must be ok because there was no over-revving.

She did it, rode out of the city, turned around and came back in over the George Washington Bridge. The city welcomed Her home by totally overwhelming Her with traffic. She swayed through the spiral off the bridge and was funneled onto the West Side Highway, heading downtown. Her field of vision went no farther than the tons of metal that whizzed a few feet all around Her unprotected body. She sweated in Her jacket, white knuckled the handle grips. She was doing it, though, riding on Her own. Success. But where the hell was She? She looked around and saw that She had overshot Christopher Street and now the financial district was coming up. Signs slid by. Slow down—try to think. Stay to the right, go into the parking lot for the Statue of Liberty. Shit yes, turn off the engine, turn the key. Shut the gas valve. Stop. Just stop and try to stop vibrating. Rest and think, ease the ache in tense arms.

Fucking A. Her hands trembled as She lit a cigarette. The insides of Her thighs ached from hugging the tank, or was that from fucking? Anyway, She was hurting and exhausted and She wanted to leave the lovely bike and take a cab home. It was work now and only some fun. It was that work for survival that drained Her. She had worked to survive on that bike, doing what needed to be done to stay alive. It did and would take everything She had until She mastered it.

Survival? Survival for what? Her work, the new stark images of women had been put aside. She hadn't been working, only fucking, running, testing out relationships. Relating. The life of an artist, or a bum—whatever it was it meant that She had to live. It was material to use, experiential fodder to be translated into the work. Not translated, it wasn't that simple. No direct correspondence, and more than creating—a word everyone used—it was atoms that changed you, physical change of doing, action that you took inside.

Did She fool Herself with thinking She needed it, and disguised laziness with artistic need? Run away on a motorcycle. Run away from living. Run to death. And She threw away the cigarette and started the bike. Aching muscles, tense, She wheeled it out, missed a car by inches and throttled up and shifted hard, lurched the bike.

Goddamn, help me. She needed to get home, park the beautiful machine, rest ...

The red tint from the woman's ass dripped down her legs. She watched it, knew She had mixed it wrong, but watched it anyway. Leave it. She made multiples of the print, did not rest. She had not rested a throbbing body before She started work in the darkroom. Seven images, change the size slightly on each, change the exposure slightly. Make it look like she might be moving, just a little, when the prints are seen left to right, or right to left.

The woman She had shot so long ago for these photographs had presence. Her eyes bored out into the camera's lens at the viewer. A tight but not thin body, one foot reached for the first step of an old-fashion oak library ladder leaning against scarred brick—her foot did not quite touch. The lift of it allowed one to glimpse between her legs, from behind. And her upper body turned as far as it could, one breast in full view, the other's roundness and nipple, just behind. Her face fully seen, those eyes firm, a look of fierce expectation, waiting, both hands on one side of the old beautifully-crafted oak ladder, waiting, challenging, one foot poised above the first step.

Crisp, grainy, crisp again in each photograph, with each. That woman, Martha, had been a good model, penetrating eyes She could command, and smooth brown bobbed hair like in the 1920s. The red wash on the first print slid down her legs, and her look told you she didn't mind. In the next, She focused on her lips, brushed them delicately with blue, the red on her ass concentrated now, red with an under-blush of blue-purple, like a blue blood. She worked, She worked on it without breathing without blinking, hunched over. The fine brush in Her hand moved slowly, rapidly, testing, finding.

The phone rang quietly—volume turned down—but repeatedly in the five or so hours She worked. She heard the click of the machine answering but there was no volume at all, no distraction.

Not finished with two prints, thinking about starting the third, She realized her arm was going numb. Take a break. Still with Her cowboy-used-for-motorcycle-boots on, the helmet and leather jacket on the floor by the door, She dragged Herself to undress, take a shower. But when She saw Her naked reflection in the bathroom mirror She stopped. The aches and pain She had been feeling and ignoring glared at Her. Ugly bruises covered the outside of Her left leg where She had fallen. Her left forearm was black and blue from elbow to wrist, a place hard to bruise. The insides of both thighs were marked ugly from straddle walking the bike into parking spaces. Then there were the bruises on Her knees and on the inside of Her right leg and ankle from fucking RoTina on the couch, that leg braced for pressure against the metal frame of its fold out bed.

She looked like She had been beaten. Seeing it made Her suddenly admit the pain She had avoided feeling by working now, finally working. Six aspirin, a cleansing shower that actually hurt on Her skin, then a soaking bath. Forget the calls on the machine.

She smoked a joint in bed and watched cartoons, a habit She picked up from Jean. Jean was the only person She could have tolerated seeing Her like this.

- 1986 -
AND MARGRET?

The letter from Margret made Her cry. Not hard, but a soft and sad crying. If She had read those words, had heard them, ten months ago it would have changed her life. Now She did not want Her life changed. She didn't want it changed by anyone except Herself.

"Too late," Nance said. "Not too little, but too late. Too bad, because she's feeling like shit, like it's all just hitting her now."

"I know that. What the fuck can I do about it?" She spit out the words, but edged them with anguish.

"You can see her."

"It wasn't a goddamn question, Nance. You don't have to fucking answer everything."

"Touchy, aren't we?"

She was sick of Nance being right all the time or trying to be. Margret's letter was upsetting enough. She flung it across the sticky table where they were sitting in the WaWa Hut on Avenue A, drinking in the afternoon. Nance didn't pick it up, didn't want to touch it, but read fast and in snatches.

"You're all I want … You gave so much to help me grow … and I …"

Those were words She needed to hear, but long before now. She grabbed back the letter and shoved it in the envelope. She crammed it into Her jacket pocket.

"You going?"

"Not to see her. What the fuck would happen to my head? I've got to work."

She refused the last of the scotch and went home. She went to work in the studio. When Jean called later, She was doing enough with Her prints to feel all right about it—exposing perfectly, burning and dodging just the way and where She wanted, brushing the colors on the final prints. They felt right.

Jean called, and She let her come over so she could watch TV or do whatever she wanted. But She went back to work on Her art—She hoped it was art. And She could work with the girl there. It was a first. Company. Comforting, no demands. She worked. Jean puttered back and forth to the refrigerator, laughed out loud at the TV, turned it off, read, listened to music, and still She worked. The photographs came to life, finally. The series of stills began to breathe and move.

And when Jean finally decided to go home to her own place up on 14th Street, She called RoTina. They made love again, did not fuck. Her bruises kept Her from too much activity anyway. And when RoTina saw them, she ran out and bought Tiger Balm to warm Her aching muscles and even for the bruises. They were too far advanced for any ice treatment to do any good, but RoTina gently cared for them as best she could. Just the feel of her comforting hands helped.

Phone calls from Olivia recorded regularly on the machine and She ignored them, kept RoTina in Her arms through the night. Something was different with her and She wanted it, wanted the feeling, but was afraid of the situation. Too close, too close. She knew, was reminded by this, that She had to see Margret. She had to face it, sooner or later. Nance was right, again. Even as She took—and more surprisingly—even as She gave to RoTina She knew She had to see Margret.

And if I want to be alone, who will let me? That is a cry, a silly whimper, while they are fixing the cords. There are knots with glass sticking out, when they tighten them, they cut. Drops of blood. Tie me down, and when you are finished will you leave me alone? Only a few moments, solitude, before darkness. I will hum my own songs, no one to keep time.

I long for Plato's cave. Shadows of my own reality, made by me. To be tied like that, unloved, before darkness.

RoTina loved Her too well, like Olivia needed Her too much. She didn't trust anymore, not like before. RoTina would say she missed Her when she didn't see Her for a few days, and She missed her too. But even so newly into the affair She began to do strange things She hadn't done before with so much deliberateness.

She let a few days go by. Then She called and actually made a date that She actually wrote down to remember to show up.

"We'll meet at the movie, ok?"

"Right."

She made the plan, but She had time. She took Her helmet and went to practice with the bike first. She had time.

But not enough time. She never showed up. RoTina was hurt, then alarmed until she finally found out that She was all right—She was all right but lost to everything else when She got on that bike. And She made it up to RoTina the next day, though, fucked her brains out with a body still ravaged with those bruises. Fucked her in pain, to pain.

But they stopped doing it. All of a sudden it seemed, She was not available, said She had to work. Even before the end of days of isolation, though, RoTina knew there was a problem, and surmised that she was the problem. Each person's own insecurity can always be counted on to give you guilt, make you take responsibility for problems that aren't yours. And She tried to tell her, but RoTina was beyond listening to much of anything.

"It's not you, it's me," She said.

"Never mind. Work it out, I'll give you space. Call me next week, or something." RoTina was caustically cheery and left Her alone in Her apartment.

Immediately, without waiting a beat, She left and went to ride the bike to exhaustion. Most of the night, from East Village to West, roaring up, drinking, roaring away. But, surprising the next day She called RoTina. She was coked up for energy and using it to mask a morose mood.

"Hey, Ro', want to fuck?"

Surprised, yes, RoTina was. But she answered Her, she did want to and she would. And they met and She gave it to her and refused to take anything for Herself. And then She left again.

The challenge of the bike took Her heart. Mesmerized by the challenge, the austerity of the machine that would not yield and demanded concentration, demanded fidelity, that was love, a love hard to attain. She rode in anger, hating the submission this learning took but She loved it, the mastery that came so slowly and the symbiosis with the machine. She could glimpse that reward, worked for the day when finally She would be one with it. She needed that solitude, ran toward it, but was too weak to cut away people who loved Her. Free of love, or free from love.

Mother fucker, come on, lose the fear. Wind it out to fifty, sixty.

She did, hit the mark on the speedometer over sixty-five and screamed into Her helmet the ecstasy of speed, of control on the edge of destruction. She held it until She was bursting with the feeling, then slowed. Down, down to fifty-five, forty, downshift again, laughing. And She made a mistake—popped the clutch, lurched the bike, hit a pothole … and dumped, hard.

Goddamnit! Down again.

Pavement skidded across the helmet. Could have been Her head. Instant pain in Her knee. Rolling, rolling toward the bike screeching on its side. Finally stopped, stopped, dazed and stunned. She got up, slowly, yanked off the scraped helmet, righted the bike, shed tears for its new scratches, the dent in the tank. *Goddamnit!* Walked around—or tried to, Her leg shot with pain. She ignored it, shook out Her body, tried to check for broken bones. Cursed Her stupidity. She couldn't pick up the bike, the pain wouldn't allow it. A guy in a truck saw Her struggling, stopped, helped Her. A sweetheart, an ex-biker, of course. He held the bike steady, which embarrassed Her, and She got on and settled Herself as best She could, took a breath, focused, patted the tank as if the bike were a horse, and rode home slow and carefully, wincing with every gear shift, every brake press or pull.

Ice on the knee that swelled like a frantic cry. Elevate it, rest it, avoid the messages piling up on the machine tape. By evening She could barely walk, hardly move. RoTina called twice, Nance four times with variations on *where the hell are you, bitch?*

"Being an asshole," She said to the empty apartment.

There were more calls. Jean wanted to come over. And Margret called once, for dinner. *No* to them all, without bothering to voice it. *No* to everything, except for the pain in Her leg.

The next day She wanted to work. Impossible. The pain was worse.

The day after that, She propped up Her leg on a chair and insisted on balancing Herself on the tall stool She used so She could see Her prints better, do some work. She tried to get comfortable, almost fell on the floor.

Fuck me! I've got to work! Work, fucking Goddamn me!

Glass shattered into a million pieces against the wall. Three days of pain and no work made Her throw the glass. She had taken Her last handful of ibuprofens. Glad not to have a cat, any animal to worry about hurting itself on the shards. So many, big chunks and tiny evil splinters, they covered the wood floor like sand on a glimmering beach. It made Her think of the snails in Provincetown that She and Margret had seen exposed at low tide. Margret? Always Margret. A black spiral of depression moved down on Her, wrapped Her. For two days She had locked Herself in, ignored the phone, smoked dope and found remnants of smack to snort to ease the pain in Her knee and leg. Ease the pain in Her mind. Now, She hobbled to the phone and called.

"Yes," Margret said She would come to talk.

And as long as She was up She filled another ice pack. Three days since the dump and hiding away to alternate ice and heat packs hadn't worked. Maybe finishing with Margret would be the magic, the dues-paying that would release Her from the pain.

She yelled "come in" when Margret knocked. It hurt too much to try to stand at the door waiting for her to climb the stairs after limping there to buzz her in. And when Margret saw Her, so banged up, she went to Her, touched Her face gently, fawned over Her. She did everything, brought Her cookies and Coca Cola and anything She wanted from Her barren kitchen. And then, they finally talked.

"I was under pressure too," Margret said. "You were so distant I needed something else."

"Yeah, but you didn't stop. You kept sleeping with— Never mind," She said gently. "We fucked up together, didn't we?"

"Always together," Margret whispered.

They were quiet, careful with each other. No will to fight, no anger left. And She felt sorry for Margret now because She had gone on, or was trying to, but Margret was just realizing how completely She was lost to her. She looked miserable, tired, her pale fingers fidgeted with a rubber band, then doodled with a pen on the back of an envelope. She wished She could hold her. She wished time had never happened to them, that it was sometime last year, before everything. Sometime a world ago before everything, and that Sam and so many, so many, were still alive.

She took Margret's hand, given eagerly. It felt luminous, wondrous. But time had happened to them. It was awkward, and it was somehow like before. Those years they had together vibrated between them. They were stacked tall and precariously there in the air between them, and they could not be ignored. Not Her heart, not Margret's, could ignore all that was there that they couldn't see, but felt. She began to feel a part of it now, was beginning to sense the awkwardness, the not feeling good enough, terrified of failure in Margret's eyes.

"We can do anything we want," Margret said. "Together."

"Theoretically," She said with a hardness that surprised Her, and grew. "But you've already got something in mind, right?"

"Just that we can decide together, on anything we want."

Evasion, how She was tired of that—it erupted inside Her. Margret's dodging now made Her remember all the times She had needed direct emotion from her. If she had only come back before, appeared at the door with a suitcase, a bottle of champagne, or a joint, anything to make up with. But no, Margret's romanticism had not been that clear for years, if it ever had been. She had been more than romantic, enough for the both of them, and still was. The romantic, the fool. It still made Her feel terrible, thumped a heaviness in Her chest, made Her take a deep breath … Her throat closed. It wasn't like She would burst out crying but She felt a sadness that was profound, ineffable, and She felt the meaning of it. All this again. All this still. She wasn't free.

Light griefs can be expressed but deep sorrow has no words.

It was what Montaigne wrote, or close to that. She had learned this, too, from whatever quotes She could remember that Sam had said. But She couldn't speak, only felt deadness on Her skin, in Her heart.

"There are good things that came out of this, change is always good."

She said "yes" to agree with the abstract, not believing it for Herself or for them. With Margret, talk was always in the abstract and it spurred Her to call her on it now to break the long silence.

"What are you saying, you want to get back together? What does that fucking mean?" She said it quietly, a tone of dark calmness.

"It's not in those terms," Margret took a teaching tone. "It's more what we can do, discover together. We have to get to another level, think about it differently."

Hearing that tone, that distance, for the first time in a long time, the old anger came back to Her. The hesitation, the dodging, the detachment. She had never thought of Herself as conservative, but maybe She was now when faced with Margret's verbiage. Why should there be this examination, such scrutiny? You're in love or you're not. You feel passion or you don't. It shows, it just comes out. It doesn't have to be discussed to death, viewed under a magnifier.

She struggled to arrange Herself on the couch, picked up Her leg at the knee with Her hands to move it to a more comfortable position. Margret shot up from the couch, fussed without touching Her, made motions to help. But She moved Herself, motioned for Margret to sit down again. But, "no no," she didn't want to trouble Her and that made Her angry. Like so many things Margret insisted were for Her own good, but weren't, now She had to look up uncomfortably to talk to Margret where she stood.

"You know," She said, "there's a point where intellectual feminist bullshit has got to stop and you just have to go with feelings. I honestly don't understand what you mean now. Because you know, absolutely, that I don't want to, and have never wanted to, examine my every action with you. I just wanted to do, to be, to live without analyzing every fucking move. Period. Just live."

That was what She wished for, that kind of freedom. She was still lying, denying that She obsessively rehashed Her faults. But the calmness in Her voice, and a kind of control, made Margret shift position and move back a step. When she met Her eyes, it was a little anxiously.

"No, it's different." Margret was being logical, lecturing. "We did, and we still can do, what we want—anything we want—together. But if we just try."

"And here we are talking about it, aren't we? It's what always happens. How many times over this year I just wanted you to come back, fall into bed with me. That would have said it all. We might have talked, later. But it's always been your way, the talking comes first and it kills me. Do you get it? It kills me. It sure as hell kills any feeling. There's something Artaud said about if your life lacks fire it's because—"

"Stop it! Everything can't be a fairytale, or a movie like you want. Living is hard! We have to be so careful, so careful to live."

"No!"

She exploded. She was pushing against the couch to get up, stand up and face Margret. There was no going back now, that was obvious. "No" to everything. "No" to lying on the couch, and She kept trying to rise. "No" to the carefulness that was so saccharine, and that She felt churn Her stomach. It was why She wanted to conquer riding a motorcycle, do drugs, pick up women—thrill seeking, risk taking through fire and brimstone to fucking live. There was something about brimstone in Her life, something Sam had told Her that was by Antonin Artaud, but for Herself She knew it already. It was something about being alive, by proving that death exists. How much sweeter the end will be having really lived, really sought. Living on the edge of death means living to the extreme, hanging your feet over the edge of darkness means you've got life at your back, have pushed through to the last degree. The trick, the supreme trick is getting back, coming back from the brimstone and living with the knowledge of that success. Is that Faustian?

But Margret was talking again. *Stop! Stop,* She wanted to scream even though She hadn't been listening. It didn't matter. She didn't care anymore. She only cared about getting off this too-soft, too yielding couch She was flailing against.

"... all our years together, we can't just throw them away."

"Oh crap. I used to think that, but you did it. You threw them away, already."

"No I didn't! It was just something I had to do because of *your* craziness. I had to accept what you needed and what you had to do for yourself!"

"What? I never left you."

"And I didn't leave you!"

She lurched off the couch, wavered, Her arms reaching to break the fall that was coming. Margret rushed to Her and held Her, steadied Her and gently helped Her sit, upright, Her leg on a chair she dragged to the couch.

"See? Talk is cheaper than action. But you still keep saying that, that you didn't leave," She said quietly. "You were living with someone else. Someone else, babe, and you started a serious relationship. That's what you did and I know what it made me feel, and I'm not being talked out of my feelings anymore. I don't have to explain them, my feelings are as valid as yours, and I deserve the same respect I've had to give to your boring analytical minutiae."

Silence. She was so calm, with such unemotional reflection evident in what She said and in Her tone there was no response to be made. She had stated facts not open to debate, that's what it was. Margret was not at all used to this kind of grounded-ness from Her, this calmness.

"You should see a doctor."

They sat in silence, sad. Margret was uncomfortable, but not Her. Did Margret sense that this lack of displayed emotion was worse than shouting rage? She knew it, though, for Herself. She could tell because She didn't hurt, didn't feel like trash, didn't feel like She had to throw up at the images of Margret and Bitsy together, and didn't want to know if they still slept together—didn't care. Progress, growth is what the correctos would call it. But Margret wouldn't let it be. She had to try her line again.

"We can find another way to be together, to learn the good from this. There is good if you just allow yourself to think about it, just open up to being together in a new way instead of being so judgmental—"

"Why are your labels the only valid ones, the correct ones? The painfully correct ones, all on your terms ..."

She didn't have the energy to go on. She didn't have the desire to argue because it didn't matter anymore. She had made it not matter so that She could look at Margret's exquisite face, her eyes, watch the hands She had loved so much, those sensitive hands of an image She had wanted—She didn't long for it anymore. There was only sadness, and resolve.

Margret got ready to leave. She muttered something about they could "talk again" to see "what would happen" between them.

She didn't bother to answer in words but made a sound that seemed indeterminate or even agreeable like *umhmmm* and let it go at that. Then She pushed Herself up and limped with her to the door. Margret didn't mention that She could barely walk, but looked sad and preoccupied as if there were something else she wanted to say. But She was used to this tactic and knew Margret wanted Her ask "what's wrong?"

Then she would want Her to wait in silence for an answer. This time, though, She didn't even attempt to coax one from her. She opened the door. Margret was still silent, looking as though she wanted to say something. It wasn't until She made it obvious that She was going to shut the door, really, that Margret finally spoke.

She turned and said to Her, "Never mind."

"Ok," She would not take the bait. "See you around."

She was supposed to ask, was expected to ask, "Never mind what?" She had been through this control game of Margret's too many times. Now She was different, She had changed, and She was goddamn not going to play that game again.

When Margret was finally gone, when she finally edged past the door and was out in the hall, She took a breath. It was rapid and satisfying, and She felt and heard it. It was as if the action woke Her and She realized She had not been breathing while She watched Margret's uncertain, unreliable exit. She closed the door and leaned against it. But there was more to do, and that determination drove

Her. She reached up, steadying Herself on Her bad leg to reach up higher than Her injuries made comfortable, and turned the tumblers on both of the door's Medeco locks, then below them, She took the chain lock and slid it across into its long slot. And finally, bracing Herself for the effort, She used both hands to turn the center knob on the Fox Police Lock to slide its heavy crossbars, to the left and right, into the metal strike plates set into the doorframe on both sides.

Tears came, but not sobs. Quiet, sliding tears She allowed to fall, did not brush away. Then She limped to the couch and made a decision: it was time to see a doctor. It was time to make time to take care of Herself.

- Tock Tick -
COLD FIRE

And I feel like I have been, am being, saved. Why else do I see these things around me? Why was I allowed to see death? Is it that if you live long enough you see it all? Not like this, not watching the boys die the way they do. I feel I'm being saved, I don't know what to do. Completely helpless. Death in the tower, the penthouse, Sam's death. The boys die and no one helps. Why was it only me? I brought Sam the books, the food, anything he wanted. And he needed a fan for that ninety-degree weather last September. Nowhere to be found because of the heat wave, but I found one. I walked with a display model I made them take from the hardware store window on University Place. I walked with it right along Eighth Street to Fifth Avenue, the fan head moved from side to side as the wind turned the blades. Relentless oscillating action, like my life.

The boys go in and out of lucidity. Sam languished. He ate soup and ice cream, sometimes. Egg salad and chocolate malts from the good coffee shop on Bleecker near LaGuardia Place, when he could get them down. At least he ate, sometimes. But he would forget things. I didn't know what to do. Tell the doctors to let whatever happens, just come. Death takes its ways.

Every night and every day I wondered if he would still be alive. Then I forced myself to think of next year with him at Fire Island. We'll all be there. Sam will look healthy again, the ugly purple Kaposi's spots will be gone. He will be gracious like he always was, at least to me, and handsome again. We will all be healthy. We'll all be healthy and play in the waves on the ocean side in Oakleyville or the Pines.

And the goo-goo kitties he loved so much will no longer languish as they did when he was so sick, draped listlessly over chairs like they had never done before. Poor cats. Poor men. Oh the death in the tower on Fifth Avenue. It followed him home from the beach, the Sunken Forest. The sand soaked with death followed him, like I did.

Crutches. Goddamn, She needed crutches to get around, to rest the torn cartilage, the chipped bone in Her knee. Fluid was drained off twice, painfully.

"I twisted my knee running down the stairs," is what She told everyone.

She hid the bike. She made sure it was in a good spot on the sidewalk, covered and tucked safely close to Her building. She gave the Super of the building ten dollars to keep an eye on it. And from Her front window if She leaned way out She could glimpse part of its grey cover five stories below, safe.

Jean came to help Her out, slept chastely in Her bed and made RoTina jealous. But She needed the girl. How was She going to climb up and down all those steps? And She was more at ease with Jean than anyone. Not in love with her, but loved her. She wasn't afraid of Jean, but She was afraid of RoTina. RoTina with a mature love, a willingness to accept Her, care for Her, who had a passion for Her. She didn't drown Her or stifle Her like Olivia wanted to do. But She didn't want to fall in love. That was what frightened Her, virtue. She was afraid of anything that was too good.

Woodstock retrospective on television. We were dazed—all of us—in that time. Disgusting Eighties now, aching Eighties. It's painful to watch the way we were. Doing things, anything, because they felt good. Feeling good was an important enough reason for anything. So stoned. Watching people talk to the camera on acid. So obvious, so out of it. You couldn't be teary, happy-jumpy like that today. Jumpy but coping.

If you feel like experimenting only take half a tab. Remember? If you're not down from yesterday's hit only take half a tab, save the rest for later. Remember no fear? Open your mouth and stick out your tongue baby.

I can't stand seeing the young Joan Baez from those days. Are we so old now? No, just fucking no, because that's where our heads are, still fucking searching.

Young Joan, toothless Ritchie Havens singing about freedom. How much better then than now. Now yuppie, no voyagers. No trippers, only trips.

She made Jean go home for a night and invited Ellen for a visit. It was hot—Ellen and the sex—even with Her knee that shouldn't have gone through a night of fucking, although they tried to be careful. She wanted Ellen's newness, liked the fact she was getting back into women because of Her. And She liked her brooding intelligence. So She had Nance come over to be her friend, her muse, her selfish sounding board—and to deliver an ounce of grass She desperately needed. She rolled and told Her stories about Her girls while Nance walked around inspecting the funky space, and probably to show off walking while She was still a gimp.

"Shit," Nance danced over and air-slapped at Her. "How do you do it? You should be resting. How do you get them to keep coming around when you're a fucking invalid?"

"Better than a regular invalid."

"Shut up," Nance grabbed the joint. "You should stick with RoTina anyway, she's hot."

But it was too soon to be with any one woman. And it was too scary. It didn't matter what Her friends counseled or yelled at Her. And when later on Kelly came by to bring Her food, she taunted Her.

"Where's the manual you've been reading that tells you how to keep women hanging around."

"Sensitivity, baby, that's all. Listening to heads, listening to bodies instead of just feeling them up."

"You're high," Kelly said. "I bet there's a girl you can't get."

"Again? Remember you lost on that Bardot-blonde woman with the giant girlfriend at that club on Christopher."

"Gawd, that was scary. You never called her, right?"

"Nope."

"Wuss."

"Fuck you. Who you got in your evil little mind now?"

"You don't have the time," Kelly goaded. "And you can't even walk. Stick with RoTina, she's nice."

"And hot."

"'Nice and hot'? I hope you're delirious. You'll never get this woman I know, not with shit like that."

"Come on, who is it?"

They ping-ponged with *faux* arguing, playing until Kelly finally capitulated. They made a deal. She would give Her phone numbers and introductions to two of Her girlfriends She was no longer seeing. In return, Kelly dangled a blonde reward.

"It's Louise, who gives ice in July and great suction. I bet you can't get her into bed."

Louise was definitely a prize, if a bit flawed. Blindingly blonde, beautiful, total bitch.

"She just broke up with her girlfriend, and the deal is twice," Kelly said. "You've got to do it twice because—don't say anything to Nance—even I've had her once."

"Then she was through with you? I guess you don't want anyone knowing that."

"Fuck you."

Kelly stopped straightening up the pile of newspapers and magazines on the floor by the couch. She had a penchant for cleaning that, watching her, She thought She should take advantage of more often—invite Kelly over more.

"What do I win when I win?"

She grandly flicked an ash on the floor. Kelly was so disgusted, and so quick, she almost caught it before it hit.

"If. If you win," Kelly muttered at Her. "And I'm not worried that you will. But having her is enough."

"What? No, no, what do I get besides that? I need dinners and motorcycle gloves and maybe a helmet."

"What the hell for?" Kelly stopped in mid-ashtray cleaning.

"In case I ever get a bike or something." She coughed, pretending it was from a toke and not from blundering into honesty. "We got a deal or what?"

They argued about it for some time more because Kelly loved to argue about anything. They drank, they smoked, they laughed and finally they shook on the bet. There was no time limit because Kelly agreed She had to heal enough to at least be able to walk without crutches, walk downstairs. She had wanted to include some definition of Her being in "top form" but Kelly wouldn't go for it. Fun, Kelly was a welcome nutty diversion. It was something to look forward to, if She ever did it at all—but that didn't matter. It was fun to think about. Something to look forward to, mindless fucking to counteract the lovemaking with RoTina. Too good. *If your life is without fire ...* What was that quote Sam recited?

It was something She couldn't remember. And it was too bad because She needed something to hang onto, to have some direction. Song lyrics helped—but She knew that was too pathetic to admit. So She needed friends and lovers, the intermittent pop-ins of Her scraggly and magnificent clan of misfits that fit right in on the Lower East Side.

"It's been weeks, why is she still practically living here? What's going on with you and Jean?" RoTina was ending an uncharacteristic rant, trying to control her anger. "I'm not going to be part of your string of girls you parade through here."

"String of pearls, not girls, is the expression," She joked back with a smile.

"Fuck you!" RoTina exploded.

"Anytime."

And she slapped Her, slapped Her a good one right on the cheek. Hard, openhanded smack that left a mark. It was perfect, and it stunned Her.

"Jesus fucking Christ, RoTina!" She yelled it, surprised and really hurt.

"That's right, you better get ready to do it with Jean or whoever because you're not getting me anymore."

RoTina yanked open the door, but surprise, Jean was on the other side. She had the keys in her hand, ready to let herself in. She smiled wide and innocently and danced past RoTina. Lousy timing— She couldn't believe it. She wanted to call after RoTina to at least ease over what just happened. But Jean was already in mid-story and high energy, chattering while she emptied the bag of groceries she brought. When she noticed She didn't respond, she finally stopped.

"Did I walk into something?"

She shook Her head and took a long toke. "What did you bring to eat?"

And then they, like a couple, with Her leaning on Her crutches while Jean worked around Her—they made dinner together, talked, completely at ease together. Everything else receded from them, from their togetherness.

"Am I fucking things up with RoTina?" Jean said when they were eating.

"Don't worry about it."

She felt mean, energized by the slap, which had stung for a longer time than She wanted to admit. The slap justified Her feeling mean. It blunted the blade of responsibility She had begun to feel at Her throat. She had been slapped. She could cop an attitude now with justification. It put a wrinkle in the relationship with RoTina, slowed it down and gave Her a reason to back off from Her. Her ego did not allow Her to consider the reality that RoTina had already retreated from Her, the reality She felt in a stinging cheek.

But, when in doubt, flirt. And when frightened, pick a fight—but be the victim. It gives you space, some freedom. It can make things exciting. Can't be bored if you don't let it get boring. That was what She convinced Herself of, and She'd stick to it. Or at least try—no boredom, keep moving.

I am really alone, have been for some months. Start feeling me. What dreams I have lately, vivid.

On a windowless small, cluttered dark basement apartment. An attractive short-haired blonde, Margret and me. The blonde talks to me, looks me straight in the face. Smooth, roundish, her face. Then they are talking, excluding me. We sit at a table, they are across from one another, talking only to each other. Then I notice they're holding hands. Margret's peeking from under a black square briefcase. I think: should I leave? And it seems I've thought that before. So I just get up and put on my coat, get my gloves. Margret looks upset, asks, why am I going? Don't go. The blonde says, don't go. But I leave. Winter outside. I climb steep, narrow broken cement rectangular steps. Grass and weeds grow in between. It's icy, so steep I use my hands to crawl up sometimes. So high. It's in Harlem. I look down and see there is a straight flat sidewalk just below, going to the same place because these steep steps are like a pyramid, go down on the other side after sloping up to a plateau, mountain on the right. Why didn't I take the easy way? The black guy with the long coat and big hat in front of me says, this is cooler. This be what you want. Cool.

She couldn't see as many women, couldn't get around with Her bad leg. Weeks dragged by and She thought about the motorcycle outside that was now in a parking lot where She had Her old friend Alan take it. The Super of the building couldn't keep it in front of the building any longer, so Alan came and moved it to a regular parking lot. She had to pay twenty dollars a month to keep it in one corner of the open lot over on Houston. At least that was taken care of, but She was still anxious to ride, wanted the mastery.

But being stuck at home, forced to stare at the studio without so many women around, the thread in Her work—the strength of women She showed in mood and color on black and white prints. Maybe it was Her need to get out the strength She didn't have Herself. It was that work, important, She had started before She felt the need to follow farther. She wanted to work. It was time, the prints, Her photographs, were coming to life. The technique She used for the first series was used on them now, more refined. She spent all Her time in the darkroom.

I dreamed I was with Nance and couldn't find my way up her stairs. And we were in a vacant lot, broken glass, weeds, and fat, big bugs with transparent skin filled with white and brown pudding-like insides. Someone threw one at me and it landed backwards, pointing away from the direction the other bugs were headed. Then I was in a car, going over a suspension bridge, but I was driving on the swaying pedestrian footpath on the outside. Water beneath, and I said, damnit how do I do this? The traffic is moving much faster on the real roadway, the inside lanes. Behind pedestrians where cars shouldn't be driving, it was slower but more scenic. A little scary, very sway.

She told Nance about the dream. But she wasn't surprised.

"It's like the other dream, same thing. Paths, wrong paths."

"Give me a break. Where've you been, in a gypsy storefront? You're some kind of fortune teller now?"

"No, bitch, you are. You're throwing your life away, and you're telling it to yourself. And why? So you can prove Margret was right in your sick little mind because you think you don't deserve better? You fucking deserve to be left."

It was worse than the slap from RoTina. She tried to struggle to her feet, but couldn't. She grabbed one of Her crutches and hurled it at Nance like a javelin.

"Fuck you."

Nance dodged the crutch and yelled a reactive "shit!" Really angry, she dropped the sandwich she had been making for Her and headed for the door. She left the food she brought on the table still in the bag. That wasn't good. Her crippled state was still being catered to by Her friends. But Nance, the most loyal, She was driving away. She needed her, how Nance always stayed to talk while She ate. But she was at the door now, ready to leave.

Nance turned and said, drolly, "I never saw you this bad. You can be a real bitch, no kidding. You're unhappy? Think you're the only one? Let RoTina come and take care of you. Get rid of Jean and your one-night ego boosts."

"Leave me alone, would you? I need to fucking work. Go, I need to be alone." She said it angrily. She said it bitchy.

For some reason She needed to say it. For as much as it hurt Her and Nance, something made Her blurt it out, be so ugly to Her best friend. Something had changed in Her, and She suddenly didn't need to talk in the way She had before. She needed to show Her feelings in Her work now. They emerged on the papers as she processed the prints. They glowed under Her brushes, moved on the images and they talked for Her. They told Her stories.

"Can I see what you're doing in there all the time," Jean asked, only once.

"No!"

"Calm down. Sorry I asked."

The girl annoyed Her. It was the first time She wanted her to shut up, get out of Her space. She hobbled around on her crutches and snubbed her. She wanted to ignore her laughter that was too loud, movements that were too broad and energetic. Distracting. Finally, She told her to *go home* with a strength that surprised them both.

Alone, just alone was all She wanted. Be careful what you wish for, rattled in Her head. Like that old picture of Dorian Grey, the cat might be listening and grant the wish that will haunt you forever. Damn, was the spirit world so unforgiving? If She railed to the heavens for solitude, it was only the retribution She needed for having given too much of Herself. Did that deserve the eternal punishment of solitude? Only sometimes, only sometimes She wanted, needed to be alone. She needed intimacy too. All on Her terms.

Come and be with me now. Go away, I can't stand the sight of you, the feel of your presence in my space. My space. My life.

Selfish bitch. But She didn't know how else She could work except to be alone. How else could She have the support to work except with a woman's love? Selfish, necessary.

She wanted a wife, everyone did. A slave. Be here, go away. Do the bidding of your owner. Slave masters were no fools, they had known the freedom of power for centuries. And if they were artists they knew the freedom part. But if they were stupid then they must know only the constriction of staying in the role, master with servant, never let down your guard. Masters ended up strangled in the night, or knifed. A wife, no involvement. Keep Jean the tease because she wanted no involvement. Easy. The easy way out. Avoid RoTina and her intelligence, the seductive equality of minds that frightened Her more than flirting with a May-December romance.

How the politico-correctos would howl. The most conservative would say only men—or only gay men—were so incorrect as to love very young men. They would say that only men dabbled in sadomasochism, only men lived through their genitals. *Yeah, right.* All that those painfully correctos accomplished with the straightness in their gayness was the reaffirmation of the myth of women's nonsexuality. No need to enjoy sex, oh no. *Fuck them, bring on the girlies.* But not right now, maybe in a minute again. And how the correctos would hate the words—girl, girlies—the lighthearted words that were not descriptive of reality but of a state of mind would make them shit. Of course She meant "women," and using "girls" was Her fun word, Her affectionate—yes, sex-focused word. So what? Politicos be damned, hung by their straight laces.

Bring on the girls, but in a minute. She had to think about work, wanted to finish Her work. There were too many involvements to sort out, and did She really want to deal with them now, or at all? Five weeks, She was still hobbling around on crutches, but better, able to move around. She was able to get down the stairs, slowly, and out to check on the bike now and then. She might be able to ride it if Her left knee would only bend so She could shift gears. If it had been Her right knee She could have ridden, could have used only the front brake on the right handlebar without operating the rear with Her foot. Maybe, maybe it would bend enough. But She couldn't even get on the bike. Crutches flailing in Her way, unable to put full weight on Her left leg. Ridiculous.

It was a new distraction to keep from working, or dealing with Herself. Women, motorcycles, drugs. Her digressions—entertainment. Now She was doing none of them, except for the prescription drugs codeine and Percodan, which were worse. She was left, when She stopped running, with Her work and Her self.

Goddamnit, She had to ride. Like a sailfish caught on a line, She wanted to leap and twist, strain at the bond. Get away, break away. Go to emptiness, be alone, be free of ties, of the hook of love. Be free of the terrible, tearing, maiming barb that rips the reddest of soft moist flesh.

Paranoid. Yes, paranoid, but usually right. And macabre. A macabre sense of reality. There was nothing to fight, no sinister forces. Maybe. She crutched in from visiting the bike, no one would stop Her from getting on and riding off, if She could. She lit a joint and paced, which meant lurching back and forth for two or three steps. Some smack in a packet that She had hidden away, maybe. If She found any She should shoot it instead of snort it. No one would know. Get really high and call some girls, run through them again, one after the other, and fuck their brains out. If She could do anything at all with the pain in Her leg. She could. She could do anything.

Fuck this ...

But She did nothing. Coward.

Fantasy, someone told me I had an active fantasy life. The same thing others call paranoia. Fantasy, Freud said it is the root of all creativity. Artists are like neurotics, he said, because both can't get what they want in life. So fantasy is used to create a work of art. The artist driven by instinctual art is the way to glory and women, and it's a road block to reality. Sounds like fun. Artists experience pleasure through their own works of art, he said—but why the hell shouldn't they? The only problem is that people don't want to reveal themselves in art, not too much, although some sure as hell do. Why not reveal, why not expose? What's the horror? Yes, what's the horror? Exposure. Exposure is risk, risk is death. Or risk, if done properly, should be death.

Where do you think you're going? That's really the question.

A dot of bright light in the sky blinks on and off. Circles, comes toward me. They're going somewhere and I'm not. I lie, waiting. It's not lying in wait. There is too much silence for that, inside me. But there should be silence. Otherwise you can't hear. They say.

It's the waiting. Harold Rosenberg wrote, you loiter in the neighborhood of a problem and pretty soon a solution strolls by. Waiting for solutions. Waiting for Godot. *But what are the problems? Is silence enough? Hello, is something there?*

There was huge red full moon in the sky before. I told a friend about it on the phone. By the time I was through it was no more. Higher, white, a more normal moon. Truth depends on time. Truth depends on context. Time changes them both, truth and its world—the world and, of course, truths.

Time is waiting. Time is waiting and I'm waiting. Does that make me time? I am a concept that clicks on, knowing itself only through change. That's why the waiting is so hard. I don't change. I get bored. Get frightened. A sense of myself slips away. Nothing happens.

Death must be the ultimate boredom; nothing changes. Thrill-seekers probably tempt it most when they're the most tired of change but don't know it. Or, like me, they're more afraid of the aware immobility than the dumb deathness. At least you don't know when you're waiting. Waiting. Not going anywhere when everything else is. When you're dead you have an excuse for not working. When you're alive the frantic wait consumes you. Will I ever think, create again? Will the waves of wanting ever part to allow a free thought to come through? Is my silence my lot, forever waiting for time to make waiting a legal truth? Waiting to work. Is this really work? If it isn't, then why does it feel so bad, so good?

- What If It Were Only Sun and Moon?
No Industry Selling Time -
FUCKING MEANING

"She can accomplish anything She wants," She remembered hearing him, a teacher, friend of the family, talking about Her. But Her dream didn't tell Her that, or maybe it did. The failure dream, Her grandmother saying to Her, "You sound like you should have been somebody."

Should have or could have been, She wasn't certain now. And it didn't matter. It was a question of cowardice, always was. She would rather put Her body on that motorcycle, torn up knee, ripped muscles and all, than settle down to work, work at success, or stay still long enough to be loved. Escape on the bike.

But She couldn't get around. Seriously immobile, experiencing disability for the first time, She withdrew into Herself. Except for borrowing money from friends, a little at a time, shuffling credit cards to live, making a shaky existence like that, off friends and plastic, She was alone. She stopped looking forward to Jean's long stays, did not share with Nance Her every mood swing, and She stopped returning phone calls from women. Kathryn with the Harley pursued for a time and then stopped calling. Ellen tried every few days. Olivia left long messages, orders with what to do about Her leg. Those, She especially ignored, could barely stand to hear her commanding D.A. voice before pressing the erase button. Saint Carmen of the Screams wanted to see Her but She avoided even her. And RoTina, RoTina waited. Maybe she was letting Her simmer in the memory of the hunger they satiated so exquisitely, the seclusion of that lovemaking, the whispers that urged more, and still more somehow. It was a closeness from which She ran. And She ran even from the easy ones now.

Jean stayed away and soon took up with another friend who filled her time—the gossip was on a message She actually listened to entirely. The girl would never learn fineness of art from the mediocrity of that other woman she took up with. Too bad; her problem. Not sparked by infatuation with Jean as She had been, She didn't care if her puppy cuteness degenerated into crudeness with someone else who couldn't teach her about art like She could. She was sure it wouldn't happen, couldn't. Let her go. And although She felt badly for Margret, because Margret felt so badly for herself, that wasn't Her problem either. Out of the slideshow of women in Her life, the only one who came without problems was RoTina. And it was RoTina She felt stirrings for and ran from every time. Now She was alone.

Colors brushed on carefully, or tints laid down vigorously then studied, and reworked—or not. Work. She worked again. She took those stacks of prints that loomed untouched for months and brought them to life. She put Her life into them. It was suddenly there. *Let it out.* She knew She couldn't hide now. She had always hidden before but with a new eye, a new touch, She opened up—exposed Her love for women. But was it complete? Were the women in those shots she had taken before, were they objectified alone, with Her outside, the creator at a distance? It struck Her one day in Her new work on those recently-old shots as She looked over them laid out on the big worktable.

The series with Martha by the ladder, the first of the newest hand-painted work, was good, made Her smile. Other series, some with Martha, some with other models, were dramatic nudes that were not completely nude with pieces of clothing—jackets, belts, gloves— all had been shot outside more than a year ago in the beautiful filth of alphabet city against brick walls, on roof tops, or at night on street corners where Her lens had caught those used to being unseen by surprise. They were like movies, still-shot stories, each print colored by Her hand. Except for that, Her eye and Her hand, only Her intentionality was there in relation to the women, but not Her. They still existed alone, Her subjects. Her subjects: that was Her relationship to women since the shock of Margret's betrayal. Margret's surprise that was forced on Her, there it was in Her work.

She sat down, felt knocked down. Kicked in the head. Goddamn, there it was. And She cowered, staring at the work. She sat, smoking, for hours. Thinking about it. Liking it.

A grasp of identity. A grasp at revelation.

I'll remember this. What it feels like to look in a mirror. Smile. What it's like. No other images. No need to fear the feeling on stage.

I want it to be good. Not what I have to do. What I want to do. Really want to do. Why not.

Why do I always forget philosophy?

It wasn't fear of failure, or fear of success, at all. It was fear of self, of giving. Exposure. Risk equals flirting with death. Risk equals death. But exposure is worse. Giving, risking with relating, opening to people wasn't the same thing. It was more frightening. Crutch out to the bike, ride it. Get away, fast. Do some coke. Dull the pain, lick shards from forgotten smack packets. Do more coke. Get away.

The guys at the parking lot asked if She needed a hand. And she said, "Yeah thanks," and let them. They held the crutches, steadied the bike while She got on and helped Her right it.

"You sure you're ok?"

"I'll be fine. Can you hand me my helmet, please?"

They watched Her start the bike, get as comfortable as She could. She moved Her left foot carefully under and over the gear shifter, going from neutral to first, then first to neutral to see if She could do it. She grimaced, a little pain that the Percodan masked pretty well.

"Ok."

The guys waved a car out of Her way as She eased the bike forward under a slow but constant throttle. It was difficult to balance with Her feet down since She couldn't really extend Her left leg to the ground very easily or with any quickness. She knew once She started riding She would have to keep going, or stop completely, and when she did eventually it would have to be with all the weight resting on Her right leg. Traffic lights were going to be a problem. But She didn't think, just rode. Her crutches were left behind with the parking lot guys.

Where to go? She craved the country, trees, solitude on a country ride with only Her and the bike. But this was Manhattan, worse, LOSAIDA. To get out, She would have to fight narrow streets and crammed traffic to a bridge or tunnel, neither of which She had experience with except for that one time over the GW bridge for a hot minute out and back. She wondered about the Lincoln Tunnel for the quickest way out, closer to where She was downtown. In the tunnel at least the road surface was familiar, smooth, did not really change. All She would have to deal with was exhaust fumes, claustrophobia and tailgating or being tailgated by behemoth trucks and busses. On the bridge She had learned for Herself there were those slippery and jarring expansion grates. And She replayed stories remembered from the biker girls.

"Ride the grates at a constant speed if you can, get forward on the bike and get low, don't hold the front wheel too tight. You've got to let it vibrate and wander a little with the grates when they move, and just relax."

Relax? Not likely, not today, not with Percodan, old leftover heroin bits and the coke mixed in Her. It was no way to ride a motorcycle, strung out and hardly admitting it, never mind the leg that still throbbed and shot a jolt through Her every time She shifted.

She headed for Central Park, the closest place to country She could handle. Maneuvering uptown through traffic on Third Avenue at eleven in the morning on a weekday wasn't as bad as it could have been. Difficult, but manageable. The Percodan and smack kept Her laid-back loose, the coke kept Her alert and made Her feel happily invincible. It was totally stupid, of course, but at least She had ingested an optimal drug mixture to function. Stopped at lights, She primarily used the front brake lever at the right hand grip. The rear brake that was at Her right foot She used only until She had to support the slowed bike with a leg, and that had to be Her right leg instead of the customary left. She managed.

The park was green, cool, aromatic and beset with yellow cabs and random cars rushing through the winding hilly roads—hillier uptown past the 90s up toward 110th Street than anyone thinks Manhattan is, or should be. She dealt with it, leaned with the curves, accelerated up hills. Once She got a little comfortable She laughed like a fool and slalomed the bike tightly in Her lane. Hit the throttle, feel the vibration between Her legs, hear the engine respond, feel it. Take off, no barriers. No barriers? What a joke.

She turned into the bridle path and crossed where it was almost level with the track that runners used around the reservoir. The engine with the seat and her, leg bandaged at the knee, illegally stopped in that place. She watched the people. People running, moving and She was chained to the bike, could walk no more than a few steps without crutches. Stark. There it was, one of Her diversions and the tangible result, immobility.

But the physical immobility, fortunately for Her, would pass. The homeless woman who made a statement with her existence, though, she showed Her how much worse Her psychic immobility was. She had seen the woman a few times before, recognized her, but She had always seen her downtown. She wore a camisole-type sheet over her clothes, white, and it was embellished with new wave images. It was an intriguing art that she wore. Not obvious, not blaring the condition and content of homelessness, it was just good. You wanted to look at those symbols, those individual drawings and figure them out. They pulled you in, like good art does. And the woman, asking for money, would explain "it's nice to look at, isn't it?" No bullshit. She liked the way it looked as much as the people who saw her did. She liked it, people liked it, and she would talk about it. Her art, no bullshit.

She watched from Her bike, smoked, and was coming off the coke high. Should have brought the bottle with Her, She realized. Watching, watching the runners, dog walkers, solitary readers, watching. She felt furtive. A fugitive, escaping from the self. No escape, though, what a jerk. What the hell was She doing? She looked at everyone going by and was irritated. Wasting time, She was wasting time. There in them, in the calm reservoir waters lined by Fifth Avenue apartment buildings, in the tufts of trees peeking from austere penthouse roofs, in all of it She saw Her work. Color She could use, texture.

For too long She had forgotten to notice all the sensations She had blunted, left behind while She was laid up or getting laid. *Fuck this*. What was She doing chained to this engine under Her? There were Her photographs, Her work, the series, little stories She had started to tell. Something to say, but what? Was it important? Who cares, just do it, do it like that woman who wore her own art. Do it because you love it. Fucking do it, worry about its meaning in the world later, if ever. That was how She fucked women: do it easily, joyfully, worry later if you have to. So why couldn't She work that way? Just fucking do it. Don't evaluate first, scaring the shit out of yourself with, is it good, what does it mean?

Just do it, fuck it. Really, just fuck it.

She righted herself, started the bike. She burned out of there throwing dirt from behind the sliding rear wheel. *Fuck it*. Get home, get to work.

Yin and yang. If there is a thrill of victory, there is also a thrill of defeat. We get used to the level we're at, and there is a fear of change. Addiction to negative feelings, addiction to worry, addiction to keeping things the same. Goodbye, risk.

But we have to create. Create a positive space for yourself, for saying it. Expression. Exposure. Must trust your instincts, trust standing on your own in whatever way that is.

Fear of failure. Fear of success. Fear of the critics.

- Betting On Time Speeding Up in Hell -
BRIMSTONE

She shot two women together. Laconic but iron-eyed Martha and a fire-eyed blonde.

When She hand-painted the series of stills, many series, She changed them. She changed their mood, the feeling that once had been obvious, to its reverse, with color. Or changed it to a half-step difference in exposure from what might have been expected, with Her own intention. She played with the reality of what She had posed, shot, by using color, texture. She added grain or softness in elevations on the prints. They became *bas-relief* photographs, but so very subtlety, elusive enough to invite inspection to make sure you really saw what you did really see in and on them. There were layers of reality now because of the doubling and redoubling of intentionality, or the confusion of it. It's what She wanted, what She lived.

There was a series where Martha, brunette with deep eyes, passed a doorway, an open door, through which she saw the lean blonde reflected in a mirror. That was the obvious reality, the pose She created for them. It took hours to shoot, an afternoon and part of the next morning. She had a lot of shots of this first scene from which to choose and a number of every other of the *tableaux* She set up and had shot over ten days. The other shots for the first series continued the theme of Martha walking past the door, the blonde turning and looking away from the mirror toward her, as if to see where she had gone. Martha rotated to find the empty mirror, then a shot of the doorway from inside the room, the back of the mirror partially seen. The halter top Martha had been wearing was on the floor. The next *tableau* was as if the previous action had never happened, Martha outside the door and continuing to walk away, slightly farther than before, and the blonde looking, this time in the mirror but her eyes directed to the reflection that had been behind her, now gone.

These were painted with shimmering washes when the women were farthest apart and with cool, cool metallics for their skin tones and hues of the print when they were closest, their eyes met, or when it was implied they were together. A judicious, uncomplicated, spare use of texture, a scrap of luxurious ermine She got from a friend at FIT became the rug the halter-top lay on. The halter remained black and white, grainy—a photographic image resting on a hint of sensuous fur, a rug, meaningless in itself, but not. And in another series the rug was photographic and the halter was made of aluminum, tawdry and unmistakably repellent. The intimate made repulsive, the mundane lavish, at odds with its own image and meaning, and at odds with the concept of the piece itself in each series. Did they glorify sensuality or mock it?

In another series, lazy Martha and an African American woman whose every gesture and glance were compelling enough to stop any gaze, they were shot in crowds on the streets. They pressed against each other through filmy dresses, a hand on a breast or buttock, as they stood in the midst of lunchtime crowds waiting to cross uptown Madison Avenue. Or they kissed, open-mouthed, tongues hinted at, blurred, the large image of them hazy while the interior of the church where they stood was in sharp focus--and then the sharpness and soft focus were reversed in other prints. These shots were washed with sepia tones and weird pinks, a faded look that contrasted with the activity of the crowds. But they were also pointed with a metallic detail or single line: silver paint in Martha's languid eyes or real paper-thin copper arms on the sensuous woman who was feeling her up. Then the story would be punctuated by shots of the women alone, suddenly naked, looking away from each other, sometimes trying to touch intimately, but maybe not.

She had forgotten how hard She had worked before Her life stopped a year ago. She had moved the stacks of prints and contact sheets without looking, packed in boxes and stored in Her new apartment while She went a little crazy because of Margret and Her reflexive escape into women. It was as if She was discovering someone else's work, and She liked it. It was good.

She worked hard now on those photographs from the base She made for Herself and had abandoned. She transformed them. She made the textures that were velvet, satiny lush or else studded them with spikey, tiny, ugly nails. She made colors that were lethargic or eye-burning. When they were soft they invited you to enter bedrooms with them, when abrasive they invited touch just to prove they could really be as awful, as painful as they looked.

Working on the prints, printing some from negatives for the first time, brought Her back to all the locations where She had shot. She used the feelings She remembered. She used languid colors that hinted, were so very soft they invited you to enter the bedrooms in prewar buildings on the Upper West Side with them. Or the romantic, old train compartments She had found at an eccentric collector's place in Amherst. A ship's cabin in a yacht at the 79th Street boat basin that She filled with exotic flowers Sam had gotten for free from a rich friend. The velvet petals She spread thick on a narrow berth that showed the impressions of lithe women who had lolled there deep in the caressing petals, but who were now gone.

In these places the women did not touch, or like the ship's cabin were no longer seen. When they were there they stared out at the camera, or down or up, anywhere but at each other. She tinted their skin so that it seemed to corrode, transparent flesh tone over liquidly purple-pink that was the color of a woman's open and ready sex. She made their eyes gleam with transparencies, hot, or dull leaden grey. But they never looked at each other, never touched. Only in those shots with the crowds, then they were hungry for each other. But in the fantasy or the realness of their being alone together, then there was distance, real distance in the intimacy.

She worked like this, with this theme, completely absorbed in it. Hardly eating, not needing much sleep. She barely smoked any grass, except to get some sleep, and did no other drugs. She was working. Too many cigarettes and a torrent of work.

- No Time. But All the Time. -
YES, BRIMSTONE

"You're playing with dreams alternating with reality, or a twisted kind of reality. But which is it?"

It was sleek Judy, ebony Judy, with the same slow deliberation she had used to examine Her work for the journal so long ago it seemed … It was Judy again, studying Her photographs, and it took a long time. And She finally decided, in all that time, it didn't matter after all, the realness or not.

"The intentionality in these is that you want to create that confusion, don't you, take it somewhere indefinable, eliminating words?"

"Kind of."

She said "kind of" because She wanted them to be so much more than the art critic's definitive, constraining words—so Judy was more right than She thought, or admitted. She wanted the pieces felt, loved or hated didn't matter to Her as long as they were reacted to so strongly that they couldn't be forgotten. She wanted viewers hooked on their own experience with the images.

Don't talk about it, just fucking feel it. How She wished She could follow that voice in Her head.

And the way Judy talked about them, Her photographs, too long and too slow there in Her studio, made Her glad She hadn't gone to bed with her before when Judy was editing the journal with Her work. Probably as pedantic and precise as her reaction to the new work, that was Her excuse to not kick Herself for having missed something with her. And now, it didn't matter if she had to give words to the emotions

She didn't want to be named or didn't want to be so clearly exposed, that was what happened when the work was out there: reactions, critiques. At least Judy got it, she got the impact of it right.

"They're powerful pieces."

That was what She wanted to hear. Nothing else she said to Her mattered as much.

Serendipity had brought Judy there, to see the work. She had run into her on the street while She was out buying cigarettes at the corner *bodega*. One thing led to another, a little flirting but not really. It was the more the civilized exchange of art world jockeying: business. Each of them was sensitive to what the other could do for her. It was the kind of business usually conducted at openings, parties and sometimes at chance meetings like this. It was the game She had not been willing to play for a long time. It was a game that had frightened Her into paralysis, into running from it.

But Judy asked about any new work of Hers, and for the first time She said that She had been "working hard."

More than that, She was surprised that She had said out loud She felt "good about it."

It was only down the block, did Judy want a first look? Serendipity, the alignment of stars, just dumb luck or the enticement of making a discovery, she hesitated a moment then said she had *a few minutes—* and that was that. They went to Her place. And She was more excited than She had thought She could be. No one else had seen the pieces. For two months She had kept everyone away. To have a well-connected player in the art world who had the eyes to know good work was phenomenal. Too good to throw away. Her response was valuable and maybe She wouldn't be able to ruin it no matter how much her defensive bullshit got in the way. She got real: Judy's reaction was important.

Work. She was amassing a body of work again and She wanted it shown. Judy could help. In return she might receive the reflected glory of having brought the work out as a discovery to her art establishment cronies.

"You would be ready for a show in the fall if it worked out?"

There was ringing in Her ears all of a sudden. Like a movie where the sound goes off and the camera zooms in on a face, astounded, aghast, agog—or something. Anyway, silent except for that damn ringing. Until, *wham*, it stopped.

Shit, She'd be ready in a month at the rate She was working. But not really. There was framing and presentation yet to think about, because She wanted any framing to be part of the pieces, to make a statement instead of only being containers. She thought three-dimensionality or maybe giving them the illusion of being open on one, maybe two, sides. It could be done with glass ends that were transparent to appear as if there were no barriers there. One shot in the series could lead into the next, in either direction, or vertically too. The frames could restate the dualities of the content, reinforce it, be part of it. Anyway, She would have to see what it felt like, feel it.

And in Her ears now, not ringing, but something—something happy, whatever it was. She wanted to talk, to be with people. Softness, friendship, closeness, openness. It had been too long. The avoiding calls, the cursory answers of *yes I'm still here and yes I want to see you, but...* That time was over and She had new needs, the old needs.

That was why She wanted to see RoTina again. She thought She could test the exhilaration of the work, not by talking about it but by letting the mood spillover. She wanted to feel again. In the last few weeks She saw Jean for the first times in a long time, and not often. It was good with the girl, no matter what, but when She was working like this She couldn't have her around like before. No one could be around when She got really serious with work, not even Jean the puppy.

RoTina was hot. Everyone said it, her sensuality couldn't be missed. The energy in her every move was vibrant, and in lovemaking it was overwhelming. When She called her, she came right over, no malice from all the weeks apart. She gave herself with passion, clean, no attitude. RoTina wanted to be with Her, wanted Her, didn't bother to hide it with games or act cool. She saw it and appreciated it. Honesty was the jewel in her. They fell into a lovemaking that was graceful in its tenderness, elegant in its tender force.

When RoTina told Her no one made her feel the way She did, She believed it. She believed it because She felt the same. It was different than before. She wanted her not to prove Herself as She did with so many women, all of them probably, but because RoTina meant something. What exactly, She didn't know. How and why eluded Her. There was only the feeling, a feeling of wanting her, and a calmness. It was meaningful because She felt it, and it really didn't need justification beyond that. She didn't want to examine it. It felt perfect in just being there inside Her, felt.

"You're different you know," RoTina said.

They were lying on sex-soaked sheets, their fingers trailing over bare skin. Quiet.

"My hair got longer."

"Easier to pull out by the roots now."

"Am I going to get slapped again?"

"Not when you're human, baby, and treat me right. That's the difference I'm talking about. You seem better somehow or other. Happier."

And She saw the warmth in her eyes, the realness. No bullshit, no games. Was it that She was finally ready to see it in someone else, or that RoTina was the only woman to really offer it to Her? She didn't know, didn't care. They kissed carefully, with gentle pressure, just enough, and it was enough.

"Where's the bag of new toothbrushes you used to keep for your tricks?" RoTina called from the bathroom. "Your string of girls dump you?"

"Very funny. I've been working. You're the only one who's been here."

"Right answer."

She could just make out RoTina's murmur from the bathroom. It made Her smile. For as much as She had wanted to think she really cared for Her before, She believed it more now.

It was the work, the lack of women, fewer drugs, and the fact the bike was collecting dirt in the parking lot. Everything was different because of the work. No escape, but an old reflex made Her try it again.

"You know I'm not ready for a relationship." It brought RoTina out of the bathroom, wrapped in a towel. She looked quizzically at Her, then smiled.

"I only asked for a toothbrush."

And she laughed at Her so that She had to laugh back. She knew the limp lack of conviction in Her voice had been lame, see-through.

What happened to death? What happened to fear and risk-taking, rather be dead than bored? Boredom had been Her cover for fear, and now somehow She was less afraid. Afraid of what, not afraid of what, She didn't know. Like a pinball at Her favorite Mars Bar machine, She had been ricocheted off flashing lights and bumpers before but now She was not in the game anymore. It was still exciting somehow, even more, because She had something to say, was saying it. And She started to tell RoTina about the work, what She was trying to do. She took her to the studio, showed her the new work, the stories in the photographs, the exposures of Her life.

RoTina was touched, amazed. She clung to Her more tightly the more she saw of the work, heard Her talk about it—Her life. Exposed. The risk of failure, looking stupid, being odd, being laughed at, being hated. The risk of exposure, worse than death. And RoTina understood.

"Don't say anything," RoTina said, "And don't freak out. But I think maybe I could love you. No strings. No bad ones anyway."

"Yeah right," She said gently.

"Just me ... don't want to hear about anyone else. Is that a bad string?"

RoTina kissed Her very lightly and turned away to go back to the bathroom, towel still around her. As She watched her walk away She finally remembered the quotation She had been trying to call from Her memory. The one She tried to tell to Margret. It came back to Her all of a sudden, maybe because She knew RoTina was not walking away forever, or because she wasn't staying too close. Whatever brought it back to Her it was in Her mind now, repeating.

When RoTina returned, dressed and ready to go it was easy. She kissed Her goodbye lightly, but somehow seriously. She told her She was going to *get back to work* and She didn't need her around to *distract* Her.

"When you want to show me more, call. Don't worry, I'm here for you. Just keep working, it's really incredible stuff. Just keep getting it out there. It makes a difference—in you mostly."

They kissed, deeply this time. Then RoTina pulled away carefully, cast a glance over the messy coffee table and made sure there were enough jumbled packs for Her to have enough cigarettes to work through the day and night. Then she left.

In the quiet the words wouldn't leave Her. The quote She had been trying to remember came now in the peaceful scream of a siren outside, the rumble of deep voiced men arguing from the street, someone clumping up the stairs out in the hall. It was New York quiet. And the words came.

If our life lacks brimstone, a constant magic, it is because we choose to observe our acts and lose ourselves in considerations of their imagined form instead of being impelled by their force. That's what Sam had told Her. It was Artaud, and no wonder She hadn't been able to remember it. She had been living its opposite, talking instead of acting, afraid to take the risk of living, of losing. Now She was compelled to live, to show Herself. And there was a thrill in it. No need to escape, but She did escape anyway. After all, She was in love. But it was different.

She went to Her big studio table and took the photographs She had been working on, spread them out there. There was a progression in them. It struck her clearly now and She had to smile, lit a joint and a cigarette while she arranged them. She alternated smoking one then the other to and from the astray as she concentrated. She moved a fuchsia-tinted couple leaning from a fire escape here in the line of prints, then an ample cyan-washed nude reclining against a dark elevator there ... She arranged, moved and re-moved, and She found a pattern, a sequence. She took a breath and looked. It was a long time before She realized She had not breathed again, and gasped in more air.

There was finally Margret. There she was in the print She had assembled from two photographs. She had merged them. She took the one She created of Margret tinged with regal translucent purple—that one She burned into a print among the trees in central park. Margret's fluent hands were just barely caressing their leaves.

She saw the progression. It moved from the dualities and dependencies of couples. But She was in love again. There was a problem, though, and it was there in the sequence. She was alone in Her love and, with the clearest of ringing silence, She knew that was finally enough for Her.

Exquisite Margret, goodbye forever.

Forever? She really hadn't done anything wrong, not enough for the condemnation She had heaved at her—strong Margret. That's what She finally thought when She finally thought about it all.

But that was later. Later when She had stared at Her work until it was dark and only the city lights from outside let Her still see the images, the story of Her life there in the photographs that led to solitude. Only then could She admit what She had done to her, and what She had to do to go on, alone, even with someone else.

"I have never seen a greater monster or miracle in the world than myself."
—*Montaigne*

Endnote

The Assistance of Vice was adapted for the screenplay *F*STOP*. It won the Jack Nicolson prize in screenwriting in 2004.

It was then reimagined as a short film also titled *F*STOP* starring Rain Pryor, Emily Cline, Jody Booth, and the Las Vegas Extremes motorcycle riders.

F*STOP has screened in forty-three festivals worldwide including Palm Springs, Outfest, Frameline28, Breckenridge, Rome, Berlin, Paris, Sydney, and Jakarta.

The director's cut can be viewed on Vimeo:
https://vimeo.com/search?q=F%2ASTOP+degnore

Visit the author online at www.robertadegnore.com.

Find the author's books:

Until You See Me

Invisible Soft Return:\

Acknowledgments

I want to thank all the woman and men who were my friends and anchors to reality—or catalysts to fantastically crazed times—in the caldron of the 1980s. The Sirens Motorcycle Club, ACT UP, GMHC Caregivers Group, Judy Peabody, Illith Rosenblum for her forbearance, Alexandra Seletti, Martin Bressler, Maxine Wolfe ...

And because of Sam Wagstaff too.

For incomparable editorial assistance: Don Weise

About the Author

Roberta Degnore is the author of thirteen published novels. She is a Lambda Literary Award finalist and an award-winning screenwriter and filmmaker. She holds a Ph.D. in psychology from the Graduate Center of the City University of New York and an MFA in screenwriting from UCLA. Always moving in broad arcs instead of straight lines, she travels widely and learns whatever she can wherever she is. Based in New York City, she returns frequently to Los Angeles.

73.22
3908 95117

XT3STV2

CPSIA information can be obtained
at www.ICGtesting.com
Printed in the USA
LVHW041050200323
742011LV00007B/159